Cover created by Ashley Santoro.

ISBN

Print: 979-8-9855317-4-9

E-Book: 979-8-9855317-3-2

HOT ROD HOOKUPS

FIXER UPPER ROMANCE, BOOK #2

CASSANDRA MEDCALF

For Mary Ann

Shawn huffed in irritation.

Setting down his socket wrench, he shimmied out from under his 1954 Chevrolet Bel Air and pushed himself up to a seated position. Empty sockets stared at him from where the headlights should be. Last week, he had removed the lamps to buff and polish the lenses. Now, he studied the chipped chrome grill and the interior of the front side panels. His eyes traveled up the curved lines of the car to the open hood, wherein sat the current bane of his existence.

That engine. He'd tried everything. Well, everything he knew to try.

He'd rebuilt the carburetor. He'd cleaned and replaced all the fuel lines. He and his granddad had even taken out the engine block and honed every cylinder until it sparkled, checking all the nooks and crannies for cracks, nicks, or stress fractures. It was immaculate.

Shawn and Walter Cobb had fixed a bunch of old cars together as a hobby, even taking a few down to the raceway when Shawn had first gotten his license. But as the old man's health had gone downhill, there had been fewer excursions to the track. This car was the first one in five years to reignite that sparkle in his granddad's eye, and Shawn wasn't about to let it get the better of them.

It wasn't as if he couldn't get the engine to turn over. It would start, but once it got warmed up, it would stop out of nowhere. Without fail, when it got to the fifteen minute mark, it would choke and sputter before coming to a complete standstill. And every time, he'd have to wait a day before it would start up again.

It was *killing* him.

"And here I thought I could have this done in time for me and gramps to actually enjoy it," Shawn mumbled to himself.

"That seems a little ambitious, don't you think? It's not even painted yet."

Shawn craned his neck around the front bumper to see his sister, Melanie, standing in the doorway of their parents' garage.

"Painting is, like, the very last thing you do, Mel. I also can't do it here. I need to take it to the body shop for that, and unless I can get it running, I'm not gonna be able to drive it there. That's assuming I get a few payin' gigs and can actually afford it."

Shawn tucked his knees up and leaned on his elbow, running his fingers through his hair before remembering all the grease on his hands.

Aw, shit.

"You're a mess, Shawn. Did you wake up with that cowlick?"

"Thanks, Mel."

Melanie walked around the car and leaned forward to look under the hood. Shawn slowly got up, grunting as his knees popped and his back ached, and took a minute to stretch. Then he stood beside her to examine the engine for the 3000th time since his friend Natalie had traded him the Bel Air.

"So she's still not running, huh?"

"Not for more than 15 minutes, nope." Shawn tapped the

hood with his fingers. "I can't figure it out, Mel. No one can. I've never even heard of this kind of problem before. Of course, it doesn't help that I can't bring it in to have someone *look* at it."

Mel looked over at him. "I thought Granddad was helping you out?"

Shawn shook his head, "It's dangerous for him to work on the engine with his oxygen. He'll help me with the other stuff. Or, maybe once the weather is a little warmer, we can work on it outside." He glanced toward the closed garage door. Even with the space heater running, it was barely above 60 degrees in the garage. It was *freezing.* Unseasonably so, even for February. Shawn hadn't been able to work outside in weeks because of the weather.

He looked over at his sister and shrugged. She frowned at him sympathetically and tugged at a loose curl of hair hanging in front of her shoulder.

"You look nice. What are you all dressed up for?"

Melanie rolled her eyes, "Are you serious, Shawn? It's Valentine's Day."

Oh. Right.

"Ah. Is *Christopher* taking you someplace special?" Shawn nudged the longboard he was using as a creeper back under the car and made his way over to the tool bench to grab some wipes for his hands.

"Yes, actually!" Mel followed him to the bench. "It's a surprise. He's not telling me where exactly, but he said it's in Martinsburg and to dress up really nice for it. Do I look extra special?"

Shawn groaned as he worked a towelette in between his fingers. "Really Melanie? You know I'm not good with this stuff."

"You're a *guy,* Shawn. Pleeeease! How do I look? From a guy's perspective?"

Mel held her arms out to her sides and did an awkward little turn. Shawn held back a snort as he took in her outfit.

She looked nice, like he had said earlier. She was wearing a longer, dark gray skirt and a red sweater with lace around her neck and shoulders. She had on pearl earrings, and she had curled her long, light brown hair so it hung in ringlets down her back. When she turned, he saw a black satin bow at the crown of her head where she had pulled back some of her hair, and he noticed the rest of her accessories were also black—a wide belt and some short heels that didn't look particularly appropriate for walking around in the middle of a cold snap in West Virginia.

"You look… nice. But your feet are going to get cold."

Melanie pouted. "Should I do boots? I thought about boots. Would they be cuter?"

"They'd be warmer." Shawn shrugged. "Your hair is pretty. I like the bow."

"It's not too much?" Mel touched daintily at the back of her head and grimaced. Shawn chuckled.

"Mel. Christopher likes you, okay? If he didn't, he'd have stopped dating you by now. Haven't y'all been going out for like, two years?"

"Twenty-one months," Mel corrected. "So… cuter with boots?"

She stuck her right foot out and pointed her toes, swishing her skirt around her calves as she did so. Shawn chuckled and shook his head.

"Again, Mel, not really my thing. Ask mom."

Mel sighed. "*Fine.* I'll ask mom. What are your plans for tonight? Do you have a date? What about that Natalie girl you keep talking about? When are we finally going to meet her?"

Shawn's shoulders stiffened. He tried to hide his reaction to Natalie's name by cracking his neck and packing up his wrenches.

"She's got plans already tonight, I'm sure," he muttered into his tool box.

"I thought she barely knew anybody around here?"

Shawn winced. "You know? I might just go to the bar tonight. With all the other pathetic, single guys in the eastern panhandle."

Mel scrunched her face. "Gross. You spend too much time there."

Shawn shrugged, happy for the change of subject, "I like it there. It's fun. Bet there aren't darts and pool tables wherever Christopher is taking *you* tonight."

Mel laughed. "I *hope* not!"

He smiled at his sister and closed up his toolbox, taking one last look at the Bel Air before gently closing the hood. "Well, I'm not going anywhere before I clean up a bit. You all done in the upstairs bathroom?"

"You mean *my* bathroom?" Mel crossed her arms and raised her eyebrows.

Shawn leveled a look at her. "I believe it was *our* bathroom for a good seventeen years before you went to college and I moved out, Mel."

"Worst seventeen years of my life," she said, and then winked at him. "Just don't get it all gross! I swear, if you leave grease marks all over the sink again…!"

She walked back up the couple of stairs and through the door into the house, and Shawn glanced back at the car.

Guess I'll have more time tomorrow, he thought, as he packed the last of his tools away.

CHAPTER 2

To Shawn's surprise, the Potomac Bar and Grill was actually packed on Valentine's night. There were a few couples there, he noticed, but mostly it was the single men and women that he'd seen there before, milling about in groups around the pool tables and dart boards and a few crowded around the Deer Hunter game in the back. One of the few free chairs was in the very center of the bar by the register, and he did a quick scan of the room to see if any of his friends were around.

But even he knew it wasn't likely. He'd grown apart from most of his buddies now that they all had girlfriends or wives to hang out with, and of course, Natalie had her sexy lawyer girlfriend.

Natalie Roche had shown up in the area last fall when she'd inherited her family house after her grandmother passed away. When Shawn ran into her after work one day, she had been hell bent on giving up her grandma's house to keep her hellish job in L.A.

But she and Shawn had gotten along, and in the first week of their friendship, he had made a deal with her. He'd bet that he could make her fall in love with the place if she would let him help her fix it up a little.

Yeah, fall in love with the house, Shawn thought, shaking his head, *that's what I get for being cute about it.*

In the end, she *had* ended up staying, but not because of Shawn. Instead, she'd fallen for her family's beautiful estate attorney, and Shawn had gotten an old car as a consolation prize.

You blew your chance, dude, he chided himself. *Give it up already.*

Shawn walked past the booths through the crowd of high-top tables and claimed the seat by the register. Jess was behind the bar tonight, as well as three other female bartenders, and Dave the manager with his wife, Susan. It looked like they were training two of the girls while Jess and the other girl were handling the actual patrons. It seemed a bit chaotic back there.

"You're not out with your boyfriend tonight?" Shawn yelled over the ruckus to Jess, who was normally the one to serve him. Her back was to him; she was attending what looked like an entire tray of Jaeger Bombs. He took a second to admire the view of her ample backside before she turned around.

"Be right with you!" She called over her shoulder, before hoisting the tray of close to a dozen glasses and balancing it on one hand over her shoulder, just barely steadying it with her other hand. She hip-checked the swinging door separating the bar from the main floor and carried the tray over to the pool tables in the back.

Shawn watched, mouth slightly open, at the short, curvy blonde. She swerved her wide hips through the crowd with the ease and grace of a ballroom dancer. He'd carried shingles up a ladder before, but he'd never balanced a heavy tray of precariously loaded drinks through a crowd. It was a wonder none of the shot glasses fell into their pints. He was still watching her nimbly avoid drunk customers when the other bartender popped up in front of him.

"Would you like a dinner menu, sweetie?" she asked him.

He turned his head back around to look at her and glanced down to her name tag. It read *Sheila*, with a little heart over the "i" instead of a dot. "Uh, sure, Sheila. Thanks."

She reached under the bar and grabbed him a menu. "Something to drink? You interested in our 'Sorry Singles Special'?"

"Your what?" He blinked.

"Sorry Singles Special," Sheila said, and he dumbly mouthed the words—wondering how she didn't stutter as she spoke them.

"What's the Sorry Shing–the Sho–what's that?" Shawn flinched. He hadn't even ordered yet, and he already sounded drunk. He heard a giggle as Jess came back through the swinging door, and then walked up to Sheila and patted her on the shoulder.

"I'll take this one, Sheila. He's one of my regulars."

Sheila's brow furrowed for a brief second before she flipped her curly brown hair, muttered "fine," and walked away.

"Dave and Susan just love their tongue twisters," Jess smirked, "The Sorry Singles Special is two shots of tequila for the price of one, and you're not allowed to share." She gave him an evil little smile. "I said it should be the 'No-Share Sorry Singles Special' and be two shots of schnapps, but no one could say that without messing it up. So we had to shorten it."

"The Shortened Sorry Singles Special?" Shawn smirked. *Nailed it!*

Jess laughed. "You want one?"

Shawn shook his head. "Nooooo, no thank you. I hate tequila. I'll have whatever IPA's on tap and a soft shell crab sandwich."

"One Sorry Single Softshell Sandwich comin' up," she said

with a smile, her blonde ponytail bouncing as she punched in the order.

A cold gust of air blew past his shoulder as the side door opened. Shawn looked up.

Natalie.

Shawn gulped as Natalie Roche walked into the Potomac Bar and Grill, rubbing her hands together and shivering in an oversized navy scarf and a tight gray button-up sweater, layered over tights and a tank top. His mind flashed back to how he thought his sister wasn't dressed for the weather, but Natalie didn't even look like she owned a winter coat.

Bonnie the Lawyer came running in behind her, carrying a pea coat and a hat. He watched the two of them banter as Bonnie handed Natalie the items, and even though he couldn't hear what they were saying, he assumed that Bonnie was lecturing her on dressing for the East Coast weather.

He swallowed. He could literally see her every curve in that outfit. She couldn't be comfortable in that. She must be freezing.

He should look away.

"Here you go, Shawn," Jess said, thunking his pint glass down on the bar between them. "We're doing a team meeting—you want in?"

Shawn pulled his gaze away from the door and looked back at Jess, "Sorry, what? Team-"

"A staff shot. Jameson. You look like you could use one." She gave him a sad smile, and he didn't like the look of understanding in her eyes. She glanced over to the door, where Natalie and Bonnie were still arguing playfully.

He grabbed his beer. "Sure. Thanks, Jess."

She patted the bar beside his hand and turned back to a line of shot glasses that Sheila was filling for the six staff members, and quickly added a seventh to the row. Sheila looked at her questioningly, and Jess jerked her thumb toward Shawn.

He gave Sheila an embarrassed wave. *Great. Now I'm the sad, single guy.*

He wanted his sad crab sandwich.

He quickly glanced back over his shoulder to find Nat and Bonnie. They'd squeezed themselves into the same side of an empty booth in the corner, and he looked away when he saw them making googly eyes at each other.

"You gotta problem with that?" Sheila snapped at him as she set down his shot.

"What?" Shawn blinked.

"You know. With two girls together."

"What??" Shawn repeated, louder. "No! No, it's not like that–"

"Sheila! Stop being mean; Shawn's not a bigot," Jess said, cutting in beside her. She gestured with her own shot, and they all lifted them to their lips and tilted them back, tapping the glasses on the bar when they'd finished. "He was sweet on one of them," she gasped out through the whiskey burn.

Shawn coughed. "Hey, I didn't say—"

"Which one?" Sheila asked, eyes widening.

"It's not like tha-"

"The shorter one," Jess answered.

"The one without a coat?" Sheila gaped. "Why do they always go for the stupid girls?"

"She's from L.A., okay? She probably doesn't even own a coat!" Shawn felt his face heat as he defended her.

"Either way, it looks like she's got someone to keep her warm, huh?" Jess teased. Shawn rubbed his face with his hands.

"Don't y'all have other relationships you can talk about?"

He felt two small, soft hands grab his wrists and pull his arms away from his face. Jess leaned in close to him and stared into his eyes. He swallowed and looked away from her scrutinizing gaze, but what he found didn't do much to calm him down. As his eyes moved down, he saw she was wearing a baggy flannel shirt that was unbuttoned, but tied just above her waist. Her stomach was visible underneath was a black sports bra, which barely contained an ample chest. He'd only ever seen really skinny girls dress like that, but on Jess–*is curvy the right word for her?*–he felt like there was much more to appreciate. *He* appreciated it.

More girls should dress like that, he thought. Then his face flushed, and he darted his eyes back up to hers.

"We're not here to talk about *our* boyfriends," she said, still holding his wrists. She hadn't missed his eyes trailing down her body. "We're here to help cute, lovesick singles stay positive. Comes with working in a bar six days a week."

Shawn looked away from her and pulled his hands away. They felt a little tingly where she'd been touching them. *Cute, huh?* His face was hot, and he felt a buzz in his pants...

What the-?

It took him a second to realize it was his phone vibrating— *duh, Shawn. Of course it's your frickin' phone, you idiot*—and he pulled it out of his pocket to see a text message from Melanie. It was a picture.

He unlocked his phone screen and opened the text conversation to see a photo of his sister's hand, with a *giant* diamond on her ring finger.

ME

Jesus Christ. Is that from Christopher??

He stared down at the photo. Three dots appeared under his text.

MELANIE

Say hello to the future Mrs. Christopher Bennett!

He barely had a second to process this bombshell before she responded again:

And don't take the name of the Lord in vain.

Shawn tossed his phone onto the bar and ran his hands through his hair. This couldn't be happening. He normally didn't focus too much on romance, but in this moment he felt so incredibly single it hurt. Jess had been looking at him, and when he tossed his phone, she glanced down at the screen.

"Woah!" she said. "Who's the chick with the rock?"

"My sister," Shawn grumbled. "Apparently, her boyfriend proposed tonight."

"Well, isn't that nice for her?" Jess looked thoughtful for a second before noticing Shawn's dejected expression. "Oof."

"Yeah." Shawn met her eyes. "Oof."

Jess wiped her hands on the kitchen towel that was tucked into her apron. She looked Shawn up and down again, and huffed out a little sigh.

"Tell ya what," she said. "I *really* shouldn't do this, but how about I pour us both a Sorry Singles Special, only I swap out the tequila for whiskey, and we split it anyway?"

"Wouldn't that just be two shots of whiskey?"

Jess nodded. "Yep. And boy, don't we need 'em."

CHAPTER 3

It was a training night. Jess probably should have been focusing a little more on the new girls and helping them figure out table numbers. She definitely should have been paying attention to the tables throughout the bar, instead of parking herself squarely behind it and leaving the holiday rush to Sheila.

But she knew the look of a man in crisis. And Shawn Cobb was smack-dab in the middle of a crisis.

Of course, almost everyone in the bar tonight was having something of an episode. It was Valentine's Day, after all, and no one who was happy in their relationship (or lack thereof) was going to spend Valentine's Day drowning their sorrows in tequila at the Potomac Bar and Grill. That's not what happy people did. Jess had worked at this place long enough to know that, while most nights here offered a fun collection of country himbos out for a good time, the holidays brought a special kind of crowd—a depressed kind of crowd.

And she *should* have been making her rounds. She was the friendly face that down-on-their-luck folks needed on nights like this. She had been that friendly face for the past four years

—through the Valentine's Days and Thanksgivings and Christmas Eves. She couldn't remember the last time she'd had a holiday off.

Her phone buzzed in her pocket, and she ignored it. Of course, Kyle had wanted her to spend the holiday with him. But while they *were* beginning to get a bit more serious, she couldn't pass up on the tips that came with working a night like this. He'd agreed to stop in later to visit her while she was working, though, so she would at least get a goodnight kiss on Valentine's Day.

If not a little more.

Jess worked on all the holidays. Unlike Kyle, star pitcher of the local Community College baseball team and all-American hottie, who came from a pretty well-off family in Northern Virginia, she'd been working for as long as she could remember. Long before she'd been old enough to work in bars, she'd been helping out in her dad's garage since she could hold a wrench. Still did, too—although none of her boyfriends had ever been particularly happy about her spending her afternoons getting sweaty and greasy around a bunch of older men.

But where none of *those* relationships had panned out, things with Kyle seemed to be going somewhere. He treated her like she really mattered, like he wanted to take care of her. And after night after night of taking care of everyone else around her, it was nice to have someone return the favor for once.

Even if they couldn't spend every holiday together.

"Bottoms up!" Jess said as she handed a second shot of whiskey to Shawn. He stared at her, and she gestured again with her own full shot glass. "I'm not gonna drink this by myself, you know."

Shawn sighed. "Jess, I'm not really feelin' getting drunk tonight. I might just head home." His eyes darted once again to the booth in the back corner, with Bonnie Baker and Natalie … whatsername. Jess didn't remember.

She slapped a hand down on the bar.

"Hey!" She set down her shot glass and eyed him menacingly. "You don't mean that. You haven't even gotten your sandwich yet."

"He would have if you weren't wasting time *talking*." Sheila elbowed her way past Jess and into the conversation, depositing Shawn's dinner in front of him. "We're swamped here, Jess, and the girls don't know the table numbers yet. Help us out."

Jess flinched and shot Shawn a look before grabbing the bus bin out from under the bar.

"I'll be back—don't *you* go anywhere."

Jess hustled to the kitchen counter to pick up and distribute orders and made her rounds about the floor, checking the door for signs of Kyle and glancing back at Shawn every so often to make sure he was still there. She could be miffed at Sheila for bossing her around, but Jess knew she didn't mean it. Sheila had requested the night off so she could spend Valentine's Day with *her* boyfriend, but had been called in to help with the rush while the owners trained the new girls. Still, it was no fun working with a grump.

After checking in on all the diners, she grabbed a water pitcher and headed back over to the bar to get refills to the folks that had been cut off. She grabbed a glass for Shawn and filled it.

"So tell me about your sister. I've never seen her in here before," Jess said.

"This ain't really her scene."

"Older? Younger?"

"A couple years younger," Shawn said. He pushed the crumbs on his plate around with a fry.

"Do you like her fiancé?" Jess prodded.

Shawn shrugged. "He's all right, I guess. A little stuck-up. He's a tech guy and makes good money. He makes Melanie happy."

Jess studied Shawn's face. It was sad to see such a catch sitting all alone at the bar on Valentine's Day. His broad shoulders were hunched over the bar, his shaggy brown hair covered his downcast eyes, and he was fiddling with his fries more than eating any of them. He hadn't taken an actual bite since she'd gotten back to the bar.

Loneliness didn't suit Shawn Cobb. She reached for his plate. "Didn't your parents ever tell you not to play with your food?" She was flirting, something she'd gotten very good at over the years as a bartender. Kyle told her she flirted too much with the customers, but it was practically part of the job description. Being standoffish didn't pay the bills.

And if he cared *that* much, she reasoned, then he should've been pushing her to work more at the garage and *less* at the bar, instead of the other way around.

Men.

Shawn slumped in his seat and put his hands on his knees. "Sorry. I guess I'm done."

He was in worse shape than she'd thought.

He leaned forward and reached into his pocket for his wallet, like he was about to leave. *Fuck.*

Jess didn't want him to leave; she was still worried about him. She hadn't seen him smile once tonight, and that wasn't a good sign. Every time Shawn came in the bar, he practically lit up the place. He'd always been something of a social butterfly though, she supposed—he tended to flit from group to group; he didn't really have a "best friend" that *she'd* witnessed. The only times she'd seen him really connect with someone was...

Well, with the woman that was currently necking with her girlfriend in the corner.

Quick, start a conversation!

"When was the last time you got laid, Shawn?"

Shawn stumbled off his stool and dropped his wallet. He

flushed, and his wide eyes turned to her before he bent to retrieve it. "What're you askin' me *that* for?"

Got him.

"That long, huh?"" She shook her head, her face full of mock pity.

Shawn blinked. "That ain't your busi—"

"You can tell me Shawn; it's okay! You've been comin' in here telling me your troubles for how many years now?" Jess reached to pat his hand, now resting on the bar where he had grabbed it to steady himself.

Shawn glanced around the bar, as if nervous someone might overhear. "Jess, that ain't a polite thing to ask somebody!"

Jess laughed. "So proper! Well, fuck, I didn't realize I was in the presence of *royalty.*"

His face went from pink to crimson, and his pale blue-green eyes were wide with embarrassment.

God, he's a cutie. Why haven't I ever noticed his eyes before?

Shawn glanced back once more to the table with Bonnie and Natalie. Natalie was practically in Bonnie's lap now, leaning into her as Bonnie whispered in her ear.

Jess looked at the pain in Shawn's eyes. Then it clicked.

"Oh *shit,*" Jess hissed. "Did you and Natalie—?"

Shawn jerked his head back, "What? No! We're just friends."

"But you wanted to," Jess said.

"I didn't say that. What's got you all interested in my love life all of a sudden?"

"Your lack of love life, you mean?" Jess teased.

Shawn narrowed his eyes and pulled his hand off the bar. "Later, Jess."

"Wait, Shawn!" Jess sped after Shawn, who was already pulling on his coat as he pushed out the side door. She ran outside after him, forgetting it was eight degrees outside.

"*Fuck,* it's cold!" Her teeth already chattering, she crossed her arms over her exposed midriff, pulling her long sleeve flannel tighter around herself. "Shawn, I'm sorry—I didn't mean to hurt your feelings!"

"Yeah, well," Shawn called as he walked to his truck. He didn't turn around.

"I'm sorry!!" Jess shouted. *Fuck* she should have worn thicker pants tonight. Her thighs stung under her jeggings as the wind picked up.

Shawn opened the driver's door of his truck and gave a wave. She ran awkwardly over to the driver's side, gingerly stomping in her old boots that were not exactly appropriate for an icy parking lot. By the time she reached his truck, he'd shut his door and fired up the diesel engine, and he sat in the cab blowing on his hands to warm them.

She knocked on the window.

She saw him angrily look at her and debate whether or not to open his door. Eventually, he couldn't ignore her anymore, and he rolled down the driver's window.

"What?" He grumbled.

"Are you safe to drive tonight? You're not like, gonna hurt yourself?" Jess bounced her knees, attempting to keep herself from freezing.

"*Yes*, Jess, I'm fine. I'm not gonna hurt myself. And I'm sober, 'kay? I've had less than you have."

Jess shivered and nodded.

"Now get back inside. You're not dressed for this." Shawn started to roll up his window.

She put her hand on the glass. He rolled his eyes and lowered it again. "You sure you're good?"

She'd hate herself if he got into a wreck on the way home. She wasn't sure where he was headed, but the Potomac River wove its way through the mountains all around them, and the roads could be scary when it got this cold.

Shawn sighed. "I gotta wait for the truck to warm up, anyway. By the time I head out, I'll be more than fine."

Jess bit her lip, which was already chapping from the cold. She didn't like that response very much.

"I'm waiting with you."

"What?" Shawn scoffed, "Jess, I'm—"

"It's my job to make sure the people that leave this bar are good to drive!" To convince him she meant business, she stomped her foot. Unfortunately, the heel of her boot caught a bit of ice when she did it, and she lost her balance. Her other foot slid on the slick drive, and she waved her arms to catch herself.

Shawn leaned out the truck window and grabbed her under her shoulder blades. She looked up, hanging from his grip, and was momentarily breathless with shock. Their eyes locked. She slowly, carefully, found her legs and stabilized them once more, straightening as Shawn shifted his grip around her ribcage. Shawn didn't let go, though, and her standing brought her face closer to his as his hands securely held her sides. Their breath clouds mingled in the freezing air between them.

"Thanks," Jess mumbled, eyes not leaving his.

"Get in the cab, Jess."

"What? But I'm–"

"Look." Shawn removed his hands from her waist now that she was standing on her own. "If you gotta stay with me until you think I'm good to drive, then you ain't gonna do it out in the cold, makin' me keep my window open. Get in the cab."

Jess nodded. She *was* cold.

She elected to cross in front of the truck instead of around the back, where the piled snow from the last storm provided a crunchier, less slippery surface than the shiny blacktop of the parking lot. She opened the door and hoisted herself into the passenger side.

It was so much warmer in here than it was outside. She sheepishly looked back at Shawn.

"Sorry. Maybe I've had more than I realized. Sometimes I get carried away drinking with the customers," Jess admitted, rubbing her hands together in her lap, "Especially on the holidays. I just… I hate seeing people sad. I like to help cheer 'em up, you know?"

Shawn nodded, reaching over to grab her frosty fingers with his very large hands.

Jess swallowed. She shouldn't let him hold her hands. But she was freezing, and he was warm. How was he so warm?

"I really am okay, Jess. I'm sure there are some guys in there that need you more than I do." He chuckled. "Or, you know, Sheila."

Jess laughed and then winced. "Oh fuck— Sheila's gonna be *pissed*."

Shawn patted her fingers and withdrew his hands. The cold air rushed around her palms in their absence. She really should get back to Sheila. Shawn would be fine. He was probably more fine than she was.

Shawn sighed. She glanced up at him.

"I guess … I guess I am a bit of a wreck tonight."

Jess studied him. He stared off in the direction of the passenger side mirror, not meeting her eyes.

"I haven't really had time for relationships since high school, you know?" he said quietly. "When Natalie came here, and we started gettin' along, well… I thought maybe it'd be like those movies my sister always watches. But then she found someone else, and I guess… I mean, I'm happy for her! Really… but, now I'm back where I started."

Jess shifted in her seat to look at him better. She wasn't expecting him to actually open up like this tonight. She put her hand on his shoulder. The muscles tensed briefly at her touch, then relaxed as he turned his head to look at her.

"Sometimes it's like I just woke up and suddenly everyone had someone, you know?"

She swallowed. "Yeah. Yeah, I get that."

He nodded and looked at his dash. She wasn't sure what he saw there, but he seemed a little less lost. Her phone buzzed in her pocket–*That's probably Kyle*– and the noise brought them back to the conversation.

"Well, you still got work to do, and I probably ought to get home. I haven't even been at the house yet today, and I gotta start up the furnace before I hit the hay."

Jess flinched. "You have to start up a furnace?"

Shawn smiled at her. The cab felt warmer.

"It's ain't so bad," he said. "That's what I get for spending all day at my parents' place."

She wanted to ask him what he was doing there all day, but then he gestured toward her door.

"Oh! Right. Yeah. Back to work!" She turned to open the door, then looked back at him, "You know, Shawn, we could always hang out sometime. I'm kind of surprised we never have before."

Shawn shrugged. "Ain't no rest for the workin' class."

She nodded, and opened the door. "Thanks again for the save. And the warmth."

She didn't just mean the cab.

"See ya later, Jess," Shawn said. She closed the door and stepped back as he eased out of the parking space and onto the road.

Then she crossed her arms back over her chest and carefully stepped her way back to the bar.

CHAPTER 4

Kyle was waiting for her.

"*There's* my girl," He wrapped his bulky arm around her waist and gave her a kiss before she slipped back behind the bar. He leaned forward over the spot Shawn had just vacated.

Jess washed the glasses that had piled up behind the bar. "About time you showed up! Where've you been?"

"Picking up this."

Kyle pulled out a solitary long-stem rose from behind his back and held it out to her. Jess cooed as she accepted it, and Sheila cut between them, glaring at her.

"Alright, Cinderella, are you gonna work tonight or not?"

"Aww, come on, Sheila. Give the girl five minutes."

Kyle's eyes sparkled as he pouted at her. Jess stifled a giggle.

Sheila was unimpressed. "She just took five. She's back on the clock now, loverboy."

She grabbed a pitcher of water and bumped Kyle's shoulder as she walked past him to handle refills. He grimaced.

"What's got *her* all pissy?" he sat down and Jess poured him a beer.

"She's just mad she has to work tonight."

But Jess did make an effort to check in on the other patrons more after that. She did a loop and refreshed a few pints before circling back to Kyle. He was staring openly at her chest and exposed midriff as she washed glasses.

"Someday maybe you won't have to work so hard, Jessie."

"What's that supposed to mean?" she shook the Clorox water off her hands and reached for her dishrag.

Kyle gestured around the bar. "Look at all you do. Bartender by night, mechanic by day… you oughta take a break sometime."

"Is that so?" Jess raised an eyebrow at him.

"Yeah," He grabbed her wrist as she wiped down the bar beside him. "Why don't you let someone take care of you?"

"Anyone?" She fluttered her eyelashes at him.

"Well, not *anyone…*"

"Two burgers for table twelve!" Sheila shouted, once again bumping Kyle in the shoulder as she hustled to the kitchen. He grunted, and Jess bit back another laugh.

"Maybe someone should take care of *her* first…" he grumbled.

Jess swatted him gently with the dishrag. "How about I let *you* take care of me once my shift is over, *loverboy?*"

His face brightened considerably. "*Now* you're talking."

THAT NIGHT, she let Kyle take care of her slowly and deliciously. And when she rolled off of him after returning the favor, she set her phone alarm before curling herself against his muscled chest.

"What are you setting your alarm for, babe? Tomorrow's Saturday."

"I'm at the garage tomorrow morning," she said, lightly running her fingers up and down his arm. She loved the feeling of his strong arms around her. He made a noise that was some-thing between a scoff and a snort.

"What?"

She could see a grimace cross his face in the light of the streetlamp that glared obnoxiously through the drab gray dorm curtains.

"Isn't it kinda weird, you hanging out around all those old men all the time?"

Jess laughed. "You mean my dad?"

"Babe."

Instead of answering, he just raised his eyebrows at her. She shrugged. She'd hoped that Kyle didn't have the same kind of misgivings all of her other boyfriends had had about her working at her dad's garage. She liked Kyle. Maybe even loved him.

Why are all my boyfriends so weird about me working with other men?

"You don't have any problem with me hanging out at the bar."

"That's different. There are other girls at the bar, and besides, you get me free drinks." He grinned at her, and she rolled her eyes. "The old men at the garage… I worry about my buxom beauty getting sweaty around all of them, you know?" He squeezed her ass. She squealed.

"Are you talking about Randy and Chuck? They practically raised me. They're also in their fifties." Jess shuddered, and snuggled closer into his chest. Even the *idea* of Kyle being the least bit concerned about the mechanics at her dad's shop was laughable, if not disgusting. They were family to her. He didn't have anything to worry about.

"What about the other guy? He's only, like, 30."

"Beau?" Jess sat up, and Kyle's eyes lingered on her bare chest as she did. She smacked him, and he met her eyes, a lusty grin still tugging at his lips. "He's practically my brother. And he has a kid."

"Yeah, and you know how kids are made, don't you?" He grabbed at her ass again, and she giggled, slapping at him in a playfight.

She knew he was only trying to protect her. But she didn't like what he was insinuating.

"Kyle, it's not a problem. Trust me."

He wrapped his arms around her waist and pulled her back against him. She only fought for a second before acquiescing. "It's not *you* I worry about, babe. It's them."

"And I'm telling you, it isn't a problem."

"Babe." Kyle reached a hand under her chin and tilted her face so their eyes met. "You are the type of girl that all men dream about settling down with. Those guys–even if they *aren't* interested in you, they're keeping you away from your future. It's not like you're going to work at a garage when you're some- one's wife someday."

Heat rose to Jess's cheeks. *Settle down? Wife?*

Is he saying what I think he's saying?

"What do you mean, babe?"

"I *mean* what I said earlier tonight," he said, holding her tight against him. She could feel the curve of her stomach squish against his hard, warm chest, and she felt herself relax instinc- tively against him. "You need to stop working so hard. And let someone take care of you for once."

Jess's heart beat faster in her chest as he held her tight. Kyle had used the "w" word. Did this mean he was really that serious about her?

Maybe it *was* time to rethink working at the garage.

CHAPTER 5

The next day, Jess tinkered with the wrenches in her father's tool chest at his shop. Kyle's words from the night before ping-ponged in her brain.

Just north of the Virginia/West Virginia border, Ernie's Garage attracted the more discerning car enthusiasts from the tri-state area. Her father was a wizard with engines, gas and diesel, and he'd trained a few apprentices that earned their keep. Growing up, Jess had spent more time in the shop than she had in their Virginia home.

After her mother had died in a car crash when she was seven, Jess's dad had thrown himself into his work. Jess didn't remember much about her mother except for a few flashes here and there—her wavy, blonde hair, the old denim shirtdress she always wore, the way she made a fresh batch of cookies every week.

I wonder if dad minded her hanging out around the shop.

There had once been an old polaroid picture in the shop of her mom and dad leaning over the doors of an old vintage car they'd fixed up back when they were dating. The turquoise husk of that car had been towed back to the garage after the crash, folded and burnt, and had sat in the back lot until her father had finally scrapped it when Jess was in high school. The polaroid disappeared soon after that.

But in the more immediate aftermath of the crash, Jess had needed someone to watch her after school, so she got used to a rotating schedule of mechanics that would come pick her up in whatever car was running at the time. She'd do her homework beside the tool bench with the smell of coolant and gasoline tickling her nose, and classic rock radio tweedling through an ancient boombox in the corner.

Eventually, though, she'd finish her homework and find herself standing over the feet of Chuck or Randy or Beau, leaning against the front bumper of a 1991 Honda Civic and handing sockets over when they'd call for a different size from underneath the oil pan. Before long, she was fixing up cars herself, and when she was fourteen, her father had presented her with a nearly totaled, champagne gold Ford Escort station wagon of her very own—provided she could make her road-worthy by the time she got her driver's permit.

A smile snuck across her face as she remembered the day she'd dragged her father into the garage, parked him in front of the newly-undented bumper as she slid into the driver's seat and turned over the engine. He'd been so proud of her, he'd hopped into the passenger's seat that very night to accompany her to buy a seat cover and a set of fuzzy dice for the rearview.

So many memories in this place.

"What you over there grinnin' about?"

Jess looked up at her dad's gruff scowl peeking out from under his bushy eyebrows and bushier beard.

"Hey pops. Just thinkin'."

"Humph."

"Humph," she echoed, furrowing her brow and crossing her arms over her chest as she glared at him playfully. He chuckled and crossed over to the tool chest.

"The boys leave a mess again?"

"Not a total mess. Just a few sockets out of place. Nineteen mil where the 7/8th goes, that kind of thing."

"Humph."

"You're 'humphing' an awful lot today. Did all the guys call in sick or something?"

He sat on a stool and let out a breath. "Nah. Actually gave all the guys the day off today. It's a Saturday, after all—day after Valentine's Day. Thought they might like some time with their families."

"Well, that was awfully nice of you." She waited. Ernie White didn't give his mechanics the day off out of the blue. Certainly not for something as silly as it being "the day after Valentine's Day."

"And you know, it's been a while since you and I had some time without a bunch of grumpy old men hanging around."

Jess snickered. "Daddy, you *are* the grumpy old man that hangs around."

"Hmph."

Jess eyed her father. "What's up, Dad? Did you want to talk about something?"

Ernie fiddled with the latches on the tool chest. "I think it's time we talk about your future, Jess," he began. He pulled up a stool and sat across from her. "Now I know you think you're not going to take on the shop when I'm gone, but the me and the guys were talking, and—"

"Ooooooh no, I'm gonna stop you right there, Dad," Jess interrupted, her conversation with Kyle still fresh in her mind. "First of all, you're not *going* anywhere. And secondly... I think it's time we talk about me not working here anymore."

"Whaddya mean?" He nearly fell off his stool.

Jess sighed. "Well, I've been thinking..."

"You know that's dangerous." His eyes twinkled a bit at their old joke.

"Dad. Come on." She rolled her eyes and took a deep breath. "I was talking with Kyle last night—"

"That the lacrosse player?"

"Baseball," Jess corrected. Ernie grunted. "Come on, dad. We've been dating six months. And he's expressed–well, not just him, almost everyone I've dated has said something like this–it's a little weird that I spend so much time here."

His bushy eyebrows pushed together in a scowl. "You work here."

"I know. But I'm not always going to work here," she twirled a tire pressure gauge between her fingers. "Shouldn't I find another place to work? Someplace where I fit in a little better?"

"You've got a place right here!" He placed a large, calloused hand on Jess's shoulder. "Jessie, is this Kyle guy putting ideas in your head? You haven't even brought this kid around to meet the other guys—"

"Dad, I'm not one of the guys!" She winced. She didn't mean that. "Kyle's not a kid. And I'm not a guy. I'm a grown woman. I grew up here, so of course I ended up hanging around, filling in and learning the ropes, but now…" Jess found herself rambling.

The truth was, she liked working at the garage. She loved the cars, the dirt, the grease–tinkering with tools and puzzling through problems. She'd been doing it for so long that she hadn't ever imagined her life *without* exhaust fumes in the air and grit under her fingernails.

They *were* like a family here at the shop. But none of the guys she'd dated had ever been comfortable with her working around a bunch of dirty old men, even if her dad was the owner. And if she were ever going to have a family of her own, a man of her own…

She studied her rough, dry hands. Between washing glasses at the bar and digging around in engines at the shop, she couldn't remember the last time her nails hadn't been chipped.

"I like working at the bar. I like talking to people. I think maybe I'm good at it, you know? Maybe that's more where I belong. Like the guy in *Cheers*."

"You wanna leave your family to swirl schnapps and talk to drunks, huh?"

Jess studied him. He was trying to hide his disappointment with his joking tone, but she could tell he wasn't thrilled by the prospect.

"Daddy, eventually I'm going to have to move out, you know. And if I'm ever going to start my own family…"

"Whaddya mean?"

Jess fiddled with a socket wrench. *How serious are Kyle and me?*

"Dad, Kyle mentioned that he's uncomfortable with me working around the guys all the time."

Ernie snorted. "Sounds to me like Kyle's not a good fit for you." They shared a look. He shrugged. "You don't have the best track record with guys, you know."

She threw down the wrench. Ernie picked it up and placed it where it belonged. She fumed at his indifference.

"Daddy, it's not fair of you to judge me for the guys I date."

"That's a little rich," he huffed.

Jess bristled. "It isn't! And if you really wanted me to stick around, you should be a little more respectful of that!"

He looked away from her and stood, shoving his hands in his pockets. "If you're so eager to get out of here, then maybe you should go ahead and move out. You're twenty-two now, after all. It's not like you're in college. Maybe it's time you made your own way."

"What, now?" Jess backpedaled, "I thought I'd save up a bit before I started looking–"

"How are you gonna save enough money to move out if you're not working at the garage? You plannin' on paying for an apartment on a bartender's paycheck?"

"Well… I…." Jess stumbled over her words. This conversation was not going at all how she'd planned. But if this was how he really felt about her and her boyfriend?

Maybe it was time for her to have her own space.

"You know what? Maybe you're right. I'll start hunting for a place. I can live on my own, Dad. It's not like I've never had to take care of myself." Jess pushed herself away from the tool chest and out of the garage toward her station wagon.

"Jess, wait a minute!" he shouted behind her.

But she didn't wait. She wrenched open her driver's door and climbed inside.

He didn't think she could live on her own, huh?

Well, I'll show him.

She ended up at the bar, several hours before she would normally get there for an opening shift, to take advantage of the free coffee and wifi. She sat in the half-lit, empty restaurant, scrolling through Craigslist at the various posts for affordable apartments within a half-hour drive of her job. There wasn't much.

She sent off a text to Kyle, telling him about the fight.

BF KYLE

Woah. Ur moving out?

ME

Guess so.

So that means I can start sleeping over at your place ;)

Assuming I can find a place I can afford…

I wish you could just move in with me. Maybe I can hide you under my bed?

Ha ha.

Jess considered asking around to see if anyone she knew was in need of a roommate. She wasn't looking to rent a whole house. She worked practically all the time, which meant she didn't spend much time at home in the first place. *Although, if I'm not at the garage anymore...*

She bit her lip as she scrolled. She wished she could just live with Kyle. That would be easier. She really only needed a bed and a shower, and maybe a shelf in the fridge.

Apartments in Virginia were all stupid expensive. The West Virginia apartments were all a little too rough-around-the-edges. And the places in Maryland... well, there were better options within her budget around there, but she also didn't know the neighborhoods as well, and they were farther away from Kyle's dorm. She didn't know how he would feel about driving an hour to get home from a booty call.

Jess slumped against the back of her bar stool, crossing her arms and glaring at her laptop.

"What are you doing here?" Jess heard Dave call out to her as the rest of the lights flickered on in the Potomac Bar and Grill. "You're not scheduled to open today."

"Hey Dave," she sighed, closing her laptop resignedly. "I know, but I needed to take care of some stuff, and I didn't want to do it at the house."

"Something wrong?" Dave walked up to Jess's table and plopped a box of napkins and silverware on it. She shifted her laptop into her bag on the floor to make room and helped Dave wrap table settings.

"Dad says I need to find my own place."

"Really?" Dave raised his eyebrows. "That doesn't sound like Ernie. I've always gotten the impression he liked having his little girl around."

Jess grimaced. "Dave, come on. I'm no one's *little girl.*"

Dave snorted. She wasn't sure if it was because she was just shy of five feet tall, a veiled criticism of her weight, or if it was meant to be a criticism of her sex life, but either way she let it slide.

"Or… at least, I'm not *his* little girl anymore. No matter how much he wants me to stay here for the rest of my life."

Dave looked up at her from his folding for a second. "Wants you to stay? I thought he was making you move out?"

Jess sighed, and met Dave's gaze. "I told him that I can't work at the garage anymore."

"I thought you loved working at the garage?"

Jess buffed a water spot on a spoon with the pad of her thumb. "Well, it's all I've ever really known. But maybe I've outgrown it. Kyle and I are starting to get serious now, and…" Dave didn't say anything, allowing her to reorganize her thoughts.

"He's being unreasonable, right? I mean, Dad had to know I wouldn't want to work for him my whole life. I mean, a girl's gotta do her own thing eventually! I want—"

She paused. What *did* she want, exactly? She loved having someone pay attention to her like Kyle did. She had been taking care of herself and her father for so long, on top of working two jobs. Maybe she was tired of always being the one to look after everyone else. And at the end of the day, it was nice to have someone taking care of her.

Dave continued to fold napkins. Jess paused in her wrapping, sifting through the muddy river of her feelings to try to unearth a nugget of clarity. The silence stretched; her prospecting was coming up short. Finally, Dave looked up.

"You know, Jess," he said at last. "It's not a bad idea to strike out on your own. But you should do it because *you* want to. Not just because your boyfriend or Dad is making you. You've never lived away from home, right?"

"No," Jess said, fumbling with the little sticky strips of paper they used to hold the table settings together.

"You learn a lot about yourself living on your own." Dave

handed her a stack of folded napkins, gesturing for her to keep wrapping. She did.

"'Course, you might need a roommate at first, and that's okay too. It'd be good for you, actually, maybe another girl your age. You don't really hang out with other girls much, do you?"

Jess shot her boss a sizzling glare, "You trying to say something there, Dave?"

Dave put his hands up as if she were a cop. "No, no judgment here, just an observation." As her shoulders relaxed, she heard Dave let out a sigh. "But you could stand to make some real friends. It's gonna be tough to find your way in the world without any."

Jess finished wrapping the remaining silverware and strapped her laptop bag across her chest. What was Dave even talking about? She had friends. Sheila, for one. And…

Well, she was dating Kyle, but he counted as a friend too, didn't he?

"I'm not working until eight tonight, am I?"

Jess had, in fact, known she was scheduled for the late shift that night. But she hadn't chosen to spend her day at the Potomac Bar and Grill so she could fold napkins with her boss. "I'll see you later, Dave."

Dave watched silently as Jess stomped her way toward the door. Maybe she could hang out at the dorm before her shift, instead.

CHAPTER 6

The fire had gone out. Again.

Shawn grumbled at the wood furnace in his grandpa's cabin as he once again loaded the nooks and crannies of the stove with kindling and newspaper balls. He needed to get the bigger logs to light before he could leave the house for the day, or else he'd come home to frozen pipes.

Despite its issues, Shawn loved living in his grandpa's old cabin in the woods of Harpers Ferry. When his grandfather's health had declined and he'd moved in with Shawn's parents, he'd asked his only grandson to watch over the home that he'd built for Shawn's grandmother over 50 years ago. It was a meticulously crafted one-story Adirondack-style chalet in the West Virginia mountains, complete with twenty acres of virgin forest and even a bubbling creek that ran through the property. The beauty and tranquility of the property was more than enough to make up for the mid-century appliances, finicky water heater, and antiquated electricity.

He cursed to himself as he lit a few matches and nudged them strategically into the wood stove. What he really needed was a better way to heat the cabin.

But heat pumps and mini-splits all cost money, and cash was something Shawn was regrettably short on at the moment. He'd made the impulsive decision last fall to trade the cost of his labor for his steadiest gig (updating Natalie's house in Maryland) for the vintage Bel Air that had been buried in her garage. So he hadn't made nearly as much money as he'd hoped to this winter.

Of course, there was still the occasional window replacement or painting gig that kept fuel in his truck, but those weren't enough to really build the handyman empire he'd dreamed of. His savings was the lowest it had ever been. And now it was February: smack dab in the middle of slow season with a record-setting cold snap that had seriously dampened his clients' enthusiasm for window replacements.

Shawn's phone buzzed. He caught some kindling on a teensy little flame and fed it into one of the newspaper balls before reaching into his pocket to check the message.

CUTIE FROM MCDS

Hey! Are we still painting today?

Natalie was checking in on him. His eyes flicked to the time in the corner of the screen. Shit. He was already half an hour late.

Yeah sorry, furnace went out. Just getting a fire going before I head over.

The paper in the stove had ignited, sending white tongues of fire lashing up the flue. He prayed the smaller logs would catch.

Oh shit. You okay? :/

Shawn smiled at his phone. One of the things he loved about Natalie was the fact that she genuinely cared about him. People say that city folk can be cold, but he hadn't found that to be the case with Natalie. The two of them had clicked since the moment she'd arrived in town last fall, and working with her on her house had been the main thing keeping him from going crazy all winter. She was his best friend.

And I'll never find another girl like her.

He frowned as the newspaper smoldered again. He blew against the charred remnants, ressurecting an echo of life back into the few remaining embers. He stacked in another couple of logs, opened the vents, shut the stove door closed, and prayed that it would last the day before finally heading out into the cold winter morning.

NATALIE HAD ALREADY GOTTEN STARTED when he arrived.

"Woah, Nat, what's all this?" Shawn laughed.

Natalie paused with her long-handled paint roller, attempting to manage the dripping paint as she struggled to find a safe place to put it down. "One second…"

Shawn grabbed a still-in-its-packaging drop cloth and ripped open the plastic wrapping. "You're supposed to lay these out *before* you pour any paint, you know." He unfolded the sheet in front of her, securing it to the floor by gently placing the over-filled roller tray on its corner. "I asked you to wait for me!"

She set down the sopping roller and its extension rod gratefully.

"It's painting, Shawn, I figured even *I* couldn't mess that up!" She put her hands on her hips and gave him an exasperated look.

He attempted to hold in a chuckle at the ridiculous picture she painted, in her tattered sweatpants, stained tank-top, and cheap plastic safety goggles. Her hair looked like she'd slept in it for three days straight, with locks of dirty blonde sticking up around her face and coming loose from the drooping bun that looked about three minutes away from falling out entirely. She was the most beautiful woman Shawn had ever seen.

And the most ridiculous.

"Did you at least watch the video I sent you?"

Natalie sighed. "Honestly, Shawn, I think you're making this more complicated than it needs to be." She reached for the roller. "Now can you help me take off this extension handle? I thought it'd make it easier, but I've almost knocked over the paint can, like, three times already."

Shawn slapped her hand away and carefully unscrewed the handle, bracing the roller against the side of the paint tray with the built-in hook. Natalie's eyes widened.

"That's so cool! I didn't know it had a *hook!*"

Shawn tipped his head at her and stifled another laugh. "That's why you shoulda watched the video, Nat."

A flush of red blotched her face as she sat back on her heels and wiped her sweaty bangs out of her eyes. "Fine, oh Great Master Painter. How should we proceed?"

Shawn began to reorganize the pile of painting supplies that he and Natalie had bought earlier that week. He noticed that the sander he'd insisted she get was still wrapped in its cardboard cover.

"Natalie." He nodded at the sander. "Did you sand before you started painting?"

Natalie winced, looking at the wall, and the haphazard swipes of paint she'd put there. "No?"

Shawn sighed.

"Well then *first* we have to wait for this paint to dry," he said. "And while we do that, we're gonna watch the videos I sent you."

Four hours, three sanding discs, and several YouTube tutorials later, Shawn and Natalie were finally ready to paint the dining room. No sooner had the doorways and windows been neatly framed with painter's tape, when they heard a couple of bangs on the front door.

"Food's here!" Bonnie's voice rang through the hall, as well as the crinkling sound of take-out bags. She parked a small feast of Chinese food on the counter and she and Natalie arranged the buffet of containers and sauce packets. Shawn lingered in the dining room, putting away the sanding supplies and tape to give the girls some time to greet each other before he made his way into the kitchen. He wasn't eager to watch them kiss hello.

"Sha-awn, *food!*" Natalie called.

"Coming," he shouted back.

"Will you at *least* think about it?" Bonnie was saying when Shawn finally made his way into the kitchen. He grabbed a paper plate off the stack that Natalie had set out and some chopsticks and began piling noodles and chicken onto it.

"I have to live here, Bons, remember? Part of the will conditions and all?" Natalie shifted in her chair, poking at her lo mein. "Your place is great, but I'm finally starting to feel at home here. I don't want to deal with the headache of moving again."

Shawn froze with a serving spoon of sweet and sour sauce suspended between its container and his plate. "Nat, you're not thinking of moving, are you?"

The mounded glop of sauce teetered precariously on the edge of the spoon as Bonnie and Natalie shared an uncomfortable look.

Finally, Natalie sighed. "Bonnie wants me to move in with her."

"Like I said, if I hadn't signed the full year of the lease, it would be a no-brainer for me to move here!" Bonnie said. "But it would only be for six months. You'd still be working on this place, so it's not like anyone would challenge you about the will."

Shawn just caught the spoon before the sauce dripped onto

the counter. He swallowed. This didn't seem like a conversation he should be a part of.

When Natalie had inherited her grandmother's house last fall, there had been a stipulation that Natalie had to live in the house. Otherwise, it would be left to her half-brother, who had almost driven Natalie out of the state with his personality alone.

But Shawn had convinced her to give the house a chance, and after a few improvements (and falling in love with Bonnie, of course), Natalie had decided to stay. She'd even been able to smooth things over with her half-brother somewhat when they settled the estate.

"Look, since Christmas, things with Ethan have gotten better, but they're still not great." Nat picked at her food, "I don't want to ruin the truce we've got going on. Besides, my budget's already starting to run low. I need to do as much of the work myself as I can on this place, which is way easier if I don't have to truck back and forth every day. And I really ought to start paying Shawn soon. Right?" Natalie turned to him. "You've more than earned that old car by now. I should be paying you your rate for all that you're doing, especially since you *still* haven't seen the boost in business that I promised you."

Since she'd decided to stick around, Natalie had been helping Shawn with his "online presence," as she'd called it. At first, it had seemed to be working. But then the holidays, followed by this record cold snap, had completely tanked his growing numbers. In the end, it didn't matter what kind of ads or specials he ran: nobody wanted to take on construction projects in the dead of winter.

"Aw, Nat," Shawn said. "It ain't your fault that it's the coldest winter in a century. Nobody wants work done on their house right now. And even if they did, I'm not so sure I'd want to be the one havin' to do it."

Natalie put down her fork. "But until you get some actual

good paying jobs, neither of us are making money. I'm about to start cold-calling places to see if they need a handyman!"

Shawn shrugged. "That ain't a bad idea, actually."

Natalie pondered it for a second.

"Natalie. Just... think about it, okay?" Bonnie seemed to concede temporarily, then slumped back in her seat and shifted her attention to her crab fried rice. Natalie picked up her chopsticks and they ate in silence.

Shawn shoved a few stick-fulls of lo mein into his mouth before finally realizing he couldn't take the tension anymore.

"Ah shit, ladies, I'm sorry, but I just realized how late it is. I have to stoke the furnace or I'm gonna come back to a freezing cabin—again." Shawn set down his Chinese and checked his watch, "Nat, can we paint tomorrow instead? I told my folks I'd check in on Granddad tonight."

He hadn't, but he had been meaning to catch his grandpa up on all the work he'd been doing on the car. He figured that the old man wouldn't mind him using the occasion as an excuse to get out of the most awkward dinner of his life. Natalie looked at the microwave clock.

"Aw man, it's practically dinner time, isn't it? I'm sorry, Shawn. This is all my fault. I promise I'll watch those videos again tonight so I'm ready to go tomorrow!" She smiled at him. "Thank you for all your help. Seriously."

Bonnie set down her plate. "Yeah, Shawn, we really couldn't do it without you."

Shawn's jaw twitched. "Right. Well, have a good night, y'all."

"G'night, Shawn!" Natalie stood and gave him a quick side-hug as he reached for his coat.

He didn't have it in him to squeeze her back.

CHAPTER 7

*J*ess spent the majority of the afternoon holed up in Kyle's dorm room, searching for apartments. But she soon realized that a building full of noisy, sweaty college students wasn't the best atmosphere for concentration. Especially when one of those students kept distracting her with his roaming hands. But he did buy her lunch while she was there, and they even fit in a quickie between his classes.

Eventually, though, Kyle left for training, and she didn't want to be stuck with only her boyfriend's awkward roommate for the next two hours.

So, she was back in the bar, cozied up in the corner of the floor between the overflow storage and the walk-in. Her laptop was perched on her knees, the hood of her sweatshirt was pulled up over her head, and she scrolled and dissected Craigslist ads for rooms to rent. She'd already looked over the same handful of places at least a dozen times. There just wasn't much inventory in her price range. Apparently, mid-February was not the time to find a new place to live.

She pulled on her hoodie strings and chewed on one of the ends.

"You know the floor is absolutely filthy down there, right?" Sheila paused on her way to the walk-in, propping a hand on her hip. "It's also 7:30. You're relieving me in half an hour."

"Right." Jess closed her laptop and stretched out the kinks in her shoulders and lower back. "Shit, how long have I been sitting here?"

"Two, three hours?" Sheila crouched down, a look of concern on her face. "What's up, hon?"

"Nothing." Jess tried to sound as nonchalant as possible, avoiding Sheila's eyes while she packed up her backpack. "I'm hungry. Are there any rejects in the kitchen?"

Sheila grinned. "There's an overdone steak that table six sent back. I was gonna feed it to Rufus when I got home."

Rufus was Sheila's eight-year-old English Bulldog.

"I'll just get a chicken sandwich or something before I clock in," Jess decided, smiling at Sheila. "I'd hate to deprive Rufus of a steak dinner."

"He might never forgive you. After all, he probably doesn't have too many of those left."

"Nah, he's a fighter. He's gonna keep trucking for another 20, 30 years at least."

"Want me to put in that chicken sandwich for you?"

"Please," Jess said gratefully. She climbed to her feet and swiped at the years of dust clinging to the butt of her jeans. "I'm gonna change for my shift."

"You got it."

BY THE TIME Jess had pulled on fresh jeans, yanked off her hoodie, and swiped on a bit of mascara in the employee bathroom, her dinner was waiting at the bar. She checked the time on her phone.

All right. Ten minutes to eat.

She had just taken a massive bite when a strong hand rested

on her shoulder. The scent of woodsmoke tickled her nose as a tall man leaned into her ear.

"That looks good. What is it?"

Jess jumped and whipped around. It was Shawn.

"Chi-hen." Wet crumbs flew out of her mouth and landed on Shawn's chest. Mortified, she wiped her hands on his shirt to brush them away, and got even more flustered when her fingers lingered on the deceptively firm muscles of his chest. She covered her mouth with her hand. "Shorry!" she said, still chewing.

Shawn raised his eyebrows at her and she swallowed.

"The signature chicken sandwich—it's great," she finally choked out.

"Is it hard to chew?"

She blushed. *I am making the biggest idiot of myself.* "N–no, you just took me by surprise..."

Realization dawned in his eyes. "Oh, shoot, no, I didn't mean anything like that!" Shawn rubbed the back of his neck and gave an awkward laugh. "I'm picking up dinner for me and my granddad. He can't chew too good anymore, but he misses the food here."

Oh. Jess blushed again, but not out of embarrassment. She hadn't known Shawn was so close with his grandpa. *That's really sweet.*

"What about the crab cake sandwich? It comes on sour-dough, usually, but you can get it on a regular bun. That should be a little softer."

Shawn's light eyes sparkled, and he gave her that smile she'd tried to get out of him the other night. "That sounds great. He'll love that."

Jess observed Shawn as he flagged down one of the new girls to place his to-go order. His light brown hair was longer than usual, the wavy locks beginning to fall into his eyes every so often. He seemed a little more tired than she remembered. His shoulders slumped forward when he backed away from the bar and found himself a stool beside her.

He met her scrutinizing gaze. "What's up?"

Maybe it was the fact that she wasn't clocked in yet, maybe the weight of her earlier argument with her father, but Jess couldn't seem to summon the unflappable, happy-go-lucky bartender persona she usually kept in her back pocket.

"I had a fight with my dad this morning," Jess sighed between bites, and set down her sandwich. It wasn't quite hitting the spot anymore. "He says I should move out."

She didn't mention anything about Kyle or her job at the garage. Shawn's eyes widened. "Aw man, really?"

"Yeah. So now I gotta find a room to rent. In February." Jess rolled her eyes. "I didn't realize what a tall ask that'd be around here."

Shawn nodded. "Yeah. Most of the rentals around here flip over in January or August—every now and then you can find a summer rental by the water…" He trailed off. "Sorry, a few of my clients own cabins."

Jess tilted her head. "Do you know anybody who might have a room available?"

Shawn frowned, scratching his chin. Jess stifled a giggle; she'd never seen someone her own age make such an old-man move look so genuine. It reminded her of the guys at the shop. A brief pang of nostalgia squeezed her heart.

The feeling passed as quickly as it came, with Shawn giving a sad shrug and shaking his head. "Nah, I can't think of any. But I'll keep an eye out for ya. Sorry you're dealin' with that."

"Thanks, Shawn." Jess gave him a sad smile, checked her watch, and wiped her hands on her napkin. "I gotta clock in real quick, but I'll be right back. 'Kay?"

She scooted her barstool back and grabbed her plate on her way to the kitchen. She passed the new girl (*Bethany? Beckie?*) walking out with a plastic bag in her hand.

"Two crab cake sandwiches?"

Jess looked back to see Shawn take the bag across the bar. He waved at her.

"Catch you later, Jess."

She raised her hand in a half-hearted wave, not sure what to make of the disappointment lodging itself in her chest. Not that she had time to reflect too critically before Sheila bounded up to her, handing her a bunched apron and an order pad.

"Just gave menus to tables fourteen and three, and seven's orders should be coming out any minute. Augie's waiting outside. Do you mind if I peace out a second early?"

Jess nodded, pushing thoughts of Shawn from her head and taking the order pad and apron. "No problem, girl. Have a good date!"

Sheila winked at her. "Oh, I plan to."

CHAPTER 8

Shawn knocked on his parents' front door. For once, the driveway was noticeably empty; his parents had decided to take Melanie and her fiancé out to dinner to celebrate their engagement.

"It's open!"

A wracking cough followed the gruff voice that drifted through the door. Shawn quickly made his way into the house and down the hall to the living room in time to pat his grandad's back encouragingly.

"I can't seem to shake this damn cough," he grumbled, wheezing slightly, "Whadja bring me?"

"Crab cake sandwich," Shawn held up the bag tantalizingly.

A sigh of happiness squeaked past his grandfather's cracked lips. "You've always been my favorite grandson."

Shawn smirked. "I'm your only grandson."

Another cough wracked his lungs. Shawn winced. "Still… counts." He choked out.

Shawn set the takeout bag on the coffee table and held the travel tumbler of water his mom had left by his grandpa's chair out to him. He took a sip from the proffered straw, and then held up his hand to say he was done. Shawn set the cup down and went to get the TV trays from behind the couch.

"So who's playing tonight?" Shawn called to him. "And don't shout, I can hear you just fine."

His grandpa took a slow breath. "Virginia Tech and WVU."

"Aw shoot, that's tonight? What's the score?"

"Still nothin'," he said as Shawn set up the tray in front of him. He pulled the top styrofoam container from the bag and opened it on the tray, then went to get napkins and silverware from the kitchen.

His parents house had an open layout, with the kitchen counter curving around into a peninsula to look out into the dining area and living room. A big screen TV hung on the wall opposite the kitchen, which made it perfect for watching football.

But since Grandad had moved in, there hadn't been as many game nights at the Cobb's house. Most nights, he was in bed before nine, and too much excitement wasn't ideal for his heart.

Shawn looked out into the living room and watched his grandpa fiddle with the cannula in his nose, removing it so he could eat his sandwich. Shawn hurried behind the couch.

"Wait, Grandad, I got you a fork and a knife."

"I can eat a sandwich, son," Grandad said softly. He paused to catch his breath.

It killed Shawn to see him like this. For as long as he could remember, his Grandpa had been the strongest man he'd known. He built the cabin Shawn lived in with his own two hands—had even chopped down the trees for the posts and beams himself. This was the man that had taken him racing for the first time, the man who had once manhandled a V8 engine block into an old '69 Mustang by himself, while a six year-old Shawn had looked on in amazement.

Twenty-four year-old Shawn bent over him now, placing the fork and knife on a folded paper towel on the side of his tray. "I know, Grandad. But the PB&G makes some pretty messy sandwiches. *I* was even thinkin' of forkin' this one." He smiled at him.

Grandad gave a cheerful wheeze. "Nice try, kid."

But after he sat down on the couch beside his grandpa's LaZBoy, Shawn saw his weathered hand reach for the utensils.

Shawn picked up the remote to turn up the volume on the game, but Grandad swiped a hand at him, gesturing for him to turn it back down.

"No, no," he said, "Tell me about the car."

Shawn muted the game and turned to his grandpa, removing his own sandwich from the bag. "The Bel Air?"

Grandad nodded.

"Ugh," Shawn groaned, "Well, it's in pieces right now,"

Grandad grunted around a bite of sandwich. He gestured with his thumb towards the kitchen, where a door led to the garage.

"Your mother was griping about that earlier," he said finally. He gave a small cough. "Could you...?"

He gestured weakly towards his water cup.

Shawn got up and held the straw out towards him again. His mom had bought Grandad one of those giant, 40-oz steel-walled tumblers for Christmas when the doctor had commented that he wasn't drinking enough water. The thing was, when it was full of water, it was too heavy for his Grandpa to actually lift. Shawn wondered with a pang of guilt how long Grandad had been waiting for him to bring dinner over. He waited for him to finish drinking, and then set down the tumbler.

"You want a different cup?" He asked.

The old man nodded.

Shawn went back to the kitchen and rifled through the cabinets to see if they had any styrofoam cups with the plastic lids left over from when Grandpa had first been released from the hospital. His mom had moved them all the way into the corner cabinet behind the cereal. Luckily, there were still a few left.

He grabbed one and filled it with water from the tap on the refrigerator. He didn't put any ice in it. Grandad hated ice.

He grabbed a silicone straw from the silverware drawer and plopped it in through the little fold-back tab on the lid. He set it down on the front edge of the TV tray, so it was well within his grandpa's reach.

"Thanks, Shawn," Grandad said. He looked at him with his watery blue eyes.

Shawn's grandpa didn't wear glasses. Except when he was reading, he didn't need them, even since the heart attack. Shawn sat back down on the couch and reached once more for his sandwich. At the last second, he remembered what he'd said and grabbed the fork and knife he'd gotten for himself and cut into the soft bun.

His grandpa's eyes didn't miss the gesture. "So it's in pieces?"

"It won't stay running." Shawn shrugged, cutting up his perfectly bite-able sandwich. "I figured there might be air in the gas lines, so I thought I'd take them all out again so I could clean 'em good…"

He shrugged, and forked a square of sandwich into his mouth. It was cold. Good. But cold.

His grandpa nodded, closing his eyes as he chewed. Shawn heard him pause to take a deep breath from his nose before he continued. He studied the TV screen without seeing the game.

"Carburetor didn't fix it?" Grandad asked.

"Nope," Shawn said around another bite, "I rebuilt the carb."

"All the cylinders firing?"

Shawn nodded, "As far as I can tell. When it *does* run, it seems fine at first, but then just sounds… choked. But the engine seems fine."

"Huh."

"Yeah."

They both chewed in silence for a minute, observing the game with the volume still muted. Shawn knew their heads were both in the garage.

Virginia Tech scored. Grandad shook his head.

"I'm not sure what you're doing wastin' a..." he took a breath, "Saturday night with *me.*" Shawn's grandpa gave him a look that 82 years hadn't withered. "Don'tchya got a girlfriend to spend weekends with?"

Shawn snorted, "Nah, not at the moment."

The look remained.

"Weren't you helpin' a pretty girl fix up a house not too long ago?" Grandad's lungs quaked with another breath as he steeled himself for another bit of crab cake.

Shawn sighed. "Still am. But she's got a gir–a sweetie already," Shawn saved at the last moment.

Despite his feelings for Natalie, Shawn had no problems with her sexuality. His family, however...

Well, Shawn thought, glancing up at the crucifix hanging above the family portraits beside the mantel, *no need to cross that bridge without reason.*

Shawn's grandpa harumphed into his styrofoam. Shawn continued.

"I was there earlier, actually. We're friends, ya know? She's helpin' me with my business, too—teachin' me Facebook and marketing stuff. But with the weather... well, can't blame her for the weather, I guess," Shawn chuckled, attempting to lighten the mood.

Grandad's hand shook as he reached out for his cup. Shawn watched him out of the corner of his eye in case he still needed help, but he was able to navigate the straw and the lighter cup without incident. He sat for a moment after that, before eventually wrestling the cannula back under his nose and straightening slightly in his recliner. Shawn reached toward his tray.

"You all done, Grandad?"

Those blue eyes lingered on their grandson a moment. Shawn froze. He wasn't used to this level of scrutiny from his grandpa. But then again, with his parents or part-time home health assistants always milling around, he really hadn't had one-on-one time with him since his heart attack.

"You're too good a man sometimes, Shawn," he said at last, his voice less wavery, his eyes insistent. "You take care 'a yours, an' you're there for folks. You oughta have..." he paused to stifle a cough. Shawn reached out to pat his shoulder and the old man lifted a wrinkly hand to wave him away.

The fit passed, and he took another breath.

"Who's takin' care of you these days?" he finally asked.

Shawn looked down and shook his head. "Aw, Grandad, you know I don't need–"

"I didn't ask if you *needed* takin' care of!" The old man barked, sounding almost like his old self again. Shawn's head snapped up and caught a flicker of a familiar fire in his grandpa's eyes. He tensed, expecting another coughing fit to overtake the man, but none came. Instead, Grandad's spine straightened as he poked a gnarled finger into Shawn's forearm. "You need someone to look out for you for once, kid."

Shawn just nodded, eyes wide, not sure how to take this sudden resurgence of his grandpa's spirit. After a second, he grabbed the takeout box and silverware on the TV tray and carried it back into the kitchen. As he put the leftovers into the fridge, he spied a quick glance into the living room. Grandad was back to resting into the recliner with his eyes glued to the game: third down and three, WVU.

Shawn didn't think he needed someone to take care of him. He actually enjoyed taking care of his friends and family. And while he knew that Grandad was grateful for him, he wished he could find someone his own age who could appreciate him.

At the beginning of their friendship, Natalie had been that person. She'd been super grateful for all his help—still was, really. They'd helped each other: her with his website, the car, and managing his social media, and him with her house.

But with fewer jobs to do, there were fewer pictures to take, and less material to market. Now here he was, keeping himself busy by tweaking a car he couldn't pay to fix, heating a house he couldn't afford to repair, and spending his Saturday night making sure his Grandpa had dinner while the rest of his family celebrated his sister's engagement.

He knew he had more to give, but he was tired of only giving to family or friends, without getting much in return. What he really needed was a partner. Someone who was a real match for him, like he once thought Natalie could be.

Is there even another girl like that out there for me?

He helped his grandpa get ready for bed after the final quarter, and once he was safely tucked into his hospital bed and his parents had come home, he drove his rickety truck the twenty minutes back to his cold house and its dead furnace.

He resurrected the fire and curled up alone on the couch in front of the woodstove for another night alone.

CHAPTER 9

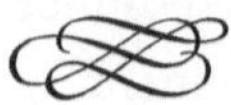

The rest of Jess's shift was a blur of rowdy tables of community college students, fried nachos, and Jaeger Bombs. Between training the newbie (*Elizabeth! But goes by Liz. Beth? Fuck.*) and juggling the onslaught of Valentine's Day rejects hovering over the two of them behind the bar, Jess didn't have a second to spare worrying about her housing issues.

It wasn't until Jess noticed that she was alone behind the bar and most of her clientele had headed out for the night that she looked at the big, neon Budweiser clock above the liquor shelves. 1:42.

"Last call!" She hollered over the lingering noise of the jukebox and an impromptu pool tournament. The announcement went largely ignored, which she was grateful for. It was never fun to cut somebody off and call taxis when it was negative balls degrees outside.

She glanced around to find Elizabeth to start going over closing responsibilities.

Huh. Where'd she get off to?

A quick scan of the floor didn't yield any different results. After drumming her fingers on the bar top for a minute to make sure there weren't any last call stragglers, she walked over to the swinging door that separated the front of house from the kitchen.

She peeked her head in. "Elizabeth?"

"Beth is fine," a small voice floated from the corner near the walk-in where Jess had sequestered herself with her laptop earlier. Jess walked over and crouched down to see Beth, curled up with her knees to her chest and her hair covering her face.

"Beth, honey, what's wrong?"

The tiny girl sniffed and pushed some brown strands behind her ears. Her cheeks were patchy with red, and her eyes swollen from crying. Then Jess heard someone call out from the bar.

"Stay right there." Jess crossed back through the swinging door and donned her bartender face again. "Closing your tab?"

"What happened to the other girl?" The guy was leaning too far over the bartop, and looked like he could use a shower. Clumps of his hair stuck to his forehead and the oak bar groaned as he pushed his full weight into it. "She said she'd give me her number."

Ah. So he's the cause of the waterworks. "Did she now? You sure she didn't say she'd get you the number of a barbershop for that situation on your head?"

Two other guys waiting to close their tabs sniggered. Greaser seethed.

"Why don't you get her out here so she can tell you herself?" He sneered. Jess snorted.

"Yeah, that's gonna be a no from me," Jess answered, "But tell ya what: if you settle your tab, get your credit card back, and head home without being any more of a bossy pants I won't call the cops on you."

"You little bi-"

"Woah now, Garrett." Kyle wedged his way through the group that had gathered along the bar and placed a large hand on Greaser's shoulder. It looked like the whole community college's baseball team was gathered around the bar. "She probably headed home already. It is closing time after all."

Jess shot him a grateful smile.

"His tab is under Miller," Kyle nodded to her.

"You got it," Jess said, ignoring the glare on Greaser's face.

She finished up closing the tabs, and let Kyle and the rest of the baseball team help usher out the stragglers. At 2:06, the place was just about cleared out.

Kyle came up to the bar across from Jess after the last customer had shuffled out the door.

"They really oughta have someone working security when it's just you and the girls working," he said to her. He leaned his elbows on the polished oak and gave her a concerned look. "Some of these guys can be real jerks."

Jess grabbed a towel and dried glasses while she responded. "Did you see him say anything to Beth?"

Kyle shrugged. "He wasn't hanging out with us. I've just seen him around campus. He's a weirdo."

"Thanks for the save."

"Well, yeah," Kyle eased up and slowly worked his way around the bar. He lifted the divider, crossing behind her and placing a hand on her waist. "I care about you, babe. The last thing I want is to see you get hurt."

Jess stiffened in his hold. She wanted to go check on Beth, and with all the hubbub Jess hadn't gotten even halfway through the closing checklist. She set down the towel and the shot glass she was polishing and turned around to face him. She placed her hands on his chest.

His eyes sparkled and crinkled at the corners in response.

"Thanks, Kyle. Really. But I gotta close up here. Check on Beth."

The sparkle snuffed out. "She's still here?"

"Yeah. And it's late. You should go home." She patted his pecs and turned, pulling away from him. He grabbed her wrist.

"Jess, why don't you come over again tonight?" He asked quietly. "I miss you. We could replay our adventures from this afternoon…"

Jess let him pull her back into his arms. He'd protected her tonight, and she was grateful, but she wasn't in the mood to spend another night smooshed in Kyle's twin bed, getting jerked awake by his roommate's sleep apnea.

But it wasn't all bad. She'd have her boyfriend, and she wouldn't have to risk running into her dad. She wasn't ready to face him yet, and was too proud to admit that he'd been right about how hard it would be to find an apartment.

Jess weighed her options.

"Yeah. That'd be nice."

Kyle's face lit up. Then he scratched at the back of his neck and gave an embarrassed chuckle.

"Um, gimme an hour to pick the place up? We all pregamed there before watching the game…"

Fantastic.

"Of course," Jess sighed, "It'll take me about that long to finish up here."

"Perfect." He bent down to give her a kiss at the same moment she'd bent to pick up a toppled shot glass, and his lips landed on the side of her head. He laughed, and grabbed her up again in a hug, planting her with a firmer kiss. She returned it, then disentangled herself to get back to her closing tasks. "I'll see you soon."

He practically skipped out of the restaurant. She shook her head and locked the door behind him.

Time to check on Beth.

CHAPTER 10

Something smelled.

Jess squinted her eyes against the too-bright winter morning sunlight streaking in through the curtains. The only thing keeping her perched on Kyle's extra-long twin bed was his extra muscular arm wrapped around her tummy pouch, squeezing her bladder uncomfortably and pinning her ass up against a *very* apparent erection.

She stayed as still as possible, legs and torso still half-falling off the edge of the bed while her eyes darted about the room, attempting to locate the source of the odor that had awoken her. At last, they settled just below her to a small trash can that had been kicked over in front of the nightstand, spewing forth several blackened banana peels, roughly two cases' worth of empty beer cans, and, she winced, what seemed to be more than a dozen used condoms.

Okay, I need to get out of here.

Delicately, she moved Kyle's abnormally large hand down her leg and slowly off of her body, relieving the pressure on her bladder slightly. Luckily, her weight was already mostly off of the mattress, so it didn't shift much as she rolled onto the balls of her feet and caught herself with her hands on the cheap carpet. She swiftly gathered up her bra, flannel, jeans, socks, purse, and boots and snuck out of the room before Kyle could wake up.

Once out in the hallway, she bolted in bare feet to the dorm bathroom, keeping on tip-toe to avoid making too much noise. Then she slid into the handicapped stall to put on her clothes.

I can't wait until I don't have to sneak around like this anymore, she mused to herself while she dressed in the echoey restroom. The swinging doors leading out into the hallway were left propped open all hours of the day and night, making this only a temporary hiding place from the dorm's many male residents. She was mostly concerned about running into any of the exes she'd spent a night with in this building.

Christian. Devon. Jeremy. Hayden lived on the 3rd floor, so she wasn't likely to run into him at this hour. Plus it was a Sunday, so she reasoned she was pretty safe from running into any college boys while she ran to her car at—she checked her phone—6:48 a.m.

She fired up her Ford Escort and let the engine warm up in the extra-frigid morning. She shivered in the driver's seat while the car slowly acclimated. The fans rattled loudly when she cranked the heater on full blast, joining the cacophonous symphony that was the background of Jess's life. She pulled out her phone and plugged it into the charger she had permanently lodged into the cigarette lighter. Then she scrolled through her notifications.

She had a page like invite on Facebook. From Shawn.

Huh, she thought, clicking the link and looking over the posts about his contracting business, *these look good.* He was awfully talented for such a young guy. She liked and followed the page.

A minute later, as she was about to back out of the campus parking lot, her phone dinged with a message. *Aw shit. Did Kyle wake up?*

SHAWN COBB

Thanks for the like!

Jess breathed out a sigh of relief, and then smiled. She checked the time again. 7:12 a.m. So he was an early riser. She remembered their talk at the bar the previous night, and wondered how his grandpa had liked the crabcake sandwich.

JESS WHITE

Yeah! How's your grandpa?

Good! He had a good night.

Jess's lip twitched. She wondered how many nights were "good nights" for Shawn's grandpa.

Jess had never really known her grandparents. All of them had passed away before she was old enough to understand what "passing away" meant, and she didn't have too many memories of spending time with them. Jess remembered her mom, but even those memories had become cloudy and gray with mental cobwebs over the years. Her only family these days was her dad and the rest of the mechanics at the shop. And even that felt like it was rocky at the moment.

Jess decided not to pry.

That's good :) It's nice you two are so close.

Jess then sent Kyle a quick text to let him know she was sorry she had to leave early. She wasn't particularly, but she didn't want to seem rude. She just really couldn't stand the smell of his garbage can under her nose any longer.

The Potomac Bar and Grill was closed on Sundays, so she

had the day off. Her dad was likely already heading for the garage by now, as he usually worked the weekends. She'd still hunt down a place to stay as quickly as possible, but until moving day she was going to act like the responsible daughter that she was.

Which meant she would do what she always did on the weekends: clean the kitchen and bathroom and prepare a casserole to have ready when her dad got home. Then he'd realize how much he actually needed her around and would miss her when she left. And wouldn't he feel stupid.

But first, she'd shower.

Yep, she thought, sniffing the remnants of college boy sweat clinging to her Orioles sweatshirt. *Shower first, benevolent vengeance later.*

Freshly bathed, clothes changed, and face made, Jess emerged from her room like a new person. She tossed a load of laundry into the washer and loaded up the dishwasher, then chopped onions while playing music on her laptop. She scrubbed down the countertops while her hamburger casserole cooked in their ancient oven. By the time the timer dinged, she had her dad's work shirts hanging to dry in the laundry room, the kitchen cleaned, and the bathroom presentable. She pulled out the casserole and let it cool on a potholder on the stovetop.

The mindless domesticity had her in a better mood. Jess had abandoned her phone to its charger while she cleaned, and disconnecting herself had allowed her to come to peace with her and her father's fight. Nothing had really changed; Jess was still determined to find a new place as soon as possible. But she felt less awkward about her current habitation of her father's house, especially after spending the morning and most of the afternoon making it feel like home.

She stared at the box of donuts she'd picked up as a peace

offering on her way home. Her dad would probably be home any minute. She plucked her phone from the charger and checked her notifications.

A text from Kyle. The emailed work schedule for the week. A few Facebook marketplace notifications about some cars for sale. And another Facebook message from Shawn.

What does Shawn want?

Jess clicked on the speech bubble icon and brought up their conversation.

> Talked with Natalie today. She might be looking for a roommate!

Jess's eyes widened. *Natalie?* Shawn's lesbian friend from L.A.? The one he had a crush on?

> She doesn't live with her girlfriend?

> Eh, it's "complicated". Family lawyer, angry brother, long story :P

Jess pondered that. She wasn't too keen on getting in the middle of something 'complicated'. But she also knew that Natalie wasn't crazy, she lived nearby (enough), and Shawn had been working on her house, so it was probably in pretty good shape.

> How much is rent?

> Natalie's thinking $600/month?

Jess's eyes almost popped out of her head. Six hundred a month was *half* of what she'd been seeing listed on Craigslist for one bedrooms.

Jess could actually *afford* that, even without working at the garage.

SOLD.

The sound of the front door opening and closing caught her attention, and the clomping of her father's workboots approached. She looked up as he entered the kitchen and watched his eyes scan the room.

"What's all this?" he grunted, his gaze finally landing on the Krispy Kreme box in front of her.

"Dinner and dessert," Jess answered coolly. She wasn't used to this kind of tension around her dad. Normally, she'd jump up and give him a hug when he came home. But then again, they normally didn't fight.

"Is that yer famous hamburger casserole?" Her dad asked, as he clambered over to the stovetop. He sniffed appreciatively.

Jess stretched her arms over her head and closed her laptop. She got up from her chair and walked over to the counter and the stove, grabbing a serving spoon and some forks from the silverware drawer and a couple bowls from the cabinet. "I thought it'd be nice to have dinner together. So we could talk."

Ernie nodded. He took the serving spoon from her and dug in, portioning himself out a healthy mountain of beef, cheese, and noodles.

She realized with a pang that when she moved, she wouldn't be cooking for two anymore. *No more Sunday casseroles with Dad...*

Ernie handed her the spoon. She served herself and they sat together at their four-person white oak dining table.

"I think I found a place," Jess ventured as she picked at the noodles in her bowl, "up by Hagerstown."

Ernie grunted. "Not with Kyle, I hope."

Jess rolled her eyes. Her dad hadn't been involved in her love life since she'd briefly dated Randy's son a few summers ago, and nearly toppled Ernie's Garage with the drama that had ensued. While at first Ernie had been purposefully ignorant of

Jess's love life, he'd realized when he'd walked in on Jess and the boy making out in the employee bathroom of the shop one day that he needed to retain enough awareness to set some ground rules.

"No neckin' in the shop!" He'd roared at her after closing down early that afternoon to drive her home, "And no nothin' with any of my boys or their kin, you hear me??" Later that night, he'd knocked on her door to deliver a box of condoms: shoving it into her hands with a gruff, "And use these if your gettin' frisky. Make sure you always bring your own," before stomping away as fast as he could without crashing into the door.

And, for her part, Jess had obliged. She may have massaged the definition of "kin" to her advantage when she'd hooked up with Beau's first cousin at his wedding reception last June, but in the five years since she'd been caught in the employee bathroom, she'd learned to select more discreet locations for her "canoodling," as Ernie called it. And she was always safe—using condoms and getting an IUD as soon as she'd been old enough to sign off on the doctor's forms without a guardian present.

Her dad wasn't completely clueless, however. He knew that Jess and Kyle had been dating for a while, and that she spent the night with him more often than not. But for the most part, the father and daughter had elected to keep their discussion of Jess's sex life to an absolute minimum. And this suited them fine.

So Jess bristled at the offhanded commentary from her father.

"No, Dad, not with Kyle." she corrected, flustered. "A friend of mine lives in her grandma's old house—she wants a roommate to help her out with renovations and stuff. Seems like a good fit for both of us."

Ernie looked up from his bowl. Something flashed in his eyes–was it disappointment?—that Jess couldn't quite put a finger on. It was gone as soon as she tried to identify it, clouding back over with his usual surly nonchalance once again.

"That happened quick," he mused.

"I've been hunting nonstop."

That look again—so quick Jess almost missed it. Was he disappointed in her? That didn't make any sense. She'd done exactly what he'd asked: found a place to live, with someone *other* than her boyfriend. What did he have to be disappointed about?

He wolfed down the rest of his casserole in a few large bites and pushed out his chair. He patted her shoulder as he got up from the table, and paused.

"Thanks for dinner, Soo-Soo. I'm gonna miss yer cookin'."

Jess's heart squeezed at his old nickname for her. "Soo-Soo" was the name baby Jess had earned back when her dad would set her up in the Pack n' Play in the garage. Both her parents had worked when she was little, and Ernie had taken her to the garage before they could afford daycare. When she'd been learning to talk, Ernie, Randy, and Chuck would all hold up tools and try to get her to name them. "Wrench," "power drill," and "jack stand" hadn't elicited much more than a couple of confused gurgles.

"Scroo-dry-verr," Ernie had sounded out to her one day, holding a flathead above the playpen.

"Soo…"

"Scuh-rooo duh-rye verrrrr,"

"Soo-soo!" squealed the baby Jess. And she'd continued to shout "Soo-Soo!" with glee every time one of the mechanics walked by with a screwdriver in their hand. Or so the story went.

Jess watched her dad rinse out the bowl in the sink and place it in the top rack of the dishwasher. She'd hated that nickname for the longest time. But somehow, it had stuck around long enough to wear her down, until eventually it was no more annoying to her than the rattle of the heater in her Escort. It was just… a part of home.

He gave her a small, sad smile before making his way out into the living room, where she heard him click on the TV and settle into his chair for the night.

He hadn't even opened the donuts.

CHAPTER 11

Shawn looked at the phone in his hand as Natalie sprayed the paint rollers in the sink. The dining room was finally painted, and Shawn had to admit—the fresh white of the walls really did make the place seem bigger. His shoulders hurt from craning his neck in the corners when he cut the ceiling. But his day with Natalie had gone surprisingly well. Since the walls had been primed properly and Bonnie wasn't interrupting them with Chinese food, Shawn had finally had a productive day with his friend again, and he'd been able to propose an ingenious solution to her "I'm-not-ready-to-move-in-with-Bonnie" problem.

Why not get a roommate? Shawn suggested, ever the helpful friend, *it'll also help you bring in some money to cover some of these renovation costs!*

Natalie had been spending money much more quickly than it was coming in. Even with her house being paid for, she still had living expenses to consider. And as long as Shawn's business wasn't making any money, Natalie had little hope of getting a paycheck for all the marketing work she was doing for him. Shawn's solution fixed some of that problem for her, he reasoned. And, of course, kept Bonnie away.

A slight twinge of guilt poked at Shawn's throat. He didn't really hate Bonnie. He just felt that it was too soon for his friend to move in with her girlfriend. They'd only been dating a few months. Plus, Bonnie was her lawyer! Natalie was right. It would look suspicious for her to move out this soon. And with Natalie's family situation being as complicated as it was…

> How much is rent?

Shawn read the latest text from Jess. Here was the real stroke of genius to his plan: he was helping two of his friends at once. Jess needed a place to live, and Natalie needed an excuse to keep Bonnie at arm's length. Once again, Shawn was here to save the day.

"Hey Nat!" Shawn said, speaking loudly so his voice would carry over the rushing faucet, "How much do you think you'd want to charge Jess for rent?"

Natalie bit her tongue while she thought about it. Some droplets of paint-water splashed up on her face and she flinched and spit out the ones that landed on her tongue.

"Bleaugh!" she coughed, "Uh, I don't know. She'd get Grandma's room with the en-suite, so that's worth something. But we'd share the kitchen and stuff…" She thought for a second, turning the force of the water back slightly and shrugging her shoulders.

"Does $600 sound fair?" She asked.

He nodded enthusiastically.

"Let's say $600, then."

> Natalie's thinking $600/month?

The next two minutes were the longest in Shawn's life, and he held his breath for every second of it.

SOLD.

"Well I got good news for you, Nat!" Shawn drawled, coming up closer to her and rolling out some paper towels to dab the rollers dry.

"Do you?" Natalie raised her eyebrows, eyes still on the rivulets of white paint water streaming from the rollers. She rubbed her hands up and down the fluff, trying to squeeze the last of the pigment out.

Shawn swallowed, trying not to think too much about what that looked like. "Uh, yeah," he cleared his throat. "Jess White is going to be your new roommate!"

"She's the bartender from the PB&G, yeah?" Natalie looked up as she handed him the mostly clean roller. He wrapped it in some paper towels as he took it from her.

"Yeah! Her dad's kicking her out. And she's havin' a tough time, what with it being February and all."

"That's rough. She's always seemed really nice. How well do you know her?"

Shawn decided to stretch the truth a bit. "She and I go way back! She's great. Hard worker, really nice..."

Rack, he was about to finish, but instead he just let the thought trail off. His mind was in the gutter after watching Natalie rub her hand up and down the paint rollers. Besides, even though he assumed that Natalie, as a bisexual woman, could appreciate a good rack, he wasn't exactly ready for the two of them to venture into "locker room talk".

And Jess *was* nice. So nice, she'd even followed him out to his truck on Valentine's Day to make sure he was good to drive. And she was one of the only people he knew who worked as hard as he did.

"Hmm. I've never been a landlord before," Natalie mused, attacking the next roller with gusto. Shawn watched her hands pump up and down under the stream of water. With every ounce of his willpower, he forced his eyes up to her face.

"I'm sure you'd be great at it. It can't be that–" he swallowed. "–Hard."

"You know what?" Natalie turned off the water suddenly and faced Shawn. She held her arms out to him, and he panicked for a split second before realizing she was reaching for a paper towel to dry her hands. He handed one to her, cursing the heat he felt rising to his cheeks. "We should sit down and talk with her. It would be nice to have the extra income to help pay for supplies, and to be able to split utilities, especially with how cold it's been. The electric bill alone!"

Natalie smiled at him, and Shawn smiled back at her.

He had only been half listening. He'd been distracted thinking about Natalie's hands… and Jess's tits.

What the fuck is wrong with me? Both of these women are taken. Keep it in your fucking pants, dude!

"Well, great! I'll text her."

"Thank you so much, Shawn. Can you ask her if she can meet this week?"

"Yeah!" Shawn nodded and refocused on the task at hand. He was going to get Natalie a roommate. Jess was going to move in here. He was fixing Natalie's and Jess's problems, supporting them both, and being a good friend.

A really good… friend.

SHAWN BREATHED in deep when he entered his parents' garage later that afternoon, the smell of dinner cooking in the kitchen giving way to the pungent odors of gasoline and motor oil. The Bel Air sat, partially dismantled, in the far end of the garage, covered by a couple of dark green tarps. Shawn uncovered the vintage beast, once again admiring the robin's egg blue of the original paint job, the bright shine of the chrome, and the sheer size of the front frame. He raised the hood, running his hands along the sleek lines jutting out from the front headlights. Beautiful.

The engine was in pieces, stacked in an organized pile atop a beach towel so nothing would roll away. The block itself was hanging from a wheeled stand that perched in the back corner of the garage. Shawn still needed to polish it with parts cleaner and double check that everything was in order. He thought he'd gone through it with a fine tooth comb, but after talking with Granddad, he had decided he needed to take a magnifying glass to it to check the cylinder wall and the head gasket for cracks again.

"You're actually home for Sunday dinner?" Melanie walked into the chilly garage, shivering as she hunted for the kerosene heater their grandpa had used in his old workshop for as long as either of them could remember. The workshop at the cabin was chock-full of old parts, lawnmowers, and various equipment that Grandad used to tinker with. Shawn had yet to get in there to organize.

"I was inspired," Shawn said, plucking a wire brush from the tool chest and grabbing some foaming agent. "Caught a glimpse of summertime and it made me wanna fix up my new ride."

And I've got nothing better to do on a Sunday night than have dinner with my family and check on my granddad. He held back a sigh and forced a cheesy grin on his face for his sister.

"Maybe you can even drive me to the wedding in it," Mel winked at him. Shawn's already tight smile twitched. He'd almost forgotten about his sister's impending wedding.

Does everybody have someone except for me?

Mel found the heater and flipped it on. The *tonks* and *sissts* and crackles of the metal sang a percussive soundtrack to

Shawn's tedious spritzing and scrubbing, and Mel sat on an upturned bucket, watching him.

"Can I help you with somethin'?" Shawn cast her a quizzical glance and dropped a bolt in a plastic bowl of mineral spirits.

"I'm just watchin' my brother be a grease monkey," she drawled, crossing her legs at the knee and blinking innocently at him. Melanie and Shawn had both grown up with a bit of a country accent, but since Mel had gone off to school she'd lost some of her twang. Shawn noted its return, and suspected she wanted something. "Mom missed you at church today."

Shawn rolled his eyes. "Ah, Mel, you know I ain't been goin' to church for months now."

"Yeah," Mel's eyes twinkled conspiratorially, "Not since that city girl came to town."

"Her name is Natalie," Shawn said flatly, "And there's a lotta work to do on that house of hers. I been busy."

"Busy, huh?"

Shawn clunked down his wire brush. "Melanie, what the hell're you on about?"

Melanie's eyes darted to the floor. Shawn saw pink creep up her neck and to her cheeks.

"Have you… have you ever, like…" She fidgeted. Shawn gave an exasperated sigh.

"Spit it out, Mel!"

"Have you ever had," she shifted her voice to a whisper, "sex?"

Shawn blinked at her. *What is it with all these women asking me about my sex life?* He quickly looked down and picked his wire brush back up. "I skip church a coupluh fuckin' times…"

"Shawn!" Melanie's breath hitched, "language!"

Shawn rolled his eyes. "We're adults, Mel. My mouth ain't half as bad as the other guys I've worked with."

"Well," Melanie fidgeted. Again.

"And keep yer damn legs still! What's got into you all of a

sudden?"

Shawn glared at his sister. He'd mostly been in a good mood, having a mostly good day, and now he was minding his own business working on his car. He'd solved some problems for his friends, and his furnace hadn't gone out. He was about to get free dinner from one of the best cooks in the Eastern Panhandle. He was trying to keep his mind *off* of sex. The last thing he wanted to do was talk about his lack of sex life, *with his sister.*

Melanie groaned. "Christopher."

Shawn's eyes narrowed. "He do somethin' to you?"

Shawn wasn't the aggressive or possessive type, but he wasn't about to let *anyone* do something to his sister she wasn't into.

"No! No, nothing like that," Melanie backpedaled, "I mean, I love him, Shawn! He's my fiancé!"

"Yeah, yeah, we all know he's your *feeyonsay*," He said, drawing out the last word. He breathed out in relief, grateful his little sister was okay. He'd never admit it, but he loved Mel something fierce. If anything bad ever happened to her...

He took another deep breath and focused on his cleaning. "So... what about Christopher?"

Melanie's shoulders relaxed a bit. "Well. I mean, we're engaged now, and, I mean, in the eyes of God and all..."

Shawn knew where she was heading with this, but he wasn't about to make it any easier for her. He kept his mouth shut, allowing her to figure out what she was trying to say.

"I want to... I want *him* to... well," Mel let out her breath in a huff, "Shawn! You know what I'm trying to say, don't cha?"

Shawn smiled to himself as her accent returned, genuinely this time. He turned his eyes at her innocently, mirroring her doe eyes from earlier. "Whatever do you mean, Melanie?" he asked sweetly.

She glared at him. "Fine, Shawn. What's a girl do to make a guy... *feel good?*"

Ah, fuck. She got there. Shawn's shoulders tensed now that the question was out in the open. The image from earlier, the one forever burned into his brain, of Natalie cleaning the paint rollers flashed before his eyes. He cursed whatever meaty part in his head controlled his subconscious.

He swallowed.

"Ah, Mel," he went to rub the back of his neck, but then remembered his hands were covered in grease and mineral spirits. "Ain't you got girlfriends you can talk to about this stuff?"

"Oh yeah, Shawn, I'll call up the youth group."

They shared a look.

What Shawn didn't share with his sister was that he was about as clueless as her when it came to knowing about anything sexual. Probably even more so, given that *he* was single. He talked a good talk, of course—you couldn't be a teenager in technical school without picking up the lingo. But he and Mel both had been raised in a church-going family. Since he'd moved into their granddad's house and stopped going to church, he'd definitely modernized his ideas around sex: he didn't think he'd burn in hell for jerking off anymore, and he certainly wasn't about to crucify any of his friends over any of *their* sex lives. But the teachings ran deep when it came to his own comfort with intimacy.

Heat rushed to his face as he recalled Jess in the bar on Valentine's Day, leaning over the bar with her chest pressed against the wood.

"When was the last time you got laid, Shawn?"

He was suddenly very aware of the zipper of his jeans. He shifted his hips a little, attempting to be subtle while he adjusted himself.

Jeezus, don't be gettin' a chubby in front of your sister. The mental reminder of the setting helped to calm him down a bit. The pressure in his stomach lessened, and he settled into a more comfortable stance behind the workbench.

Shawn cleared his throat. What were they talking about? "Have you, uh… tried any… hand… stuff?" He winced. He *really* hated talking about this.

Mel shook her head, blushing. She fidgeted with her hands. "What… what do you—how do you—start… that?" she finished lamely.

Shawn closed his eyes. *Why* did Melanie have to ask *him* about this stuff? He cursed their sheltered upbringing.

"Geez, Mel, I don't know," Shawn replied, "I assume things have gotten hot and heavy with y'all before, when yer kissin' and stuff, right?"

Melanie nodded reluctantly. Shawn figured their conversation was already as awkward as it had ever been, he might as well jump in the deep end. What kinds of stories had he overheard in the bar about this kind of stuff?

Thinking of the bar made him think of Jess. If it were *her* having this conversation, and she didn't have a boyfriend, what would he want her to do?

"Well, next time yer kissin, and rubbin' on each other…" he swallowed, "Just… reach for it. See if… well, see if he's into it. And if he is, then… well, go for it, you know?"

He looked at her. His poor sister looked embarrassed, curious, guilty, and terrified all at the same time. He couldn't stand to see her look so helpless.

"Ah, geez," He huffed, "Mel, you like him, right? He likes you?"

"Of course!" She insisted, her voice raising, "I just want to…" She sighed. "I want to give him everything, you know?"

At her words, the image of Jess solidified in his mind, wearing her flannel shirt tied at the waist, her curves full on display. The idea of a girl like her "giving him everything" shot through his spine like a shock from an electrical outlet. The pressure in his jeans was back.

I need to hang out with more guys, Shawn decided, wincing a bit as he shifted his legs again. Between Natalie rubbing down paint rollers and Jess asking him about his body count, his brain had far too much ammunition to lob at him with this conversation. It was making it hard to think straight. He thanked the Lord God for the workbench hiding his lower half from his sister. There wasn't any pulling back this time; he could *feel* his dick pressing into his leg.

"Well, then," Shawn cleared his throat. His voice had gotten husky all of the sudden. "I mean… I don't like to think about anyone touchin' my sister, of course, but, maybe let him, uh, return the favor… you know?"

He gestured lamely with the brush and the bolt he was cleaning in his hands. Melanie looked at him quizzically.

"You know." Shawn gave an exasperated sigh. "Let him squeeze the girls a bit?" He looked away and closed his eyes. Jess's cleavage flashed before his closed eyelids, and he almost groaned.

"Oh!" Melanie's face flushed scarlett, "You mean… *oh.*"

Shawn opened his eyes and did *not* like the look he saw on his sister's face.

"Gawd, Mel, keep it in your pants!" He grabbed a greasy rag and threw it at her.

"Eew, gross, Shawn!" She batted the rag away and jumped off of the bucket to head for the kitchen. "Mom said dinner in half an hour, so clean yourself up!" She looked back at him once she reached the door. "And… thanks, Shawn. I appreciate it."

"Yeah, well," He gave her a stern look that didn't quite reach his eyes, "Don't ever ask me again, y'hear?"

She snickered as she swept back through to the kitchen, closing the door behind her.

Shawn let out a breath he hadn't realized he'd been holding. His whole lower half throbbed, and he leaned his palms on the workbench and hissed through it.

Yep. Definitely needed more guy friends.

CHAPTER 12

The next day, Jess worked the opening shift at the Potomac Bar and Grill. It was especially slow, even for lunchtime on a Monday, which Jess attributed to the weather. Despite it being blue skies and sunny for the second day in a row, it was bitterly cold. At ten, when she'd left her dad's house, the weather widget on her phone had displayed a large minus four below a graphic of a cheerful, yellow sun.

She'd kept her coat on for the first hour of her shift while the restaurant warmed up, serving only two diehard regulars the soup and sandwich special. But even after they'd eaten and left, leaving the restaurant empty once more, a draft still whistled through the rustic wooden boards of the old building. *This place is a lot nicer when it's full,* Jess thought, teeth chattering, as she pulled the air out of the draught lines. The spring lagers were already shipping in, despite the icy chill clinging to the entire Potomac River Valley.

Her phone buzzed in her apron pocket. She glanced around the empty restaurant again before taking it out.

BF KYLE

Ur checking out the new place today?

She smiled. Shawn had reached out to her that morning to set up a walk-through with him and Natalie, and she'd excitedly texted Kyle the news that morning.

That's right! Pretty soon I'll have my own place! Well, kinda.

I like this independent woman ;) Can't wait to break in ur new bed together

The jingling bells of the front door sounded, announcing a whoosh of cold air, and she looked up to see Natalie, in a big puffy coat, a thick-knit hat, and rubber boots bounce inside, followed closely by a less flamboyantly-dressed Shawn. He stomped his boots on the rubber mats by the door and rubbed his arms up and down his khaki Carhartt, ears exposed and bright red from the wind.

"It's *freezing* out there," Natalie announced, as if Jess and Shawn had not also been enduring the negative temperatures. "I do *not* remember it being this cold when I grew up here."

"You grew up here?" Jess poured two cups of coffee for the newcomers. She plopped a melamine bowl of creamers and a sugar caddy in between the mugs, and poured herself a cup to drink black. She leaned against the back counter as they settled into their stools.

"Thank you," Natalie breathed gratefully. She peeled the foil tops off of a couple creamers and plucked a plastic stirrer from the caddy. "Yeah, I left once I graduated–got into UCLA and never looked back!" She took a sip and shrugged, "Well, haha, you know. Until my grandma died."

Jess nodded. She imagined Natalie in one of her breezy sundresses she'd worn when she first arrived to the east coast, walking along the sandy beaches of Santa Monica, or the bright neon lights of the Sunset Strip. "Why didn't you go back?"

Natalie snorted. Shawn gave a wry smile and shoved her shoulder, "Cause I convinced her how great it was around here! Ain't that right, Nat?"

"I'll admit, it's nicer in the fall," Natalie's eyes went dreamy and she smiled a faraway smile, "I did miss the leaves turning all those years. Didn't miss shit like this, though." She nodded to the windows and the blowing snowdrifts outside. "But that's the price you pay for losing your job and falling in love, I guess."

Jess nodded, pretending to understand. She supposed she didn't want to move too far away from Kyle. But if she had a choice between working in Hollywood and sticking around here? She wasn't so sure Kyle would be enough to convince her to stay.

Shawn took a swig of his coffee, also black. She mirrored him, pondering. *Does Shawn have someone he'd move across the country for?*

She put down her coffee and clapped her hands on the oak bar. "So, you two. What brings you here today? We havin' lunch, or are we talkin' business?"

Natalie put down her coffee. "Both? I owe Shawn at least 30 lunches at this point."

"You do not," Shawn scoffed, "You always feed me when I come by to work."

"Yeah, and you've put in how many thousands of hours fixing up my house?" Natalie rolled her eyes. "Jess, tell this man he needs to start charging me."

Jess's eyes widened in shock. "You're *not* charging her??"

"We're bartering!" Shawn said, "I got a vintage car *and* free business stuff outta the deal!"

"Woah, woah wait–vintage car?" Jess stared between the two of them. "Gimme details."

Natalie waved a hand. "It's not that interesting."

"Speak for yourself!" Shawn bumped her shoulder as he leaned over the bar toward Jess. His whole face lit up as he described the car. "Chevy Turquoise, '54 Bel Air, coupe convertible."

Something about that make and model rang a bell in Jess's mind. But mostly, it just sounded cool. "Does it run?"

"Not yet. But I'm workin' on it."

"That is too cool!" She wanted to talk more about it, but noticed that Natalie was looking bored. She turned toward her new roommate. "And you're also doing business stuff?"

"I do marketing and promotion work, helped with his Facebook page, built him a website." Natalie tallied off on her fingers, before roping Shawn back in. "Which, sure, would be great if you were actually getting work from it, but until you do, you've more than paid off anything you've gotten from me." She started poking his shoulder. "Start. Charging. Me. For. Your. Work!"

Each word was punctuated by an angry finger.

"Ow, ow, owwww!!" Shawn flinched playfully and swatted her hand away, "Them's devil fingers, girl. That hurts!"

Natalie leaned back and wiggled her fingers suggestively, lips curling in a nefarious grin. "Thanks, I work out."

Jess shook her head. It was hard to reconcile these two bantering in her bar, when just a few days before, Shawn had been moping over Natalie in that very same chair. She felt a sting of jealousy that she hadn't been able to bring out this kind of joy in him. But she also wondered if his lingering feelings had anything to do with him not charging Natalie for all the work he'd been doing.

"So tell me about the house. I'd love to see it!" Jess said, changing the subject. "Oh! But first, what can I put in for you?"

She grabbed some menus from under the counter and placed them on the bar in front of them. Shawn waved his away.

"I want that crab cake sandwich you gave me the other day."

She smiled and turned to Natalie. "Do you need a minute?"

"Uhhhh…" Natalie stalled, scanning the menu, "What's hot?"

"The special's the Two Scoop Soup and grilled cheese," Jess suggested. Shawn groaned.

"Awww, geez, I didn't know you had the Two Scoop Soup…"

He pouted. Jess stifled a giggle. *God, he's adorable.*

"You wanna change your order?"

He nodded vigorously. Jess scribbled on her pad.

"What's the two scoop soup?" Natalie asked.

"A half bowl of she-crab soup, filled the rest of the way with crab chowder. It's like a scoop of each, you know?"

Natalie squinted her eyes as if she was trying to imagine it. "She-crab is the tomato one, right?"

Jess nodded. "We're pretty famous for it."

Natalie opened her eyes. "You sold me. I'll take it. And put it all on my tab."

"Aww, Nat…" Shawn whined. Jess went back into the kitchen to put in the order, tuning out their squabbles over the bill. Maybe this would work. Natalie seemed fun. Even if it did break her heart to see how oblivious she was to Shawn's suffering.

She walked back out and refilled everyone's coffee. Other than Natalie and Shawn, the restaurant was still deserted. She wondered if dinner would be this slow.

"How late do you work tonight, Jess?" Natalie asked her.

"3:30. Just the lunch shift today."

Natalie checked the big analogue Budweiser clock that hung above the bar. "Would you want to come check out the place and work out details when you get off?"

Shawn smirked. Natalie hit his arm.

"I swear, Shawn, you are such a child sometimes!" Natalie rolled her eyes, "When you get off *work,* would you want to come over and talk specifics? Plus, I could give you a tour of the place."

Jess giggled. Oh yeah. She could definitely get used to being around these guys a little more.

"That sounds great!"

"So tell me about yourself, Jess," Natalie said, shrugging off her parka and leaning back in her stool. She stirred her water with her straw. "Are you a serial killer or more of One-Murder Wanda?"

"Nah, she's much more sinister than that. She replaces the toilet paper with the flap *down*."

"You son of a bitch!" Jess slapped Shawn on the shoulder and he laughed. His light blue eyes sparkled mischievously, and her heart skipped a beat. "Even I'm not *that* crazy."

Natalie grinned at her. "Shawn says you live with your Dad. Have you ever been away from home before?"

"No. I was saving up to move out eventually, but when Dad found out I wasn't gonna work at the garage anymore, he said it was time for me to find my own place."

Shawn tilted his head. "You're quitting the garage?"

"Yeah." Jess sipped her coffee, suddenly uncomfortable. "Kyle said—well, it's just not where I should be anymore."

Shawn scrunched his nose, and Natalie looked back and forth between the two of them over her mug.

"Kyle is…?"

"My boyfriend. You've probably seen him around here before—he plays baseball at the Community College."

Shawn shook his head. "I dunno what his problem is. It's badass that you work with cars all day. I'd never wanna leave a job like that."

Jess felt a tug in her chest. That was all well and good for Shawn to say, but she was sure if *he* was dating her, he'd have concerns about her working in the garage.

All the other guys she'd dated did.

Natalie set down her coffee. "So that means you're down to

one income, and your dad's kicked you out. You seem to be taking it in stride."

Her pointed question made Jess more than a little nervous. She shrugged. "People make it work. Besides, I still have Kyle, and this place."

"Does that mean that your boyfriend is going to be sleeping over all the time?" Shawn cut in. Jess tried to keep her face neutral. *Fuck. Am I about to lose my only lead on a place?*

Natalie rolled her eyes. "She's an adult, Shawn. If she's cool with *my* sex life, I'm cool with hers."

Natalie gave Jess a smile, and she breathed a sigh of relief. Her new landlord seemed… *cool.* Like she had a lot of things figured out. Maybe Dave was right–maybe it *would* be good to have another female friend. Shawn shifted uncomfortably in his seat, and Natalie changed the subject.

"Okay, Jess. Real talk. Do you like Christmas decorations?"

"Ha, I mean, yeah, at Christmas time." Jess glanced at Shawn. Now he was smirking over his coffee.

Natalie's eyes didn't waver. "I *will* start decorating on November first."

"Earlier if you let her, too. She turns into a mad woman as soon as the pumpkin spice stuff starts coming out." Shawn deftly avoided a smack from Natalie.

"That is acceptable," Jess said, adopting a stance on the issue, "Provided that September and October are reserved for Halloween. You have a porch, right?"

The corner of Natalie's lip lifted, and she raised an eyebrow. "Yes…?"

"I'm thinking skeletons in rocking chairs. Fog machine. A ton of that fake spiderweb stuff. Shawn can rig up a light show. And of course, like, twelve jack-o-lanterns. Minimum."

Natalie's smile widened to show her teeth. She nodded approvingly at Shawn while gesturing across the bar. "I like her. I think this is gonna be a good fit."

. . .

AN HOUR LATER, Sheila came in for the dinner shift, and Jess and Natalie piled into her Ford Escort to follow Shawn to Natalie's house.

"Thanks for the ride," Natalie said in between giving out directions.

"No problem." It was an easy drive to Hagerstown from the bar—longer than Jess's current commute, but definitely doable. She hoped Kyle wouldn't be too upset about it.

"It's a little outside of town, past some farms and an old church."

Jess took in what she could of the pastoral scenery as the last intersections of town stretched farther and farther away in the rear view. Cornfields, cow pastures, and a few little farm stands flanked a divided highway for a few minutes, and then Natalie told her to turn right.

Jess turned onto an oil-and-stone county road. Just as Natalie had said, there was an old church on the corner, and modest farmhouses lined the drive on one side of the stretch of road, looking out over soybean fields and the Blue Ridge Mountains on the other.

"It's coming up here," Nat gestured to the left of the car.

Jess eased on the brake, and they followed Shawn's pickup into a cracked paved driveway, pulling in front of a detached garage. The Escort was sandwiched between a tall wooden fence on the right and Natalie's house on the left, with a tiny path squeezed beside the garage in front of them that Jess assumed led into a backyard.

"This is a skinny driveway for such a big property," Jess observed. She stifled a giggle as Shawn unfolded himself out of his barely-opened door butting up against the chimney. His tall, lean frame was too much for the cramped alleyway.

"Yeah, I kinda hate the fence." Natalie unbuckled her seatbelt and opened the passenger door. It almost hit the wooden planks. "But Shawn's got ideas for something less…"

"Imposing?" Jess suggested.

"Yeah. Shorter for sure. Or at least see-through." Shawn squeezed his way toward them, and scrunched his face as he thought about it. "Maybe chain-link, or a picket fence, maybe."

"As long as it keeps the neighbor's dog out of my yard." Natalie shivered. "Anyway, it's freezing. Let's go inside, I'll make some tea and give you the tour."

They side-stepped around Jess's car and made their way to the front porch, which Jess noticed was a recent addition. The clean lines of the treated wood neatly framed the front of the aging house, even if the two structures did seem a little at-odds with each other. The front door was bright white against the graying aluminum siding, and Natalie unlocked it by punching a code into a number pad.

"Looks like you've done some work on the place," Jess said.

"This is all Shawn," Natalie said. "I've helped a little–he's been teaching me to measure correctly and I'm getting handy with a circular saw, but I was absolutely hopeless when I got here last fall."

"She's not wrong," Shawn leaned into Jess conspiratorially. "She was a wreck."

Jess held back a chuckle, shivering a little when Shawn's breath tickled the hairs at the back of her neck. "How'd you afford all this?"

Walking through the living room, she was awed by the brand new windows she hadn't fully appreciated from the outside, and she smelled fresh paint. She wondered how much of what she saw—fixtures, hardware, appliances, the kitchen faucet—had been put in by Shawn, or if Natalie's grandma had just had a modern sense of style.

"Gram left me a little money to fix the place up." Natalie gave a sheepish half-smile. "I uh… I'd never realized how much she really cared about me, you know? I wish…" She stopped at the foot of the stairs, closing her eyes for a second before looking over her shoulder at Jess. "She made sure to tell me I was loved, in the end. I'm pretty lucky. But I am running low on funds. The windows just about killed me."

She led the way up the stairs. Jess looked back at Shawn while Natalie told her story, and he gave her a sad smile. Hearing her talk about her grandmother made Jess think about her dad.

She vowed to try to patch things up with him soon.

Just as they had with the downstairs, Shawn and Natalie gave her an overview of the second floor. Natalie specified which spaces were open to her and which rooms she wanted to keep off-limits. Jess appreciated her candidness; all-in-all, it felt like Natalie was trustworthy. No alarm bells, no red flags…

She hoped they'd get along as roommates.

"And this would be your room," Natalie said, pushing open the door at the end of the hallway. Jess peered inside, glancing at Nat for permission before stepping inside. Two big, new windows looked out into the backyard, letting in tons of the winter sunlight and giving her a view of the modest back deck (also recently re-done). Ivory wallpaper with purple butterflies and lavender flowers stretched across the walls. Two doors led to an attached bathroom and a walk-in closet. By all accounts, it looked like the master suite for a house of this size.

"I have my own bathroom?" Jess peered into the small en-suite, cozy but bright, with a small cabinet sink and a combination tub-shower. She briefly considered how nice it would be not to have to sneak around the dorm bathrooms when Kyle slept over.

"Yep. This was grandma's room." Natalie sat on the queen bed in the center of the room, simply made with white sheets and an embroidered duvet. A well-worn oak dresser and night-stand consisted of the rest of the furniture, along with a large cedar chest pushed against the foot of the bed. "I feel more at home in the guest room, anyway. It's where I used to sleep when I stayed here as a kid."

"Oh," Jess said. She looked around again, taking in the standing lamp plugged into the outlet by the door, the vintage hardwood floors, and the old alarm clock blinking on the night-stand. As she did, she felt Shawn's eyes on her. He'd been uncharacteristically quiet as they showed her the bedroom. "Does it come furnished like this?"

"If that works for you, it's less stuff for me to move into the garage."

"You mean for me to move?" Shawn leaned against the door-way, and shot Jess a wink.

She felt butterflies in her stomach as she looked around the room. "I like it. I like the house; it feels good." She walked over to the dresser and picked at a seam in the wallpaper. "Quick question, though."

"Yeah?"

"Would you be open to letting me paint it before I move in?"

Natalie looked to Shawn to answer. He cracked a smile. "If you're a better painter than Nat? Absolutely."

CHAPTER 13

Grandad was having a good day.

Shawn could see it in his eyes when he let himself into his parents' house that Thursday morning and walked back into the kitchen, helping himself to the sludge in the bottom of the coffee pot. He was on his feet for once, shuffling around the granite-top kitchen island with his walker. Shawn worked around him as he fired up another pot, happy to accommodate another person.

"Lookin' good, Grandad!" he said.

"Had my Wheaties this mornin'," he grumbled back with a smile.

"Breakfast of champions, that," Shawn agreed, scooping grounds into the filter. "You gonna want any of this?"

"Nah, you're just makin' for you today, son."

Nary a wheeze. And he was *standing*.

Shawn hid his excitement for the positive direction of his grandpa's recovery. Grandad was too proud to accept any fuss about his health, except in the moments when he was too weak to refuse it. But there had been more of those in the last year than not; the once proud and infallible Grandpa Cobb was fading in old age. But this morning, despite the walker, despite the oxygen tube wrapped around his ears, Shawn saw the strength of the man from his youth.

They both knew he was there this morning, and Shawn wasn't about to ruin it by calling it out.

"Nat and Jess gave me the day off today," Shawn joked, "So I was thinkin' I'd start putting that engine back together. You got plans?"

Grandad's ice blue eyes zeroed in on Shawn, creases forming in the loose skin of his cheeks as his lips lifted at the corners. "You got two women workin' ya hard, eh?" He gave a wheezy chuckle, "No game on today, and you know they kicked me outta the bridge club. I should probably make sure you don't blow something up."

"I have been known to start a fire or two," Shawn smirked, "And they're only friends."

"You gotta key to their house?"

"Well, yeah," Shawn spluttered. "I put in the doors, Granddad."

"Then it ain't friendship, it's marriage." And with that, Grandpa Cobb shuffled his walker out the door to the garage, presumably to settle in for a day of polishing metal and reminiscing on his old racing days with Shawn.

Shawn sipped his cold coffee and said nothing, letting his grandpa think what he would. Jess had a boyfriend, after all, and he hadn't even attempted to explain the full extent of his and Natalie's relationship (or her and Bonnie's relationship) to his family. The crucifix still loomed over the open room as his eyes darted to the wooden planks decorated with Psalms that lined the walls of the dining area.

Deep down, maybe he'd known that he and Natalie never would have worked out. She deserved better than to be judged by his family. The older he got, the more embarrassed he was by his fundamentalist upbringing. The prudishness. The judginess.

For years, he'd never noticed it, surrounded by neighbors and friends from the congregation. Every now and then he'd accompany his Grandpa to a race or a car show and he got a glimpse of the outside world, but he was still surrounded by a fairly homogenous group. They had never needed to talk religion or politics; everyone was on the same page.

But in recent years, before his grandpa's heart attack, there had been more flags, more hate, more openly bigoted conversations. Shawn had grown too old for youth group or Sunday School, and he found that when he'd graduated to the big service with all the other adults, there were fewer lessons. There had been a lot less Bible, a lot more politics.

Shawn had stopped going to church after that.

He'd started hanging out more at the bar, and he'd found far more kinship among the "sinners" minding their own business and just out trying to have a good time, working hard and having a drink at the end of the day, than he'd ever felt at youth group.

He was happy for his sister Melanie, that she'd found a good guy at college who shared her beliefs. Their family's beliefs. That was all well and good for her.

But even she's starting to rebel a little bit, he thought. Their last conversation made it clear that she was at least starting to question the more prudish teachings of the congregation. It had got him thinking about how maybe *he* hadn't fully escaped the influence of all those years in the church. All those teachings about sin and fire and brimstone. He didn't have the time to judge others for their sexual choices, but it was much harder not to judge himself.

He wondered how his parents would feel if he brought a girl like Jess home. Not a girl with a boyfriend, of course, but a girl that was a little more comfortable with herself and her body. Would they only see how she dressed, the grease under her fingernails? Or would they appreciate her bouncy blonde hair, her deep brown eyes, her nice, round–

His parents' fancy coffee pot dinged, interrupting his revery, so Shawn topped off his coffee and made his way out to the garage.

Grandad was already sifting through the engine parts that Shawn had piled beside the car. He pulled up an electric heater and set it a couple feet from his Grandpa's walker so they wouldn't freeze. The garage was less cold than it had been for most of the month, but it wasn't exactly toasty either.

Shawn looked forward to spring. He was ready to get to work again on some paying gigs so he could finish up the paint job on the car.

"You're missing a couple bolts," Grandad commented, tilting his head at the pile.

"What? That ain't right," Shawn countered, setting his coffee down and digging through the magnetic tray he used to keep track of the tinier bits and bobs.

"Were ya hearin' any kind a rattlin' last time you fired it up?"

"Not that I remember." Shawn rubbed the back of his neck. "What's missing?"

His grandpa pointed at the engine head and the gasket Shawn had cleaned earlier that week. "At least a handful of bolts. Just count the holes."

He did. And cursed under his breath.

"Gosh dang it," Shawn said, mindful of his grandpa, "I was gonna try to put this all back together today."

Grandad nodded, sagely, "Why don't we head on down to Ernie's Garage and pick up what we need?"

"Oh, well…" Shawn waffled. "I'm really trying not to spend too much money on the rebuild…"

"I can buy you a couple bolts."

"Are you sure?"

"You fly, I buy," Grandad jerked his thumb at the garage door, indicating Shawn's truck.

"Got a full tank?" Shawn asked, nodding to his grandpa's oxygen.

The old man chuckled, "It'll get me there."

Ten minutes later, Shawn was helping his grandpa into the passenger's side of his pickup and climbing into the driver's seat. With grandad navigating, they made their way to a giant scrapyard just off the interstate close to the Virginia border. Shawn drove to the main office entrance and parked. After unloading his grandpa, they slowly walked into the trailer that bore the sign, *Ernie's Garage - Main Office.*

The front door opened to a simple but functional waiting room, with plastic and metal chairs, a coffee table littered with old magazines, and an L-shaped desk up against the back wall. The smell of burnt coffee wafted from an industrial carafe on a filing cabinet in the corner. Walter led Shawn to the front desk.

"Ernie around?"

A large man with short, dark hair and a few day's worth of stubble looked up from a computer screen to help them. He had on blue coveralls with "Chuck" embroidered on the front pocket in a vintage script.

"Been a while, Walter. What can we do ya for?" he asked, in a surprisingly soothing baritone. Shawn hadn't worked with Chuck much. When he could afford to, he'd always brought his trucks to their younger mechanic, Beau, who had been a few years ahead of him in technical school.

Shawn's grandpa nudged him in the elbow.

"Ah! Oh, right." Shawn rubbed his arm. "I'm rebuilding a straight six for an old Chevy, and I think I'm missing a couple bolts."

"A '54 Bel Air," Walter grumbled.

Chuck's eyebrows rose for a fraction of a second, so quick

Shawn almost didn't catch it. But then he backed up from his computer and got up to walk around the desk.

"Let's check the warehouse, I'm sure we got somethin'," he said, waving for them to follow him.

Shawn and his grandpa trailed behind, a little more slowly than Chuck, who held a side door open for them at the end of a narrow hall. Shawn hovered an arm just behind his grandpa's back as he wheeled his oxygen tank across a paved section of the lot to one of the large warehouse buildings.

"Sorry it's so loud in here this mornin'," Chuck almost shouted over the sound of an air compressor and what sounded like a grinding wheel. "We keep an inventory of parts in the back; I'm sure we got what you're lookin' for."

They passed two cars on lifts, and another mechanic whose feet peeked out from underneath a black sedan. The space was huge, easily enough room to work on half a dozen trucks at once. Shawn gaped at the tall, open rafters of the warehouse, and the packed shelves lined almost to the roof. He never ceased to be amazed by this place. He thought he spotted a gray, fluffy tail—most likely belonging to the shop cat—whip around an engine block stand when the three of them crossed the burned cement floor. The sharp smell of oil and antifreeze cleared out his nose as he breathed in.

I think I've died and gone to heaven.

Then he remembered Grandad, and thought about sparks flying from the grinding wheel. Shawn tugged on Chuck's sleeve and muttered close to him, "Will he be okay back here with his oxygen?"

Chuck looked back, and nodded. "No welding on the schedule today. The grinding you're hearing is in the back paint shop."

The mechanic gestured to another corner of the massive space before opening another door, which led them to another room almost as big as the first one, filled with standing shelves that were absolutely stacked with boxes and trays. Lists of product categories and part numbers were hung from clipboards on the ends of the makeshift aisles, and Chuck scanned the third one on the right.

"Chevy engines'll be down this way."

They all jumped as they heard a chorus of metallic clangs and a high voice cry out, *"Jesus fuckin' Christ!"*

Shawn ran around the rows of shelves to the source of the sound, turning a corner to see… Jess. On her ass, surrounded by a pile of cardboard and pipe.

Shawn heard Chuck lumber up behind him.

"Jess!" Chuck bellowed, pushing Shawn out of his way as he walked toward her to help her up, "What're you doin' sneakin' around back here without even sayin' hello! What're you even doin' back here anyway?"

Jess brushed her hands on her jeans sheepishly, tugging the scrunchie out of her wild blonde hair and rearranging it into an only slightly less messy ponytail. She glanced at Shawn before looking back at Chuck, her cheeks reddening.

"I needed some boxes. Why'd we move the big boxes all the way up to the top shelf?"

"Well, if you'd'a been here at all the past week maybe you'd'a known we had to get 'em off the floor before the safety spec."

Jess rubbed her hands over her backside gingerly. Shawn's eyes followed her hands over the cheeks. "Ah, right. Makes sense."

"Found 'em!" Shawn turned his head toward his grandpa's voice from three rows back. He looked back at Chuck and Jess apologetically, and Chuck shooed at him with his hands. Jess gave him an embarrassed smile. "Hey, Shawn."

"Hey." He gave a weak wave, making sure he didn't look at her ass again, then scurried back to his grandpa.

He wasn't sure why seeing Jess made him so nervous. Maybe it was just the surprise of seeing her at the garage instead of the bar for once. Or the fact that she'd said she wasn't going to work here anymore the last time they talked. He wiped sweat from his palms as he walked past the rows.

Shawn saw his grandad eying rows upon rows of plastic bins with measurement and manufacturer labels. He blinked. The whole shop was color coded, he noticed: with Ford parts in blue bins, Chevy in yellow, GM in red, and foreign manufacturers in gray. Parts that were too large for bins were stored in their boxes with colored duct tape tags affixed to the shelf below them. The two men stared at the shelves, with something resembling awe.

"So… what are you looking for?" A sweet, female voice said from the end of the aisle.

"Uh…" Shawn really should have finished his coffee before driving over here. His brain was fuzzy. He was making an idiot of himself.

"Chevy engine bolts. Head gasket, specifically. Inline 6," Grandad grunted.

"What year?" Jess asked. She walked over, brushing past Shawn to kneel beside his grandpa, moving her hand between a stack of yellow bins. *She seems so at home here,* he thought. Not that she was particularly awkward behind the bar or anything, but compared to the girl who'd seemed so eager to impress Natalie the other day, Jess was practically a different person when she was navigating the aisles of the shop.

Why would she ever want to leave?

"F-fifty four," Shawn stuttered.

She decisively grabbed the second bin from the bottom and pulled out twelve bolt pairs, filling both of her small, delicate hands. She straightened and dropped the loose bundle into Shawn's hands, donkey-kicking the bin back into place.

Their fingers brushed briefly, and Shawn noticed that her hands weren't soft like he'd been expecting. Then again, why was he expecting they'd be soft at all? She was a mechanic.

Wait- why were you even thinking about how her hands would feel?

"I'll check you out. Chuck's taller than me, so he can get the boxes I need. That work for you, Chuck?" She called back. Shawn snapped his head up from his still outstretched hands in time to see the curve of her jaw and the tiny hairs that curled at the base of her neck, before she nodded at Chuck's answering grunt and turned back around.

That skin looks much softer.

Before he could even process the thought, she swished past him and skipped between the rows, bounding off toward the garage and, Shawn assumed, the office. The rows were so close together, her hair brushed his shoulder when she moved. He and his grandfather stared at each other for a second, before taking steps to follow her.

If he'd admired the way she wove through the crowds of patrons at the PB&G, it was nothing compared to the way she danced around these aisles. If he hadn't been keeping an eye out for tripping hazards himself, he could have stared after her all day long.

"Thanks for everything, Chuck!" Shawn called as he held open the door for his grandpa.

"Anytime, kid!"

Shawn heard one last grunt and some sliding of cardboard before the door swung shut, and the rumble of the air compressor took over.

Back in the trailer they'd first entered, Shawn towered over his grandad on the customer side of the desk while Jess tapped away at the desktop on her side.

"It'll just be 16.48 for the bolts," she said, bending back to look at Shawn. "I gave you my discount."

She winked. Shawn felt his ears go hot.

Has she gotten cuter?

"I've got it, sweetheart," Grandad muttered, pulling a twenty dollar bill out of the wallet he kept in his front shirt pocket.

The rest of Shawn's face heated. Not only was his grandpa *paying for him*, he also just called his friend *sweetheart*. He tried to give Jess an apologetic plea with his eyes.

The young mechanic was unfazed, however. She took his Grandad's bill with a smile. "How sweet! Y'all fixin' up the Chevy together?"

Shawn's grandpa nudged his grandson's elbow. Shawn grimaced. "A little bit, yeah. It's a project I've been working on since Christmas. A 1954 Chevy Bel Air. Found it in a client's garage, can you believe it??"

Shawn didn't say it had belonged to Natalie's grandmother, and instead, tried to give Jess enough details to piece it together. He hadn't told his parents or grandfather who the car had belonged to, just that a client of his had offered to trade it with him. He knew if they found out, they'd never believe that he and Natalie were just friends. And the last thing he wanted was to be forced into *that* conversation. Melanie knew, but the two of them had gotten pretty good at keeping secrets from their parents over the years.

Jess's eyes flicked up in understanding. Shawn wasn't sure if she'd put together that this was *the* car Natalie had traded for all his work on the house, but it certainly seemed to indicate she'd be checking that hypothesis with him later.

"Nothing wrong with a little trade here and there." She returned his grandpa's change with a grin. "Was there anything else we could help you with today?"

"You've been quite helpful already, dear. Give your old man a hello from Walter Cobb, will ya?"

Jess's smile tightened slightly. "I'll do that. Thank you, Walter. Thanks, Shawn. Y'all have a good day now!"

Shawn could see Jess watching as he helped his grandpa out the door. Despite his high energy that morning, the old man was beginning to fade. Shawn cursed himself. This impromptu trip and all the walking through the garage may have been too much for the guy. He would likely park himself back in his chair in front of the TV for the rest of the day.

After helping his grandad get in the passenger's seat, Shawn looked back over his shoulder through the front door of the trailer. Jess had disappeared, likely to the garage to rescue Chuck. He shook his head and climbed into the driver's seat. Walter stared at him expectantly.

"So you and Ernie's daughter seemed awfully cozy. What's the story there?"

CHAPTER 14

*J*ess let out her breath in a *whoosh* as she slumped back against the wheely chair behind the desk. She had hoped to get in and out of the garage without making too much of a fuss; ideally, no one would have known she'd been there at all.

But they had moved the damn boxes up to the highest shelf, where she was way too short to reach, and she'd made a big ol' fool of herself in front of not just Chuck, but Shawn and his grandpa.

Jess smiled a bit in spite of herself. She knew from how often Shawn picked up dinner for his grandpa how much he loved the guy, but seeing him take care of the old man was something different entirely. He didn't have a callous bone in his body, that Shawn. The second someone needed anything from him, he'd be there with his toolbox and a helping hand. She thought back to Valentine's Day, when he'd invited her in his truck to keep her out of the cold. Guys like that just didn't exist anymore.

She logged out of the register and wheeled the chair away, figuring now that the cat was out of the bag, she might as well say "hi" to all the guys. She had missed them the past couple of weeks that she hadn't been around (not that she'd tell them that). Luckily, it looked like her dad was out with Randy, likely towing some fixer upper out of a bad spot, so she didn't have to start any awkward conversations.

She walked out of the trailer office and into the big garage, where she spotted Beau's dirt-caked Timberland boots poking out from under a mid-2000's Volkswagen sedan. She kicked the toe of his boot.

"Whatcha workin' on there?" she asked.

Bang. "Ow!"

Legs, waist, and coverall buttoned torso slid out on the old longboard Beau was using for a dolly, until a curly-haired head emerged being cradled by two large arms. "You could warn a guy, you know!"

"I kicked your boot." Jess looked the man up and down, thinking of how threatened Kyle had been by him. He was a little attractive, she supposed. Strong. Tall. But she couldn't bring herself to think of him as anything other than an older brother. They'd learned the ropes together around here.

"That coulda been the cat!" Beau winced as he rubbed at his forehead, a red mark beginning to swell there. Jess rolled her eyes and walked over to the mini fridge next to the tool box and grabbed an ice pack they kept around for this kind of thing. She wrapped it in the cleanest rag she could find and handed it to him.

"Thanks," Beau muttered.

"So what's up with the Volkswagon?"

Jess couldn't resist a project. She missed hanging around the shop and helping out. Beau, the youngest of the regular mechanics and a genius with diesel engines, had been her favorite partner in crime. He'd often recruit her to help him out, especially with getting under the cars and working in tight spaces where he couldn't fit.

He sat up into a squat, then stood fully, his giant frame rising a good foot and half taller than Jess's. She leaned back against a square body pickup so it didn't hurt as much to crane her neck to look at him.

"The salt on the roads was eating up the muffler. We might need to swap out the whole thing. I'm seeing if it's salvageable."

"Original?"

"Likely."

"Scrap it for tin." Jess waved her arm. "It's what, twelve, thirteen years old?"

"Owner's a real tight-ass," Beau complained. "Doesn't want the bill."

Jess rolled her eyes. The penny-pinchers always ended up spending more for maintenance in the long run. Not to mention the extra hours they'd pay in labor for forcing the guys to jerry-rig a solution to something that could be fixed with a new part.

"Ugh, too much of a hassle." Jess stretched her arms above her head. Her shirt lifted, and Beau stooped to smack her exposed stomach with a rag. She jumped out of his reach at the last second.

"That why you haven't been around lately?" Beau said, returning the ice pack to his forehead. "Too much of a hassle?"

Jess studied her toes. "No, not that."

She didn't volunteer any more. Beau didn't press.

A few seconds passed, and Chuck burst into the room, saving her from elaborating any further. "Got yer boxes, Jess. This enough?"

He had six giant cardboard boxes pinched between his fingers as he waddled over, trying to avoid knocking into anything.

"That's great! Thanks, Chuck. I probably couldn't fit any more in the car, to be honest."

"The Escort?" Chuck frowned, looking at the cardboard in his hands. "We might need to break 'em down then."

"You movin' or something?" Beau asked, raising his

eyebrows, as Chuck started to break down the boxes. Myrtle, the shop cat, appeared at that moment to inspect the new selection of cardboard apartments.

Jess shooed her away, grabbing one and punching out the bottom. Myrtle meowed at the *pop* of the packing tape and scampered away to her kingdom of tire stacks. "Yeah, Dad said it was time for me to find my own place."

Chuck froze. Beau stared at her.

"That doesn't sound like Ernie. He said he was gonna give yo–"

Beau cut him off. "Where are you moving?"

"Hagerstown," Jess said, trying to make it seem like no big deal.

"Oh, that ain't bad. So you're still workin' here?" Chuck asked.

Jess paused. "I'm not sure that it's a good idea anymore."

"That's crazy talk!" Chuck scoffed. "Ernie loves having you around. He was about to–"

"What do you mean, 'Not a good idea'?"

Chuck shot Beau an indignant look for the interruptions, and Beau returned it with daggers in his eyes. Jess was confused. Had they had some kind of fight while she was gone?

"Are you guys… okay?" she asked.

"He asked you first, Soo-Soo," Chuck turned kinder eyes toward her.

She felt her eyes burn a little at the nickname. *Dammit!* Why did they all keep calling her that?

"Y'all and your 'Soo-Soo's. I'm not a kid anymore! I have a boyfriend, and it isn't right for me to be hanging out here all the time."

"What's wrong with hanging out here?" Beau asked.

"Oh come on. How would you feel about your wife hanging around a bunch of sweaty men all day?"

"Carly?" Beau blinked. "What does Carly have to do with any

of this? She just had a baby, she shouldn't be hanging around diesel fumes all day."

Beau studied Jess's face, then blanched.

"Shit, Jess, you're not pregnant are you?"

"What? Of course not!" Jess burst out laughing at the thought. "Are you kidding? Y'all taught me better than that."

"We also taught ya not to let any boys boss you around," Chuck pointed out.

Jess was silent for a moment. "Kyle's not a boy. He's in college."

"If Kyle's important enough to be making decisions for you, how come we've never met him?" Beau crossed his arms.

"Oh come on, we're not, like, *that* serious."

Were they?

"He's telling you to quit your job. And you're *listening to him.* That sounds pretty serious."

Jess raised her hands. "Wait a minute–that didn't come out right. He's not why I'm quitting."

"So you *are* quittin'?" Chuck's jaw dropped.

"I'm just not sure that being a mechanic is appropriate for me anymore."

Jess scuffed the toe of her sneaker back and forth on the burned concrete floor. She felt the men's eyes on her face, despite avoiding their gaze.

Finally, Beau chuckled, shaking his head and reaching out his hand to tussle her hair.

"Hey!" she shouted as she batted his hand away. Her blonde hair fell loose around her face, falling out of its messy bun.

"It looks like our sweet little Jess wants to try her hand at being a real lady, Chuck."

Jess felt her cheeks heat. She pulled the old scrunchie out of her hair and finger combed the strands back into another pony-tail. Chuck shook his head.

"It ain't gonna be the same around here without you, kid," he said.

"I'm not leaving for good yet," Jess mumbled. She didn't like how heavy the air felt all of a sudden, "I'm still thinking it through."

Hearing Chuck and Beau raise concerns about Kyle made her question her decision to quit. Why *was* he so worried about her working in the garage, again?

Her mind flitted back to Shawn, who'd just left with his grandpa, and how he'd looked at her while she'd been checking him out.

At the register, she mentally corrected. *Checking him out AT THE REGISTER.*

Although if anyone had been checking someone out, it'd been Shawn. She'd seen the way he'd looked at her in the storage warehouse. He'd tried to hide the way his eyes had flitted down her body. But she'd caught it.

He didn't seem to have any problems with a woman working as a mechanic.

She bent down to gather all the boxes she and Chuck had unfolded, and then rifled through a drawer for tape. Beau grabbed a roll of duct tape that was hanging off the safety pin in the lift and tapped her on the shoulder with it.

"Thanks," Jess said. Hands full, she shrugged her shoulders and gave the two men a sad smile. "I'll see ya around?"

Chuck nodded and gave her a distracted wave before walking back to the storage room. Beau smiled back at her.

"You'd better. And Jess?"

She turned back at the doorway, surprised to see such a serious look on the young mechanic's face. "Don't let any man convince you that you're anything but a lady."

She nodded, swallowing back the lump that had formed in her throat, and carried the boxes to her car.

CHAPTER 15

*J*ess took another sweep around her bedroom, realizing with a pang that she was definitely going to need more than six boxes. Even after tossing half her closet into trash bags to donate later, she still had all her other things to pack. Her bedside lamp, sheets, her comforter, towels and toiletries…

Kyle rifled through the clothes piled on her bed that were supposed to go into her suitcase. Jeans. Work shirts. Her ratty old Orioles sweatshirt that she always wore to bed and a mountain of other leisurewear. Overwhelmed by all the packing, she'd called on him to help her out. He'd been great at first, helping her toss the trash bags into the trunk of his car, and carrying the heaviest boxes out of her room for her. But then it had come time to pack up all her clothes, and he'd gotten distracted by her underwear.

"Kyle, I need you to focus."

He wiggled his eyebrows at her. "How come I've never seen you wear *these?*"

He held up a particularly scandalous little lacy number when her dad walked into the doorway.

"Chuck and Beau said you stopped by the shop earlier–"

He froze as he caught sight of the man in his daughter's bedroom fondling his daughter's g-string, and almost dropped the box of donuts that he was holding. His face turned crimson in under a second, and Kyle shoved the panties behind his back.

"Dad!" Jess jumped in front of her boyfriend to protect him from Ernie White's full ire. "What are you doing home this early?"

"Who's he?" He sputtered, an unflattering spit bubble forming in the corner of his mouth. Jess winced. It was never a good sign when the saliva started building up.

"This is my boyfriend, Kyle. He's just helping me pack." She put out her arms as if calming down a raging bull. Kyle lifted his hand behind her in a wave, and she caught a glimpse of her panties in the corner of her eye.

Jesus Christ, he just waved my g-string at my father.

Ernie stormed past her and snatched the lingerie from Kyle's hand before dropping it into Jess's hands like a hot potato.

"So *this* is *Kyle*–" he spat his name as if it were a species of invasive millipede, "–the one who told you you're too good to work in my garage? What is he doing in *my house,* fingering your *laundry?*"

Spittle flew out of his mouth on the word "fingering." Jess saw that the situation was beginning to spiral out of her control. "Kyle, can you wait outside, please? I'll meet you by the car."

"Uh–yeah! Nice meeting you, Mr. White." Kyle stepped gingerly behind Ernie, who Jess could swear had steam coming out of his ears. The second Kyle was out of sight of the angry man, he bolted out of the bedroom.

Jess could hear his footsteps disappear down the hallway.

She elected to answer her dad's first question and pretend everything else had never happened. "I had to get some boxes from the warehouse, yeah. Figured you wouldn't mind me helping out with recycling a bit."

Ernie fumed. She could tell it was all he could do not to yell at her.

They stood in silence for a moment, both taking in the bareness of the closet, the scattered clothes and boxes on the floor.

"So, uh," Jess started, "It's good you're here, actually, I wanted to ask—how many sets of sheets and stuff are you cool with me taking?"

Ernie's scowl deepened. "Whaddya mean?"

"Well, like, towels and stuff. Bedsheets. It's a queen size bed at my new place, so I was going to take one of your sets of sheets for it and maybe a few blankets from the hall closet. And I'll need a set of towels."

"I'm not letting you take a set of *my* sheets so you can—with *that boy*–"

Jess blanched. "Excuse me?"

"You can buy your own damn sheets." He stormed out of the room, and she followed him into the hallway.

"But Dad, you don't need three sets of sheets for just you. And we have like, a hundred towels. Why can't I have, like, two?"

"Because you ain't a kid anymore, Jess!" Ernie shook his head, and his voice softened slightly. He glanced at the donut box still clenched in his hands, the cardboard smushing in his grip. "I thought you didn't want my help anymore. You don't need your family, now that you have *Kyle*–"

"Your help? You mean like how you've helped so much with the cooking and cleaning this place for the past six years?" Jess shouted. She didn't know what kind of fucked up lesson her dad was trying to teach her here, but it was awfully self-righteous of him to try to teach her what it meant to be an adult when he hadn't cooked a meal other than a TV dinner in years. "That's great, Dad. Real nice of you to lecture me on what it means to be a family when you couldn't even feed your own kid after mom died."

Ernie staggered back as if Jess had slapped him. She felt like she had. Immediately, she wished she could take the words back.

"Dad, I didn't mean–"

"You're not takin' any of the linens," he barked. "Ask *Kyle* to pick some out for you."

Then he stormed out of the kitchen, tossing the donuts in the trash as he left.

Well that went about as horribly as it could. Jess ran in the opposite direction and out to the driveway where Kyle stood awkwardly by his car, bundled up in his coat.

"Jeez. Good thing you're moving out. You're dad's a real jerk."

The cold air stung Jess's face, and she crossed her arms as goosebumps pebbled her bare skin.

"He's just upset. I'm his little girl, after all."

"You're not his little girl anymore, babe. If you're anyone's girl, you're mine." He unzipped his coat and held it out to her, and she gratefully accepted his warmth.

"Well, he's gone now. Wanna come back in and help me finish packing?"

"I don't know, Jess...maybe it's best if I don't go back into your dad's house. Why don't I just toss this stuff in the campus dumpsters for you, and we can meet up at my place later?"

Jess pulled away a bit so she could see his face. "Those are supposed to be donated, Kyle. It's nice stuff. Besides, doesn't your roommate have dibs tonight?"

"Oh, right. Well, pretty soon you'll have a new place with a queen bed, right?"

"Yeah, and no sheets." Jess rolled her eyes.

"I'll buy you some sheets. And then I'll help you break 'em in." He poked at her sides. She wriggled uncomfortably.

"*Kyle*–I need to finish packing!"

He didn't let her go. "Why don't you come over anyway?

We'll snuggle under the covers and pretty soon you'll forget all about your jerk dad."

"Stop calling him that." Something about hearing Kyle insult her dad was rubbing her the wrong way. "I'm serious. Let me go; I need to pack before work tonight."

She knew he was trying to make her feel better, but for some reason, it wasn't working. She tried to escape his arms, but his grip held firm. Too firm.

"It's always work, work, work, with you babe. Can't you see I'm trying to make you feel better?" He kissed the top of her head.

"I know, and I appreciate it, but–"

"Fine." Cold air rushed around her as Kyle pushed her out of his arms. She stumbled away from him in the driveway, almost losing her balance completely at the abrupt loss of his support. "Let's take a break for a few days, then. You've got work, the move on your mind, and it's clear that your dad doesn't want me around for any of it. Why don't you call me when you're ready to pick things back up."

"What? What do you mean a break?" She pulled her sleeves over her fingertips and crossed her arms around her stomach.

"I'm giving you space. Didn't you ask for me to let you go?" He climbed in his car.

"I didn't mean–"

But before she could finish, his car door slammed in her face, and he sped off down the driveway.

Confused and hurt, Jess walked back into the house and down the hall to her bedroom, and sank to the floor with her back against the door. It seemed like all she could do lately was make the men in her life angry.

Did that seriously just happen?

A break. Kyle had said they were taking a break. And to call him when she was–what was it?–ready to 'pick things back up'?

Was it even possible to just drop a relationship and pick it back up? Was she just something he could drop and pick back up, as easy to hold close or toss away as a baseball?

Jess hugged her knees to her chest. Just when she'd thought they were getting serious. He'd used the "wife" word, for Christ's sake! She didn't understand what she'd done wrong.

It wasn't like she'd been defending how her dad had treated him, or anything; she'd just asked Kyle not to call her dad a jerk. The whole reason she was even moving in the first place was because of him—for them. And now, she was completely alone: no boyfriend, no dad, no sheets, and no one to help her move.

Why was her dad even putting her through all of this in the first place? It had been just them against the world for almost as long as she could remember. She looked up at her dresser, where a picture from Jess's first day of school stood in a silver frame: one of the few mementos left from the time when her mom was still alive.

The three of them, Mom, Dad, and Jess, stood on the concrete pavers outside the front of their little country ranch house. She couldn't remember who took the picture. It could have been a neighbor. They'd just moved in when it had been taken–Randy had told her years later how her mother had wanted their family to get settled in a house before Jess started school. She could barely remember the tiny townhouse they'd lived in before this place.

If it weren't for that picture, Jess wasn't sure if she'd even really remember what her mom had looked like. She wondered what life would have been like if she'd grown up with a mother. Would it be easier to bring her boyfriends home? Would she have understood how to be a better daughter or girlfriend if she'd had an actual example to follow?

Jess shook the thought from her head. Who's to say what all would have been different if her mom was still around. She and her dad still probably would have fought on occasion. Guys would still feel weird about her working with a bunch of old men all the time. Maybe she wouldn't even have worked at the garage at all, if her mom had been around to help raise her. Maybe she'd be the kind of girl to ride along in cars instead of fix them.

Either way, she'd still have to grow up and move out at some point.

Jess crawled to her feet and grabbed the picture frame, wrapped it in a shirt, and stuffed it into her suitcase. She had a lot of packing to do before the night shift.

CHAPTER 16

> Are we good enough friends that I can ask you for a favor?

Shawn had to wipe the grease off of his fingers before responding to the text message.

> I found you a roommate, didn't I?

He was pretty proud of himself for that. Shawn knew he had his faults, but he took a lot of pride in his ability to help out his friends. And he thought Natalie and Jess were going to get along real well as roommates.

> Right! Which is why I feel kinda bad asking...

Shawn smiled. Truthfully he didn't mind giving Jess a hand. She was a lot more intriguing than he had given her credit for back when he'd only known her as the bartender at his favorite restaurant.

He never would have expected to see Jess so comfortable at Ernie's Garage. He'd thought a lot about what could be going through her head since he'd seen her there the other day. She clearly belonged; even his Grandad had mentioned that he didn't realize Ernie's daughter was so knowledgeable about cars. So why let all that go? Her boyfriend?

He must be a real piece of work.

After Shawn and his grandpa had returned from their field trip, the old man had parked himself in his LaZBoy and fallen asleep. Shawn felt bad for pushing his energy as much as he had. He'd ended up spending over an hour changing over his oxygen tank and getting him settled, and hadn't gotten any real work done on the Bel Air.

And now, he was left to put the engine back together without the help of his Grandpa. He had just wrestled it onto the engine block stand when Jess had texted him.

Don't worry about it. What's up?

My boxes won't all fit in my car. Would you be
able to help me move them up to Natalie's?

Your boyfriend isn't helping you out?

Not that he minded helping, but Shawn found it odd that Jess would reach out to him for something like that. Helping a girl move her bedroom from one house to another seemed like a something a boyfriend should do.

Ugh. Let's not talk about my boyfriend. He and
my dad don't get along.

He reminded himself that her relationship was none of his business.

Shawn enjoyed a break to stretch out his back and shoulders

while he and Jess worked out the details for moving day, and parsed out a schedule for painting her room. Even though he was used to doing these kinds of things at Natalie's house, it once again struck him as odd that Jess was texting *him* about helping her paint her new apartment instead of her boyfriend.

I guess it isn't all that *weird. I am a handyman, after all.*

And there were worse ways to spend a weekend than helping out a pretty girl.

THE NEXT DAY, Shawn texted Jess bright and early to arrange a pick-up. The two of them had agreed that they'd start getting Jess's room ready this weekend, and Natalie had given them the go-ahead.

But even after stoking the furnace, heating up some leftover soup for breakfast and finishing his second cup of coffee, he still hadn't heard back from Jess. He fumbled with his phone for a moment, and checked the time.

It was already almost 9:00. The day was wasting away, and he couldn't wait all morning for her to get back to him.

His thumb hovered over the call button. Was it alright to call her? They'd only ever texted before.

Ah, hell, he thought, finally tapping the button next to her name, *it's her own damn fault for not answering.*

The phone rang six times before she finally picked up.

"Hello?" He heard a hoarse croak crackle from the phone.

"Jess? Ain't we supposed to be paintin' today?"

He heard some fuzzy rustling sounds and a muffled curse before eventually Jess's voice broke once more through the speaker. "It's fucking eight in the morning, Shawn," she grumbled.

"Almost nine. The day's practically over."

"I didn't even get home until three!"

Shawn smacked himself in the forehead. *Oh, right.* Jess worked late.

"I thought you took the weekend off so you could move and stuff," Shawn countered weakly.

"Yeah, the week*end*," Jess stressed the end of the word. He heard more shuffling on her end of the line. "Besides, I had a rough night." He pictured her still in bed, with tussled hair and her pajamas all disheveled…

Wait. Why was he thinking of Jess's pajamas? He shook his head.

"I'm sorry. Do you need more sleep? How long would it take you to get ready?"

Jess yawned loudly. "No, no, I'm up now. Can you give me half an hour? Do you care if I don't shower?"

Shawn swallowed as he thought of Jess in the shower. "No! No, I mean," he lowered his voice, which had risen to almost a shout, "I mean, we're gonna be covered in paint by the end of the day anyway, right? Doesn't seem to make much sense to clean up just to get dirty again."

He winced. Shawn hoped that Jess didn't have as dirty a mind as he did.

"I guess that makes sense," Jess said through another massive yawn. "Can we stop for coffee on the way?"

"Sure," Shawn said, not that he needed any more coffee.

"Alright, then. See you soon." Jess hung up the call. Shawn hoped she wasn't falling back asleep.

Half an hour later, Shawn pulled up to the address Jess had texted him and she ran out the door in an oversized hoodie, leggings, and Doc Martens. She had a backpack slung over one shoulder and her hair was sloppily piled into a mass of loops on top of her head. She carried a to-go tumbler in one hand and yanked open the passenger door with the other. She collapsed into the seat, shivering, and put the tumbler to her lips before even saying hello.

"You look cheerful this morning," Shawn teased.

Jess glared at him. "Are you always up this early?"

"Gotta be," Shawn replied, smiling extra-brightly just to annoy her. "Us contractors gotta get up with the sun."

"Ugh. You sound like my dad," Jess groaned, "Need I remind you I'm a bartender? I don't do mornings."

"Not for the next few days, you ain't. You're workin' with me this weekend to get your room ready. Natalie's been wanting to give that room a refresh for a while anyway. This'll be good!"

Shawn patted the steering wheel and Jess stifled a yawn.

"And Natalie's got a pot of coffee brewing for us," he added.

"Thank God somebody's got their priorities straight," she muttered.

When they arrived at Natalie's house, there was a car in the driveway that Jess didn't recognize. Shawn's eyebrows drew together when they pulled into the driveway, and he broke hard. Jess jumped as the lid of her tumbler, perched against her lips, burped and splashed her in the face with coffee.

"Yeesh! Shawn!" she yelped.

"Sorry, sorry," Shawn grumbled, throwing his hand behind her headrest as he began to reverse out the driveway and park street-side instead. "Didn't realize Bonnie would be here."

A shivering Natalie stepped gingerly out onto the front porch and waved at them as Shawn moved his truck.

"Sorry!" she called, as they got out of the truck and stepped up the frozen front lawn to the house, "Bonnie surprised me this morning. She's taking me wine tasting for a belated Valentine's Day weekend!"

Jess's teeth chattered as they hurriedly shuffled back into the house.

"It's a little early to start drinkin', don't you think?" Shawn said.

"Well, we're not going to start drinking just yet." Natalie

waved off his concern. She darted around the kitchen, grabbing her purse and a small suitcase.

"Hey guys!" Bonnie came around the doorway from the living room with a pillow under her arm. "Sorry to steal Natalie at the last minute! We were on the waiting list for the weekend, and I just got the notification last night. This winery down in the Shenandoah Valley is just starting to open up cabins. I couldn't pass it up!"

"Must be nice to get away for a weekend," Shawn said.

"Will you two be okay? Jess, you're still planning to move in Sunday, right?" Natalie asked.

Jess rubbed her eyes. "Yeah, if that's okay?"

"Totally. We'll be back Sunday night," Bonnie answered for her girlfriend.

"There's coffee in the pot, cash on the counter, and you guys can help yourself to anything in the fridge or the pantry," Natalie said as she followed Bonnie out the door. "Shawn, can you lock up tonight?"

"Yeah, yeah, no problem," he said.

"Thank you! See you on Sunday, Jess!"

And then Shawn and Jess were alone.

"I guess it's just us." Jess headed into the kitchen to fill her tumbler. "Two rejects with a job to do."

"Rejects?" Shawn leaned against the counter beside her. For the first time today, he noticed the bags under her eyes–red and puffy, as if she hadn't just been tired, but crying. "Jess, is every-thing okay?"

She barked out a harsh laugh. He furrowed his brow at her.

But her eyes remained fixed on her coffee, which she was preparing with cream and sugar.

"I thought you liked your coffee black?"

Finally, she met his eyes. "How do *you* know how I drink my coffee?"

"At the bar. You always drink your coffee black."

"Well, not today. Today I need something sweet in my life." She slurped a long drag off her cup like it was a cigarette, with her eyes staring off into the middle distance.

"Did something happen?" Shawn didn't know what to do with his hands. So he poured himself a cup of coffee.

"Well, my dad won't talk to me, and Kyle decided we need a break."

"A break?" Shawn set the carafe back on the burner. "What does that mean?"

"Wish I knew!" Jess sloughed away from the counter and over to the fridge. "Natalie said we could eat anything in the fridge right? You want breakfast? I want breakfast."

CHAPTER 17

Jess cooked eggs and toast while Shawn loaded up all the painting supplies into her room. She felt terrible. She'd been too emotional to finish packing before last night's shift, half of which she'd spent crying in the beer cooler. And when she'd gotten home, she was too wired to fall asleep. So instead, she'd packed more—until her dad had gotten up and started getting ready for work. She'd finally crawled into bed when she heard his alarm go off, and had barely gotten in a restless hour or two before Shawn had called her.

By the time he came back downstairs, she'd loaded up two plates so they could eat at the kitchen table. He approached her like she was a bomb about to go off.

"All right. Have you thought about the color you want to go with?"

They sat down.

"Not really," Jess admitted. She shoved a forkful of eggs into her mouth and chewed. She could hold it together. It was just painting. "Maybe blue? My room at home has been pink for as long as I can remember."

Shawn chuckled. "I assume you don't want pink anymore?"

Jess shook her head. "Or purple. It's all purple and butterflies right now. I'm ready for something a little less… girly."

Shawn patted her on the shoulder, and his tenderness surprised her. She wasn't used to receiving comfort from one of her customers. Usually, she was the one to take care of them. "Guess we should probably go to the store and pick something out before we get too into it. Unless you want to rip down all the wallpaper first?"

"Honestly?" Jess took yet another sip of coffee, "I'm still waking up over here. Why don't we get the paint?"

"Sounds good to me." Shawn waved an envelope that he pulled out of his pocket. "Natalie left some money for supplies."

"That was nice of her." Jess had expected to cover the cost of paint out of her savings.

"She said as landlord, it was the least she could do."

He fiddled with the envelope. Jess took another sip of coffee. "Do you still like her?"

"What?" He started. She observed his body language. He shifted a bit in his seat, but overall he didn't seem as dejected as the Shawn who'd been moping around her bar for the past few weeks. "Nah. I think that ship has sailed, don't you?"

"Unless you're talking about the S.S. Friendship, I'd say yes."

He laughed at the joke, and she laughed with him. He had a good laugh–the kind that sat deep in his chest, and resonated without completely leaving his body. Instead, it crinkled in the corners of his eyes and the dimples in his cheeks. He pulled out his phone to look up paint colors, and she studied him while she finished her breakfast.

Jess had always thought Shawn was attractive. But he was the kind of hot that could sneak past you if you weren't looking. His light-brown hair was a little on the long side, and messy— with waves that stuck up on the sides and flopped into his eyes when he shook his head, and little curls at the nape of his neck. He was hardly ever clean shaven—he usually had stubble dotting his cheeks and jawline. And because he was so tall, he was usually slouching when she saw him. She knew he had muscles underneath his flannel shirts and straight-cut jeans he always wore, but she'd never really seen him show them off.

She was sure if he tried, he'd have no problem finding someone even better than Natalie. He deserved someone like that.

"What?" Shawn asked. He had looked up from his phone and was eying her curiously. She wondered how long she'd been staring at him.

"Nothing!" she said quickly. "See any cool colors?"

"They got some ideas here that are pretty neat. So you definitely want color? Not something neutral?"

She thought for a second and grabbed up their empty plates to put them in the dishwasher. "Yeah. I need something bold. A change of pace."

"Here," he said, handing her his phone. "Why don't you check through these look books while I drive us there? See if anything feels right."

She took his phone, and their fingers brushed. She noticed that his were rough and dry like hers.

Maybe having some time off from Kyle will be good for me, after all.

JESS STOOD before an entire wall of rainbows.

"How does anybody pick a color?" She picked up two swatches of nearly identical beige. "How is there even a difference between half of these?"

Shawn plucked one of the samples from her hand, "There isn't really. They're basically the same."

"Yeah, but I like this one *better*," Jess said, snatching back the sample. She held them up side-by-side in front of her face. "Why do I like this one better?"

"I thought you didn't want a neutral color?" Shawn stuck his head between the two samples and stuck his tongue out at her.

The green in his eyes contrasted with the warm tones of the paper. Jess's throat tightened.

"The colors scare me," she said, her voice small. It felt like there were a lot of changes happening in her life, all at once. Was bringing a strange, vivid color into her new living space one upheaval too many?

Shawn laughed and plucked the samples out of her hands. After he put them back, he grabbed her by the arm and marched her over to the "Brights and Bolds" section of the store.

Lush shades of magenta, olive, and navy featured heavily in photos of massive, expensively decorated living rooms and kitchens. The overall effect of the display was more cohesive than the wall of swatches she'd been looking at. More focused. But also more intimidating.

Jess rubbed her arm while she sorted through the visual overload. All of the rooms in the display photos were rich and vibrant; they warred for her attention, and she blinked repeatedly in an attempt to zero in on a color that might make her feel less… panicked. She ran a hand over a sandwich board featuring their color of the week: Pantone Orange.

It wasn't doing it for her. "I think these couches cost more than my car," Jess said with a hollow chuckle, gesturing toward the garish accent furniture.

"If you choose the color of the week, I don't think we can be friends anymore," Shawn muttered close to her ear. "Only serial killers paint their bedrooms orange."

"What about mustard?" Jess teased, holding up a grungy looking yellow.

Shawn's mouth opened in a horrified grimace. Jess's shoulders shook, and some of the tension in her neck eased. She covered her mouth to stifle her laughter.

"Can I help you two find anything?" A middle-aged associate assessed them. Jess immediately stiffened again, and Shawn looked at her, gesturing for her to answer.

"Well, uh… I'm feeling a little overwhelmed," Jess admitted.

"Just bought a new house?" The lady asked kindly, "We have bulk discounts for those taking on big projects."

Jess squirmed under the lady's assumption. "No! No, I'm uh… I'm moving to a new place and picking out a color for my room."

She held back a wince at how childish she sounded. She crossed her arms over her chest and rubbed at her elbows.

"I've been here before with her landlord," Shawn cut in, "We have an account under Roche?"

Jess looked on in awe as Shawn stole back the attention of the lady, ushering her toward the counter. He looked over his shoulder to give Jess a wink. Her stomach fluttered.

She wasn't used to seeing Shawn as a professional. His demeanor completely transformed when he was in work mode: he stood straighter, tamped down his easy, country twang. Jess observed their interaction out of the corner of her eye while she continued to peruse paint swatches, eavesdropping while he recounted Natalie's color choices from memory, and explained the plans they had for the various rooms in the house. The longer he talked, the more overwhelmed Jess felt.

She frowned, pretending to be weighing the pros and cons between Bayside Breeze and Neptune, while her thoughts actually spiraled around a much deeper question. She'd been so busy packing, working, avoiding her father, that she hadn't yet dealt with any of her own emotions around her move or she and Kyle's blow-up. Was she even prepared to be on her own? What if her dad had been right about her all along? What if she *wasn't* ready?

What if Kyle wasn't as serious as she'd thought? Was this break actually a break-up? Had she thrown her entire life into chaos for a boy that didn't even love her?

Why else would this silly decision, choosing a color for her bedroom, be giving her so much anxiety?

She pretended not to see Shawn when he gave a parting wave to the associate and wandered back over to the display. Instead, she counted the seconds it took for her to inhale and exhale as he approached and forced her shoulders down away from her ears. She blinked back the extra moisture that had begun to pool in the corners of her eyes. *Jesus, what is wrong with me?* She took another shade of blue-green from its hook and held it in between the other two swatches in her hands, as if totally absorbed in her deliberation.

Shawn leaned over her shoulder. Jess stood perfectly still, still counting her breaths, still intent on pretending she hadn't noticed his return for some unknown reason. All she knew is that if she acknowledged Shawn, if she spoke to him, her cool and flippant performance would crack. He'd see her fall apart.

She felt his arm lift beside her before she saw it in her periphery, and her breath caught as he reached around her and pointed at the middle swatch.

"That one's nice," he murmured next to her ear.

Her eyes at last focused on the swatch beneath his finger. It was lighter than the other two. Calmer. She blinked away the impending tears, and her vision cleared. She was able to read the name of the color typed out in the corner.

After the Rain.

"It is, isn't it?" she said. Her voice was quiet, but surprisingly clear.

Shawn put a hand on her shoulder, and she looked up to meet his gaze. "Is that what you want to go with?"

Jess held up the swatch again, and looked back and forth between the small paper and Shawn's eyes. The same shade of blue-green reflected back to her in stereo.

"Yeah. Yeah, I think it is."

CHAPTER 18

This time, Shawn was determined not to let a woman ruin his day of painting. No putting the cart before the horse today; he was going to walk Jess through the process step by step to avoid repeating the dining room calamity. As soon as they carried up the gallons of paint and primer up to Jess's room, he started unwrapping drop cloths.

"We have tape, right?" Jess asked.

Shawn looked up, relieved. "Yeah, it's over there on the dresser."

"Great! Would you rather me help tape down the drop cloths or start spritzing the wallpaper?"

Jess held a roll of painter's tape in one hand and an empty spray bottle in the other. He could have kissed her.

"Uh, if you can get started with the wallpaper, that would be great…"

"Cool! Fabric softener in the laundry room?"

Shawn's face broke into a wide smile. "You watched the videos I sent you?"

"Well, yeah. You said it would make it easier." Jess looked at him as if he might have memory issues. "You feeling okay?"

"Yeah, yeah, I'm fine," Shawn said, waving her away. "Just thinkin' about how I wanna tackle the furniture. I'm good."

Jess nodded and left to fill up the spray bottle. He wasn't sure what exactly, but something had shifted in the paint store. She seemed to be in a much better mood. Maybe this weekend wasn't going to be so bad after all.

He scooched the bed and dresser away from the walls and into the center of the room and began covering the carpet and furniture with the drop cloths. Jess came back with the fabric softener and mixed up a diluted spray in the bathroom. For a while, they did the prep work in silence, until Shawn heard the spritzes stop. He looked up to see Jess fiddling around with her phone.

"Whatcha up to?" He didn't want to be a hard ass, but his momentary relief at Jess's preparation faltered slightly when he saw her on her phone after only half an hour of working.

"Picking out some music. I can't work in silence anymore," she said. "You got any preferences?"

Shawn shrugged, and he let out the breath he'd been holding. *Well, that's all right. Who doesn't like music?* "I only really listen to country, I guess, but I'm fine with whatever."

"Country it is!" Jess tapped her thumb to the screen. Instantly, the opening synths of "Man, I Feel Like a Woman" tweedled out of her phone speaker. She turned the volume up and placed her phone in a bowl she'd acquired at some point, amplifying the music even more. Jess shot Shawn a smile. "This okay?"

He laughed. "A little old school, but I'll take it!"

Jess smiled and turned around to get back to spraying down the wall. Shawn also tried to get back to his taping, kneeling on the floor and peeling off long runs of tape to run along the baseboards. But out of the corner of his eye, he saw Jess's hips swaying along with the beat of the music. With her back to him, he had quite the view.

He ripped a piece at the corner and tilted his head to check his work. At that moment, Jess planted her feet and held out the spray bottle like a gun, pulling the trigger with each guitar sting, looking as if she had completely forgotten Shawn was even in the room.

Entranced, he let himself watch as she strutted up and down the length of the wall, and then snatched up a scraper off of the floor beside her. She flipped her hair as she rose, making the move part of the dance. When the bridge of the song started, she sang along, wedging the scraper into the edges of the wallpaper with each thump of the kick drum and shimmying her hips to the lyrics.

Shawn couldn't have looked away even if he'd wanted to. He sat up and leaned his back against the bottom edge of the wall on his side of the room, enjoying the rest of the show. When the final chords of the song rang out from the phone on the dresser, Jess finished off her performance with a high kick and spin, landing in a triumphant pose with her holding the scraper like a microphone above her head. A bit of wallpaper fell off the blade and onto her lips, and she winced, blowing off the wet paper and shaking her head.

Shawn clapped. Jess jumped at the sound and looked over at him sheepishly. She gave a little bow and he laughed.

"I didn't realize there was choreography involved today; now I feel unprepared."

"What, I watched all your videos and you didn't study the choreography?" Jess smirked at him. She was *definitely* feeling better. He felt heat rise to his cheeks, and he turned to get back to taping.

"It's better with a mop," Jess said.

"Huh?" Shawn looked over his shoulder, confused. Jess grinned.

"When the bar closes, and I clean up for the night, that's one of my favorite songs to mop to. I work faster when I can have a little fun, you know?"

Shawn pictured her dancing around with a mop in her hands instead of a scraper, belting out Shania Twain in an empty bar.

"I bet it's quite a sight," he chuckled.

She threw a wallpaper ball at him. He ducked.

"Now get back to work, buddy. Show's over." Jess gave him a wink and turned back to the wall, bopping her head to another song that had started playing.

Tempted to ogle her a little more, he tore his eyes away from her wiggling backside and back to his work.

A few songs later, Shawn had finished taping and Jess was almost done scraping the wallpaper off of the first wall. At some point while they'd been working, Jess had taken off her sweatshirt, leaving her in just a sports bra and leggings. He got up off of the floor and stretched his back a second, then moved to examine Jess's work.

"Not bad, Jess. You make a pretty good assistant."

"Assistant?" Jess narrowed her eyes at him. "Hey now, I may have never painted before, but I think I've proved myself to be a little more useful than a mere assistant." She poked him in the chest. "Look at this wall. It's beautiful!"

Shawn picked at a stubborn patch of paper that was still stuck to the wall just above his head. "I don't know…You might have to grow a couple more inches before I can promote you to partner."

Jess put her hands on her hips. "Promote me, huh?"

Shawn nodded, looking her up and down in mock appraisal.

Jess shifted her posture slightly, and Shawn's breath caught. Whereas before his gaze had been playful, Jess's movement had pushed her hips out, and accentuated the dip in her waist. As he trained his eyes back up to her face, they swept over her chest, which looked to be straining against the tight sports bra. He swallowed.

"Well… I mean, Natalie did leave me in charge…" he said weakly.

Jess narrowed her eyes again. She'd caught him looking at her chest, he knew it. She was about to call him out on it. Heat crept up his neck as a second passed. Two seconds.

Jess rolled her eyes and let out a small "hmph," and reached her arm in front of him, standing on her tiptoes to scrape at the piece of paper he'd pointed out. Her shoulder bumped his chest, and he caught a whiff of her shampoo as she bobbed in front of him. Even stretched out to her full height, she struggled to reach it.

"I can get it, Jess," he said, grabbing the scraper from her hand. When his fingers wrapped around hers to take it, she stumbled off her toes and bumped against him, pushing her hips into his.

"Oof!" she squeaked. His other hand wrapped around her waist to catch her.

His fingers grasped at the exposed skin of her waist, sinking into the softness of her stomach. His chest tightened, and he froze with her body against his, cursing the thinness of the fabric between them, as he felt the involuntary reaction in his lower body.

Quickly, he set her onto her feet and backed away from the wall, stumbling over the bed in the middle of the room. He allowed himself to fall back onto it, shifting in his jeans as he sat down to hide the evidence of his… well… his…

Shawn gulped. "Sorry!" He said, too loudly. "I didn't mean to grab at ya, I just um… I can reach…"

"Yeah," Jess said, nodding and pushing some stray hairs behind her ear, "Why don't I cover the lower half of the walls, and you take the parts closer to the ceiling."

Shawn bit his tongue at the mention of Jess covering the

lower half. He felt a twitch in his jeans. "Mm-hmm." He nodded emphatically. "Sounds good! I'm gonna grab another scraper."

Quickly, he stood and walked as normally as he could out of the room.

"Shawn, there are already two up here!" Jess called after him.

He pretended not to hear her.

CHAPTER 19

Jess wondered if the dancing had been too much. While at first she'd just wanted to blow off some steam, after she'd noticed Shawn looking at her…

After all, she and Kyle were on a break, right?

She walked over to her phone and changed the radio station to classic rock instead—something she was used to listening to in the shop. She figured maybe if she felt more like she was in the mindset that she had working with her dad and his mechanics, she might have an easier time controlling herself around Shawn.

But I felt something with him in the paint store. Jess began spraying the next wall to soften up the glue underneath the wallpaper. She waited for it to permeate, smelling the "Spring Breeze" scent as it wafted up into the slightly musty room. Shawn still wasn't back. Had she scared him away?

She bit her lip. Jess hadn't fallen on purpose. She had been pushing him a little with the dancing and reaching in front of him. But she honestly hadn't meant to lose her balance and literally force herself on him.

She'd had a moment of clarity while they'd been driving

back to the house from the paint shop. She needed a distraction. All of the stress with her dad and Kyle—she deserved a bit of a break from it all. And Kyle had given her that, hadn't he? A break?

What better way to get over a break-up than a little rebound sex?

And Shawn was the perfect candidate.

It's not as if Jess was at any risk of falling in love with him. Shawn probably wanted a sweet girl he could take home to his parents and move to a little cabin he'd built himself in Tiny Town, West Virginia, where they'd pump out a million babies. Like everyone around here. A nice guy like him wouldn't be interested in something serious with a bartender and mechanic. He'd said it himself: they both worked all the time. Who had the energy for working around both of their schedules?

But she hadn't expected him to be so spooked by her advances. When she'd been dancing to the music, she'd seen him looking at her. And then they'd started flirting. He was the one that had caused her to lose her balance, after all, when he took her scraper. So why did he run away like that? What had she missed?

She looked down at her sports bra and leggings. Was she being too obvious? She'd packed all of her clothes already, and she'd warmed up fast while she'd been scraping the wall, so she didn't really feel guilty about losing her sweatshirt. But she supposed she was showing a little more skin than Shawn was maybe used to seeing. But then again, he grew up with a sister, didn't he? It's not like he wouldn't know Jess wore a bra.

Jess snorted, looking down at her massive chest. As if she could get away with not wearing a bra. Honestly, crammed into the super-support sports bra she was wearing, the overall picture was far more modest than had she worn any other bra. And her leggings were high-waisted, so...

She caught sight of her reflection in the full-length mirror that hung from the bathroom door. Her blonde hair came up in a halo of wisps around her face, traces of her eye make-up were splotchy and smudged along her eyelids, and her eyelashes clumped with leftover mascara. She had massive circles under her eyes. Her rounded stomach peeked over the black waistband of her leggings and creased under her sports bra, and her pale freckly arms looked bulky, causing little pockets to form in the crease by her bra straps.

Jess wasn't one to shame herself, but she acknowledged that she hadn't put much effort in this morning to look particularly good. And she had straight up admitted when they texted that morning that she hadn't showered. Maybe…maybe he just wasn't interested after all.

She sighed and started scraping the second wall, resisting the urge to bop too much to the music. She was at it for half an hour before Shawn finally came back into the room, empty-handed. She opened her mouth to apologize, but he spoke first.

"Lunch is here. I realized it was already 3:00, so I picked up some pizza. Sorry I didn't say something…" Shawn rubbed the back of his neck. "It's downstairs if you want some."

Jess suddenly realized she was starving. "That sounds great." She put down the scraper and walked toward the door. Shawn stood in the doorway, unmoving.

"You said downstairs?" she clarified. He nodded.

But he was still in her way. He looked down at her. She met his eyes and licked her lips—they were suddenly dry. The apology she'd planned stuck in her throat.

He was so tall. Probably a whole foot taller than her, or more.

"I…" Shawn cleared his throat. "I couldn't find another scraper."

Jess opened her mouth. "Yeah. It was already up here."

"Oh."

He continued to stand there and look at her, and she saw his cheeks tint a light pink underneath his stubble. Their eyes stayed locked on one another for a moment that could have been one second, or thirty.

"Well, should we get some pizza?" Jess finally said, her voice coming out a little hoarse.

"Yeah," Shawn said, breaking himself out of their momentary trance and shaking his head. "Yeah, let's eat."

Shawn finally backed out of the doorway, and Jess followed him down the hall, cursing herself.

Oh dear. The dancing *had* been too much. She'd broken him.

CHAPTER 20

*S*unday morning arrived with a chill in the air, and Shawn awoke to a dead furnace once again. He grumbled to himself as he bundled up in his flannel and heavy sweatshirt to go outside to the wood pile to get more logs and kindling. *I need to figure out a better heating situation for next year,* he thought, poking scraps of cardboard and wadded up newspaper in between sticks and bark in the wood stove. He lit a few matches and placed them strategically among the kindling, until finally he had some flames to nurse into coals.

But even his morning fight with the fire was preferable to the impending task of painting with Jess.

Not that Jess was a bad worker. On the contrary, he and Jess had made great progress the previous day, managing to remove all the wallpaper, clean, putty, and sand the walls to be ready for paint. But after their–Shawn struggled to come up with a word to encapsulate the full disaster of him getting a full-blown erection when he caught Jess as she fell against him–*incident*, he'd been unable to say two words to her without the image of her gyrating to Shania Twain replaying in full technicolor inside his brain.

What was even worse—now he had an idea of what her body felt like against him. Her *skin.* He'd felt the softness of her waist when he'd caught her, pressed himself against the generous curve of her ass, and had been far too close to letting his hand travel up her body. If he hadn't managed to pull away when he did…

He closed his eyes and let out a breath. He'd avoided coming into contact with her for the rest of the day. They'd eaten pizza in near silence, finishing the sanding late into the night before he'd had to drive her home. He'd blasted the truck radio the entire ride home, but even that couldn't completely drown out the tension in the cab.

When he'd finally gotten home, he'd taken the coldest shower he could stand to assuage the ache in his groin. Even then, his thoughts had kept him half hard until he'd finally fallen asleep, and he'd been at full attention when his alarm had jerked him awake.

She has a boyfriend. She. Has. A. Boyfriend.

But did she? After all, she'd been crying all night before he picked her up yesterday because he'd told her they needed a "break". What did that even mean?

As he dusted off wood splinters from his hands and closed up the furnace, he climbed once more into the shower. He wasn't sure how he was going to make it another day. It had been a long time since Shawn had felt like he'd needed to stay away from a girl. He stood under the warm spray of the showerhead, looking down at himself, once again hard as a fucking rock.

He leaned against the shower wall, silently arguing with himself. Why was this so difficult? He'd thought about Natalie a hundred times while he'd masturbated in the past year and managed to keep it together around her. Was Jess just that much more attractive to him?

Or was it the fact that he and Natalie had never really…

touched? Sure, they'd had the odd hug here and there, she'd kissed him on the cheek once, but both of those interactions had been entirely platonic—even if not at first in Shawn's mind, certainly in Natalie's. He could imagine what Natalie might feel like, but deep down, Shawn knew that fantasies were the most those thoughts would ever be. They were… generalized. Fuzzy. Non-specific, with no real inspiration to ground them.

He panted a little as he worked himself, his thoughts turning instead to the way Jess's body had felt against his. The phantom memory of the tiny bit of contact his fingers had had with her skin carrying the fantasy further than Shawn had ever been able to before, the pressure of his hand transforming in his head to the feeling of her ass against him. The dip in his palm changed into the hollow of her thighs. The warm water beating onto his scalp became her fingers running through his hair.

Shawn grunted, his orgasm crashing into him hard as he imagined pushing himself into her, his cum spurting in waves that diluted with the water and swirled away down the drain. He steadied his forehead against the shower wall. He breathed heavily, sanity slowly returning along with a creeping shame. He couldn't think about Jess like this. Not if he wasn't certain she was available.

Could he?

SHAWN PULLED into Jess's driveway and jumped out of the cab to open the tailgate. By the time he'd folded it down, Jess was walking out with the first box.

"Thanks so much for doing this, Shawn." She stood on her tiptoes to haul the box into the bed of the truck. He grabbed it from her, hoisting it up and sliding it toward the front. "I know we haven't hung out all that much, but I really, *really* appreciate all your help."

She touched her hand to his arm, and he looked down at her. Shawn let out a breath as he saw the smile in her golden-brown eyes. *God, she's stunning.*

"Well, of course, Jess," he said, "I mean, no use takin' three separate trips for six boxes, right?"

She chuckled, and Shawn's shoulders relaxed. *Okay,* he thought, *I can do this. We're friends. It doesn't have to be any more than that.*

They loaded the rest of the boxes into his truck and then he closed the tailgate.

"You comin' with me?" he asked.

"No, I'll follow behind in the Escort." She took a deep breath and put her ungloved hands in her coat pockets. "After all, tonight's my first night in the new place!"

"That's right," Shawn nodded. He looked back to the house. "Do you need a minute to say goodbye to your dad?"

Jess's smile hardened. "Nope. We took care of that already."

She turned away and headed to her car. "Meet you there?" she called.

"Sounds good." He hopped into his truck, and Jess followed him to Hagerstown.

After they'd arrived and moved her boxes into the house, they climbed the stairs to Jess's room to get down to painting. With the drop cloths still in place, and the edges of all of the walls taped down, the first coat of primer went on quickly.

Once again, Jess had put on some music, but Shawn was grateful that she had toned down her dancing to a minimum. Every now and then he heard her sing along quietly to a lyric or tap her toe to the beat, but overall, they kept their conversation light, and before he knew it, they'd finished two coats and were about ready for a break.

"Well, I don't know about you, but I'm starved," Jess said, disconnecting her roller from the extension handle and carefully setting it into a tray. "Why don't we wrap these up and take lunch?"

"Sounds good to me. Got anything in mind?"

Jess chewed her lip, and Shawn looked at her for a moment, realizing as he did that he'd been avoiding doing so all morning.

Today, she was wearing skinny jeans and a baggy t-shirt. Her hair was less messy, too, he noticed, pulled back in a bun atop her head instead of the wild ponytail she'd been swinging around the day before. Shawn took inventory of his feelings as he studied her.

Was she pretty? Yes. He'd always thought her pretty. He had also come to terms with the fact that he was very attracted to her when he allowed himself to think of her in *that* way, which he'd been desperately trying *not* to do since picking her up that morning. For as long as he'd known Jess, they'd been strictly friends. He'd seen her with various guys before at the bar, and he saw what she acted like around the guys she was with. And from what he could tell, she'd never treated him like anything other than another friendly face.

Until yesterday. When she'd confused him. With the dancing, and the...

Shawn stopped himself. *No, thinkin' about that isn't going to help anything.* He cleared his throat.

"Didn't Natalie say we could help ourselves to food?" Jess said. "Why don't I go down and whip up some lunch?"

Shawn blinked. "Yeah, all right. I'll clean out the brushes."

While Jess prepared food, Shawn rinsed the primer out of the rollers and brushes, scraping the hardened paint off the handles. He always hated this part of the job. It took ages. By the time he was patting down everything with some paper towels, Jess had almost finished making a stir-fry that smelled incredible.

Shawn took a deep breath, allowing the steam from the onions and garlic and a bunch of other colorful things to clear the smell of paint from his nose. "What is that, Jess? It smells great!"

"Natalie had some peppers and stuff that looked like it had been in the produce drawer for a while, so I mixed them with some spices from the cupboard." She stirred the contents of a large pan on the stove, and Shawn heard a *ding* from the end of the counter.

"Oh!" Jess started, "And she has a rice cooker! Isn't that cool? I've never used a rice cooker before, but I've always wanted to try one!" Jess popped open the lid of the large, silver appliance and steam wafted up in a giant cloud. A huge smile split Jess's face as she reached in with a spoon to fluff the rice.

"You know what would go great with this?" Jess glanced back at Shawn.

"What?"

"*Beer*," Jess's lips caressed the word like a prayer. "Do you think there's any around?"

Shawn grinned, nodding. "There's a whole case out in the garage, I'm pretty sure. I'll check."

Shawn walked outside to the detached garage, shivering as he did so. The sun was out today at least, but the temperature still hovered just below freezing. He couldn't wait for the winter to be over.

Luckily, the garage wasn't quite as cold as outside, and the bottles of beer he and Natalie had bought for their last outdoor project hadn't frozen. He grabbed a few bottles in each hand to bring inside.

By the time he got back, Jess had served two plates of rice and vegetables, mixed with what looked like sliced hot dogs and a thin, brown sauce. He set the beers on the table and sat in front of one of the plates.

"Score!" Jess cheered, sweeping two of the bottles under the table and popping the caps off in one smooth motion. Shawn raised his eyebrows at the move. She handed him one, and held hers aloft in a toast. "To almost being done with painting!"

"Amen to that," Shawn agreed, and they clinked their bottles.

As soon as Shawn took a bite of his meal, he groaned involuntarily. It was *good.* And the hot food combined with the cold beer relaxed him in a way he hadn't realized he'd needed. He leaned forward and shoveled another few bites into his mouth before resting his shoulders against the back of his chair and humming with pleasure.

"It feels so good to sit down," he said through his mouthful, and Jess giggled.

"How's the food?"

"Amazing," he said, sitting up again to eat some more. "Are these hot dogs?"

Jess winced. "Yeah, it was the only meat that was thawed. Turned out okay, though, I think." She held up a forkful and examined it.

"Good call on the beer, too," Shawn said. "We should bring a few upstairs with us when we do round two."

"Duh!" Jess's jaw dropped and she hit her forehead with her palm. "Why didn't we do that yesterday?"

They were both quiet for a second. Shawn briefly wondered what would have happened yesterday if they'd both had a few drinks first.

They both took a few more bites, and Shawn got seconds. When he sat back down at the table, he resumed drinking his beer.

Jess, who had finished her first drink, popped open another. "How long should we wait for the primer to dry?"

"Probably another hour," Shawn said, finishing his plate. He sat back, feeling full and tired.

"A whole hour??" Jess whined. She looked at her beer. "We might need a few more of these, then."

Jess slid her chair away from the table and gathered her

dishes. "You done?" She asked, and he nodded. Shawn weighed whether or not they should continue drinking. He felt as if he was inside one of those old cartoons, the main character with a cartoon angel and devil on their shoulders.

You're an adult, why not have a few beers while you paint your friend's bedroom? The devil whispered into his ear. *You don't have to drive for hours. Plenty of time to sober up. What could go wrong?*

Yes, what could possibly *go wrong if you and Jess got drunk in her bedroom?* The angel sarcastically questioned. *You remember your performance this morning in the shower, don't you? You're begging to fuck another guy's girl.*

His shoulder devil rolled his eyes. *They're* on *a* break.

What would your mother think? The angel scolded.

Shawn shook his head to rid it of the warring thoughts. You know what? He *could* use another drink.

"I'll get the rest of the case out of the garage." He pushed out his chair while Jess scooped leftovers into a Tupperware. "There's a stepladder in there we should get too, so I don't have to reach as high. My neck is killing me."

He brushed off his shoulder, sweeping off the lingering feeling that some cartoon guardians were judging him, and rolled his arm back in a circle. Then he walked out to get the rest of the beer.

ANOTHER BEER each and an hour later, he and Jess carried the stepladder and the remaining bottles to the room. He balanced the brushes and rollers under his arm, still wrapped in their damp paper towels. He set out the tools and Jess grabbed the unopened paint cans for the final coats. She took one by the base and lid, and shook it vigorously, mixing in the pigment. Shawn looked up at the sound and instantly wished he hadn't— her chest bounced wildly with her arms. He quickly refocused on his tools, setting out the trays for her to pour the paint into.

Jess, meanwhile, was feeling much more relaxed after a few beers. She worked better with a shift drink or two, she reasoned, portioning out the pigmented paint into trays. Setting the paint can back down, she reached into her pocket for her phone to start some more music, and realized her battery was about to die.

"Oh shoot," she muttered. "I need to get my charger. Be right back!"

Shawn had already started on the far corner near the ceiling, getting all the hard-to-reach spots with the stepladder when she came back up the stairs. She took her phone into the bathroom to plug it in and started the radio again, bopping back into the room.

They worked for the next few hours in amicable silence, occasionally offering one another a beer or paint refill when one of them would get up. Jess was just about done with the second coat on the baseboard trim when Shawn stooped over her. She squinted at the overhead light behind his head; at some point the sun had set outside the big windows.

"My last spot is right above you. You okay if I park the step ladder here?"

"Yeah, that's fine," she said, spreading herself flat on her side and leaning on her elbow to make room.

At last, she swiped the last few strokes of color. "Done!" She dropped her brush into the tray and stretched out her neck. She sat up carefully and reached for the beer she'd parked by her feet and finished it, too, in one big swig. "Ugh, it feels so good to be done!"

"Aaaand weeeee are!" Shawn flourished the roller as he punctuated his last few lines with his words. "All right!" He raised his arms in triumph, tilting the tray as he did so. A large paint drip rolled out and plopped on Jess's hair.

"Shawn!" she squealed, immediately touching her hand to

her hair. She felt the giant glob ooze down the sides of her face and down her forehead.

"Oh shit, I'm sorry!" Shawn hopped off the stepladder to grab a towel. Unfortunately, he jumped right into Jess's paint tray, splashing the contents all over Shawn's pants and Jess's entire side.

He groaned. "I'm so sorry!"

She froze, eyes squeezed shut as she gingerly touched her face, now covered in aquamarine glops. "Get me a towel, asshole," she said through gritted teeth, trying to move her lips as little as possible.

"Right!" Shawn said, making blue footprints on the drop-cloth as he plodded over to the roll of paper towels. He returned and began patting at her face, gently wiping away from the center. She peeked through her squinted eyelids, amber eyes shining with amusement under her long, tangled lashes.

Shawn's stomach twisted when he met her amused grimace. He gave up trying to clean her up himself, shoving the remaining paper towels in her left hand (the one *not* covered in paint). She wiped furiously at her still closed eyes and mouth, and he held back a laugh as she spat into the towel, trying and failing to keep the paint from getting into her mouth. When her eyes finally did open, he looked away and patted a towel at the splotches of paint on his jeans, which had officially become one of his "work" pairs.

"Oh Shawn?" Jess sang out. He tilted his head just in time to get smacked across the cheek with Jess's paintbrush.

He sputtered for a second in shock and scowled at her. "That's not fair! Mine was an accident!"

"Which one?" she shot back, "The aerial attack or the cover fire from the side?" She flicked her right wrist at him, and little flecks of paint flew off the tips of her fingers and onto his chest. He looked at her, fire in his eyes.

"Oh, it's on now," he said, grabbing the tray from the floor and tossing it at her, where it collided with her chest and slid back to the floor. He choked down a laugh as paint dripped straight from the apex of her boobs down to the floor. She stared down at her shirt and back at Shawn, and his heart fluttered at the devilish look she wore.

"You have no idea what you just started, Cobb. No idea."

The next thing Shawn knew, he and Jess were a blur of flying brushes, drop cloths, and turquoise.

"Truce! Truce!" he shouted some time later, crouching behind the legs of the stepladder. He was covered in splatters: a Jackson Pollock study of latex paint.

Jess towered over him, suspending a half-full can above his head. Her hair was dripping with cool blue latex, and her baggy t-shirt clung in bunches around her frame. She eyed him warily.

"You promise?"

She dangled the bucket and he held his hands above his head, sticking out his little finger. "Pinky swear!"

Slowly, she crouched in front of him, setting down the paint can. She linked her pinky with his. "Truce."

As he pulled her into standing, her baggy shirt snagged around her knees, binding her ankles on the wet dropcloth. She careened backwards, dragging Shawn with her, and if there had been any hope of saving their pants before, it was lost when they both crashed ass-first into the blue-green puddles around them. Jess cursed.

"Fucking shirt!" She yanked it over her head, and Shawn's mouth fell open. She wasn't wearing her usual sports bra underneath her t-shirt. Instead, her breasts mounded above smooth, red molded cups, heaving with every flustered breath.

He froze. Their eyes met, and her face went red underneath the splotches of blue.

The breath left Shawn's body. Suddenly, there was far too much space between them; and the sight of Jess's pale skin flushed and exposed before him pulled him in like a winch. Every other thought left his head as he pounced on her, crashing his lips against hers. The scent of paint filled his nose as he clumsily grasped at her exposed skin, thrilled to feel her hands also clutching at his white t-shirt, pulling at the hem. He felt the roughness of her fingertips scrabble underneath against his sides, contrasting with the divine softness of her lips, her cheeks, her stomach.

God, she tasted amazing. Even the gallon of paint they'd spilled couldn't cover up the taste of her.

Hands tugged at his flannel, and he shrugged it off, his mouth still locked on hers in a tangle of tongues and teeth. She gasped in a breath, and his head spun.

The *sounds* she was making. *What other sounds can I get out of her?*

He felt his dick twitch in his jeans. Alarm flared in the back of his beer-addled mind, reminding him that something about this wasn't a good idea. He pulled away as the details floated to the surface.

"Shit! You have a boyfriend."

Jess panted beneath him, her enormous breasts threatening to spill over her sexy bra with every inhale. *Jeezus, if I could only touch–*

"No–" she sat up abruptly, and he backed away. He couldn't stop looking at her. She was mesmerizing. "He broke up with me."

He blinked. "I thought you said you were on a break?" It seemed an important distinction.

"The word 'break' was definitely involved." Jess nodded, and started crawling toward him.

He kept her at arm's length. "But are you–single?" She hesitated. And that was all Shawn needed. "We should stop."

"Should we?"

The pupils of her usually light brown eyes were blown wide

open, darkening them in a way that Shawn found shockingly sexy. He swallowed.

"Y–yes. Until you figure out what's going on with all that."

And with that, he rose to his feet, slipped some boot covers onto his shoes, and left the room.

CHAPTER 21

On Monday, Jess awoke groggily to a knock on her door. The previous night had been a late one for her. She'd spent hours cleaning, agonized over Shawn and Kyle (who still hadn't responded to any of her texts), and debated whether or not it was safe for her to sleep in a room poisoned by paint fumes. In the end, she'd cracked one of the windows, turned off her phone, and collapsed onto the bed after a long, hot shower.

Sunlight streamed through the curtainless panes in the wall across from her bed. She shivered; the thin quilt on Natalie's grandmother's bed was doing little to combat the draft whistling in from the open window, and she hadn't been able to find her favorite sweatshirt to stave off the chill. The mattress was old and stiff. The sheets smelled dusty, which was a sad alternative to the smell of drying paint that still hung heavy in the room. Although some of what she was smelling might be the stubborn clumps of blue latex that hadn't washed from her hair.

She hadn't heard anything from Shawn, either, since he'd stormed out after their kiss. Was "kiss" even the right word for it? Her stomach fluttered at the memory.

No, Shawn Cobb had not simply "kissed" her. He'd attacked her like a man starved.

In the months she'd been dating Kyle, she'd ranked their sexual explorations as some of the best she'd ever had. And Jess had enjoyed some passionate make-out sessions in her twenty-two years. She knew how to please a man, and she'd ensured that the men she'd dated pleasured her in return. Sex was great: and Jessica White had great sex.

But that *kiss?*

Shawn Cobb wasn't, strictly speaking, a *good* kisser. No, the word she would use to describe Shawn's technique was *voracious.* He hadn't "kissed" her; he'd assailed her with an animalistic fervor that had brought her entire sexual experience into question. That passion she'd felt when he pressed her into the floor, that wasn't the garden-variety horniness she'd come to expect from guys her age.

It was *need.* Shawn had *needed* her.

And then he'd walked away.

She squinted her eyes at the bright winter sun as she sat up and faced the door. Her head ached, and her stomach churned with a sour mix of guilt and unresolved lust.

"Yeah?" Jess croaked.

Natalie popped her head inside as she cracked the door. She held two coffee mugs in her hand. "Hey roomie."

Jess zeroed in on the coffee. After a night of dusty sheets and acrid paint, the tantalizing scent rising from the mugs was downright heavenly. "You're back. And you brought me coffee," she said gratefully. Her throat was still hoarse from a weekend of crying.

And her shouts during yesterday's paint fight likely hadn't helped. "What time is it?"

"Around 10:30." Natalie handed her the mug and took a seat on the edge of the bed. Jess shuffled herself to face her, grateful she'd pulled on a clean nightshirt after her late-night shower. She accepted the mug and inhaled deeply.

Yes.

"It's freezing in here!" Natalie's eyes scanned the newly painted room, before lasering in on the open window. She rose and wedged it closed, before bending to turn up the baseboard heaters underneath it. If she noticed the leftover drips on the molding that Jess hadn't quite been able to smooth out, the evidence of her and Shawn's sexually-charged paint fight, she didn't let on. "You have off today, right?"

Jess nodded. "Yeah, Dave let me take off until Wednesday so I could 'settle in.'"

"That was nice of him," Natalie said. "It looks good in here. I like the blue." The two women looked around, and Jess's eyes lingered on the bunched drop cloths and the small pile of boxes in the corner of the room. She had spread Shawn's ruined flannel over them to dry: yet another reminder of Jess's track record of rejection. She slurped at her coffee.

"How was your weekend?" Jess asked, distracting herself from her own misery.

"It was great." Natalie smiled. "I had no idea there were so many vineyards around here! Bonnie took me to this one winery where they're building a whole bunch of cabins to do events and stuff, and…"

Jess nodded and covered her mouth as a big yawn overtook her. Natalie paused and shifted on the edge of the bed, losing her train of thought. "But anyway, I was thinking. You never got to shop for a dorm room or anything like that, right?"

"No." Jess rubbed her eyes. "This is the first place I've ever lived away from home."

"Okay. What's your budget?"

"Budget for what?"

Natalie gestured around the room, "For… decor, home-y stuff. Towels, sheets, trash can… you know. The basics."

Jess let out a breath. She'd been expecting to be able to take some of that with her from her dad's place. And then Kyle had offered to buy some for her…

So much for all of that. "I've got some savings, I guess. But I hadn't really been planning to buy much."

Natalie nodded, looking around the room. "Well, you're welcome to keep using the furniture here. And there's no point in buying appliances or anything, unless there's a kitchen gadget you really need that isn't already buried in a cabinet somewhere."

Jess grinned. "I did manage to sneak out the crockpot."

"Thank God for that!" Natalie laughed. "But I know that the other stuff around here—towels, sheets, this old comforter—you deserve some of your own stuff. Especially since you painted the place, you ought to make it yours a little bit, you know?"

Jess studied Natalie. A lump rose in her throat. This person had taken her in, found incidentals for her to use while she figured out how to live on her own. The rest of her life might be in shambles at the moment, but Natalie was a silver lining.

"That makes a lot of sense."

They sipped their coffee for a bit, their conversation still a little stilted since they'd yet to get to know each other. Jess was intensely aware of the decade of life experience between them; how Natalie was almost more of a cool aunt than a true peer. She hoped that could change.

"Tell ya what," Natalie said, breaking the silence and sitting a little straighter, "When I first went to college, I severely underestimated what I'd need to feel at home. Luckily, I had a roommate with a car, who took me shopping to get all the basics for my fresh start. Whaddya say we go on a little day trip? Ever been to Tyson's Corner?"

Jess's eyes widened. She'd never been one to go to the mall

with girlfriends. And her dad thought "shopping" was a four-letter word. "No."

Natalie's smile stretched from ear to ear. "You're gonna love it."

INITIALLY, Jess wasn't thrilled about spending her one day off driving two hours to the suburbs and back, all for a shopping trip that could have easily been achieved at Walmart. But Natalie was… *cool.* And if there was something Jess White needed right now, it was a girls' trip.

Although she could also use some more coffee. Natalie agreed that that would be their first stop when they arrived. As it was, the long drive would have been mind-numbing if it hadn't been for the company and a really cool playlist that Natalie had put together.

"I've never heard *any* of these songs. Who are all these people?" Jess asked after they merged onto the beltway.

"A bunch of bands I used to work with. They're cool, right? Haha, anymore, I really only get to listen while I'm driving, because Shawn will only listen to country and Bonnie likes her whiny indie garbage," Natalie laughed. "It's not garbage, but I can only listen to so many girls-with-guitars and 90s feminist rockers, you know what I mean?"

Jess didn't actually know what Natalie meant. "Honestly, the only words I understood just now were "country" and "guitar." Her stomach twisted as her mind replayed her gyrating to Shania Twain in front of Shawn.

You're such an idiot, Jess.

Natalie's jaw dopped. "Wait, wait, wait, so you haven't heard like, any of the 90s alternative go-getters? Modest Mouse, Smashing Pumpkins, The Strokes?"

"Umm…" Jess sank into her seat. She didn't know any of those bands. *They're bands, right?*

Not waiting for a response, Natalie went into action mode, grabbing her phone out of the cup holder and pushing it into Jess's lap.

"Okay, you need to exit out of this playlist and put on my nostalgia mix. If you like this stuff, your whole life will change when you hear the greats."

For the rest of the drive, Natalie belted along with songs that Jess had never heard before. She couldn't help but absorb some of her roommate's good mood, and she was almost disappointed when they pulled into the four-level parking garage and Natalie turned the music down.

"This place is huge," Jess whispered.

"Oh yeah. Honestly, it's a shame we don't have the whole day. We're gonna get a workout here, trust me."

The next four hours were a whirlwind. As promised, the two women began with a sojourn at Starbucks, where they waited in line for over twenty minutes and made themselves a game plan for the afternoon. By the time Jess got her frappuccino and a scone, she was grateful for the extra calories. According to the directory that Natalie pulled up on her phone, the stores that they needed to hit were spread across multiple floors and sprawled from corner to corner. Natalie insisted that they try Macy's first, which Jess had heard of but never been to, and from that moment forward everything began to blur.

By the time Jess came to, she and Nat had six enormous shopping bags, more than a couple blisters, and stomachs that were beginning to eat themselves. Jess didn't want to think about the strain this had put on her savings. She'd had to rein Natalie in on a few things, but Jess couldn't justify buying matching hand towels or closet organizers when she had already spent so much on bedding and other necessities. With her relationship with Kyle imploding, and her job at the shop up in the air, who even knew how long she'd even be staying with Natalie?

The two of them collapsed on a curved leather sofa in a sitting area in the wide walkway surrounded by specialty shops. The scent of chocolates and soft pretzels wafted past their noses as their muscles relaxed. But with that brief respite, the adrenaline and serotonin rush of shopping in a new environment gave way to the inevitable crash. All the stress of the past week and her feelings over her dad, Kyle, and now Shawn, encroached on Jess, and tears threatened the backs of her eyes. Sitting down had been a mistake.

"I'm exhausted," Jess said.

"I'm *starving.*" Natalie looked at her. "Why don't I treat us to dinner?"

Jess wasn't even sure she had the energy to walk back to the car. She could feel the unresolved emotions of the weekend overwhelming her, and the idea of holding herself together for another hour in a restaurant was torture. She summoned her customer service persona. "Oh, Nat. I can't ask you to do that!"

"You're not asking. I'm offering. We need some food or we're going to pass out before we even get on the Beltway."

Jess couldn't argue with that.

"Come on," Natalie grunted, rising onto her feet and wincing. "The longer we sit here, the harder it's going to be to get up."

Jess whimpered. Natalie gave her a look and nudged her with a shopping bag.

"Okay, okay, I'm coming."

The hostess directed Jess and Natalie through the nearly empty Cheesecake Factory to a booth that seemed far too large for two people. Jess flopped herself into the seat and scanned the giant menu. She was positively overwhelmed by all of the options. Setting it back down on the table, she asked the waiter for a beer and looked across the table at Natalie.

"What are you getting?" Jess asked.

"That is the question, isn't it?" Natalie mused. "We've probably walked enough to earn some pasta, right?"

Jess nodded, seizing the path of least resistance. She glanced again at the menu and settled on the first pasta option on the list.

After the waiter delivered their drinks, Natalie broke the silence. "So how did your weekend go, Jess? How was painting with Shawn?"

Jess, who had been mid-sip when Natalie asked, coughed a little at the question. "Fine," she choked out. Natalie waited for her to set her beer down and take a sip of water.

"I'm glad that the two of you are friends. Especially with how often he comes over to work on stuff, it would be pretty awkward if you two didn't get along."

Jess nodded, air bubbles still tickling the base of her throat. "Uh-huh." She sipped more water. "You two seem pretty close," she said, when she felt like she could speak without her voice breaking. By then, their food had arrived.

"He's one of the reasons I stayed in Maryland," Natalie said, a wistful smile crinkling her eyes.

Jess twirled her fettuccine around her fork. "Was there ever anything… between you and Shawn?"

Natalie snorted. "Me and *Shawn?*" Jess frowned at her reaction. Natalie shook her head. "I'm sorry, that came out wrong."

Jess waited while her roommate chewed thoughtfully on a meatball. "Shawn, to me, is something I've never had before," she finally said. "He's my best friend. He was there for me at some of the darkest moments of this past year. If it weren't for him and Bonnie, I mean…"

She drifted off, finally shrugging as if she'd made her point.

"What about you and Bonnie?" Jess asked. "She's the other reason you stayed?"

Natalie chuckled to herself. "I didn't plan it that way, trust me. Bonnie and I weren't supposed to be forever. It just kinda… happened."

Jess tilted her head. "You think you and Bonnie are gonna be forever?"

Natalie met her eyes. Jess was taken aback at the seriousness there. She needed to know what it felt like. How did you know someone was *the* one?

The way Kyle had wanted to provide for her, take care of her, she'd thought he'd meant he was thinking about forever. And wasn't someone supposed to make sacrifices for their happily forever after? Like Natalie had sacrificed her life in L.A.? Like Jess had sacrificed her career as a mechanic?

"I do. When I'm with her, I feel like… like the bullshit doesn't matter anymore. That together, the two of us can be ourselves without scaring each other. I'm not pretending with Bonnie, I don't have to try to be something I'm not. I'd never felt that with another person before I met her." She blinked, and took another bite of her pasta. "And the sex is amazing."

Jess snorted. "Sex is sex. Sure, some fucks are better than others, but in the end…"

The memory of Shawn's kiss popped into her head, and her stomach did that twisty thing that it had the night before. She paused with her fork suspended above her plate. *Was* sex just sex? Was there something she'd been missing?

"You see, I thought so too!" Natalie jumped in, eyes going wide. She clapped a hand on the table and picked up her wine, "But there is totally such a thing as life-changing sex."

"Really?" Jess lifted her beer to her lips. She reflected back on her relationship with Kyle. They had good sex–very good sex. Jess obviously liked it, and she almost always came. But it had always been like scratching a really strong itch with Kyle, she thought. Sometimes, you just got the itch, and needed your boyfriend to scratch it. And it feels great, and then you don't itch anymore.

But that kiss...

Different. Shawn had definitely felt different. Exciting. Impulsive. A bit sloppy, really, if she were being honest. But in the way a jumpy, old five-speed Jeep Wrangler was sloppy–the kind of barely-restrained power that had you clenching the steering wheel when you pop the clutch out from fourth gear into second so you don't crash while you're offroading. Just pure wild energy and adrenaline.

But life-changing?

"You sure it's not just 'cause you're with a woman?" Jess was asking honestly. Maybe sex with women was different.

"Ha!" Natalie finished chewing and took a sip of her wine. "For the sake of all the straight women out there, I sure hope not!"

LATER THAT NIGHT, Jess sandwiched herself between her new sheets and comforter, and checked her phone again to see if Kyle had responded.

Nothing.

Jess turned to her side. The gray check mark underneath her last message informed her he'd read her question, which only confirmed her suspicions. He'd ghosted her.

Well, fine then. She'd had a weekend full of new beginnings: new home, new paint, new sheets...

Maybe it was time for a new boyfriend.

> I got myself new sheets. Looks like I won't be needing you to help me break them in, after all.

Sent. Read.

Three dots appeared for a fraction of a second, and then...

Nothing.

Jess waited another minute before locking her phone screen, setting it on the nightstand, and rolling over, ready to start tomorrow as a single woman.

CHAPTER 22

*J*ess blinked at the text message, and dropped her phone back onto the nightstand before shoving her head back under her pillow. When she'd seen the notification, she'd assumed it would be from Kyle. But once again he'd neglected her message, and she felt surprisingly... okay about it.

In fact, seeing Shawn's name on her phone screen had spurned an entirely different emotion inside of her. Maybe if she pressed her pillow down hard enough, she could snuff out the butterflies that had awoken in her stomach along with the harsh winter sunlight.

She'd yet to hang her blackout curtains, although she *had* managed to unpack her clothes and arrange the bathroom the way she wanted it. She had been hoping to actually sleep in before her return shift at the bar that evening, but it seemed that *both* of her new friends were intent on breaking her late-to-bed, late-to-rise sleep schedule.

However, Shawn Cobb was texting her again. And he wanted a favor.

Do you have to ask at the ass-crack of dawn?

It's literally almost noon.

Jess squinted at the time in the corner of the screen. It was 10:04.

I need to teach you how time works. You see,
there are 12 hours in a day…

Haha, Jess. But seriously. How good are you
with vintage Chevys?

Jess sat up. Was this about the car he was fixing up with his Grandpa? Her hands ached to get greasy again.

Any vintage Chevy, or 1954 Chevrolet Bel Airs?

Can you come over today and take a look for
me? I'm totally stumped.

Jess's lips parted in a wide smile. The butterflies stirred.

Okay, but I'm going to shower first. I'm pretty
sure I still have paint in my hair.

"OH… MY… GOSH!" Jess gaped as Shawn unveiled a near-mint original vintage Chevy. Okay, maybe "mint" was a strong word; it had clearly been sitting for a while and there were a few tiny chips and dings around the fenders and headlights. And apparently the engine didn't work.

But the body was beautiful. Somebody had loved this car, had kept this car indoors for the duration of its life, it looked like. Jess's hand trembled as she reached for the hood.

"May I...?" she whispered.

"Yeah!" Shawn gestured for her to come closer, and she slowly approached, afraid the sound of her footsteps might cause the illusion to break, that it might be some crazy dream. Something about this car made the hairs on the back of Jess's neck stand up. It was... familiar, somehow.

Of course, that feeling could have something to do with her proximity to the man who'd been living rent-free in her fantasies for the past two days. After her discussion with Natalie, their paint fight had been playing on repeat whenever Jess closed her eyes.

But this car *did* ring a bell deep in the recesses of Jess's brain. Where had she seen this kind of car before?

"Where did you find this?" she said, running her fingers along the faded paint job.

"Natalie's garage." Shawn beamed at her. Jess ignored the way her heart skipped a beat and shook her head.

"No way. Natalie's grandparents were the kind of people that saved their jelly jars and used them as drinking glasses. There's no way they appreciated the finer things like *this* beautiful girl." Jess reached for the door handle. "Can I see the interior?"

"Sure!" Shawn said. He hurried over to the passenger's side and climbed in while Jess sunk into the ivory leather bench seat behind the steering column. She looked up and padded her fingers against the white fabric shell top—the *still intact fabric top.*

"Shawn, this is unreal," Jess breathed, fingering the side-mount stick shift and palming the white plastic of the steering wheel, "This is seriously the car that Natalie just... *gave* you?"

"You understand now why I feel bad about charging her for anything," Shawn said. Jess nodded, still disbelieving her eyes.

You didn't see vintage cars from the 1950s in this kind of condition on the east coast. Maybe in California, or Utah, or places where it never rained or snowed, but here, in the Potomac River Valley in the heart of Appalachia… mountains and water ate cars like this for breakfast. For one of these to survive 60+ years in this kind of condition…

She looked up from her examination of the dash and was shocked to see Shawn's face eerily close to hers. She coughed. "What's wrong with the engine?" Jess tilted her head to gesture past the windshield, increasing the space between them.

Shawn grimaced. At first she wondered if he was disappointed that she'd pulled back from him, but then he blew out a breath.

"That's what I need your help with," he rubbed his palms on his knees. He shortened the space between them on the bench again and pointed through the dash at the half-assembled engine block. She held her breath. "I have triple checked and polished that head gasket within an inch of its life and I can't figure out why it won't stay runnin'."

"It chokes?" Jess asked, swallowing. She could smell his body wash.

"It's weird," Shawn continued, turning to face her. She mirrored him. "When you first start it, you think it's okay, but then it kinda drags, you know? Not quite putters, but… it's almost like all the cylinders are like, not sure 'bout really goin', you know what I mean? And then, after about twenty minutes, it just… stops. Can't get it to start again until the engine cools down, sometimes for hours."

Jess furrowed her brow, and shifted her focus from the close heat of Shawn's body to the problem at hand. "That doesn't make sense. If the engine block and cylinders and head gasket are all fine, that's gotta be a fuel line problem then."

"It's got all new fuel lines!" Shawn became animated, his hands waving as he continued to describe the problem, "I replaced 'em all first thing, when I got it up here. I'm wonderin' if it was a fluke, if maybe–"

In his excitement, he'd gestured a little too far and smacked Jess's boob. She jumped in surprise.

Shawn turned beet red.

"I'm sorry, I didn't mean to do that!" He scooched back, as if just now realizing how close their bodies were. He shoved his butt into the passenger door, and Jess's nervousness bubbled over in a loud laugh.

"Shawn?"

A voice rang through the garage, and Jess ducked, flattening herself against the bench seat. Shawn's head whipped toward the door to the house, and he scrambled out of the car.

As he closed the door, he saw Jess hiding, and tilted his head at her for a fraction of a second before an amused sparkle lit his eyes. He shut the door quickly, and Jess froze.

Why am I hiding?

It took her a moment to realize that her reaction had been a holdover from her teenage days, hiding from her father whenever she'd snuck one of her boyfriends into the shop. But this wasn't Ernie's Garage. And Shawn wasn't her boyfriend. So why did she feel like she'd been caught with her hand in the proverbial cookie jar?

She'd already been pressed against the seat for almost thirty seconds. Shawn was talking to whoever had come into the garage and, for some reason, hadn't acknowledged her. So not only was she hiding, but *he* was hiding *her.*

What's going on?

"So I took your advice," the new person was saying. Jess quieted her thoughts and listened in. It sounded like a young woman, someone Jess's age maybe.

"Whatcha mean? What advice?" Shawn asked.

Jess heard heels click against the concrete and a *slumph* as someone leaned against the top of the car. *Shit!* Jess thought.

Her heart was racing. In the heat of the moment, she sunk deeper into the white leather, seeing Shawn's shadow as he, too, leaned his body against the passenger side, covering the window with his back. *Good one, Shawn!* She cheered to herself, before tuning back into their conversation.

"—to let him get a little… handsy," the woman was saying. She had lowered her voice, and Jess had to strain a bit to hear her.

Had she just said "handsy"?

"Ugh, Mel!! I *don't* want to hear this!" Shawn said, and Jess imagined him covering his ears with his hands. She chuckled silently at the image.

"Shawn, please, I need your help! What do I do now? He wants… I think he wants more now!"

Jess heard Shawn groan and shift against the car. "Mel, what on earth makes you think it's a good idea to talk to your brother about this kinda stuff?"

Ah, right, his sister. She must be talking about her fiancé.

With Shawn. Her brother. Jess made a face. That was weird.

"I don't know who else to talk to, Shawn! Mom and Dad think we're waiting to do any of that stuff until marriage. My friends all go to our church, and they can't know I'm thinking about this stuff! And I don't trust the magazines—plus, mom might find them. You're a real, living guy, and I trust you! *Please,* what do guys like?? What's sexy?"

Jess covered her mouth with her hands to keep from laughing. This girl wasn't real. Seriously? What church did they even go to? She was about to get *married* and she'd never even had *sex?*

"Different guys like different stuff, Mel!" Shawn argued, "Besides, you know I don't really know any better than you do!"

Wait. What?

Quiet stretched for what felt like an agonizingly long

moment as Jess held her breath, waiting for some kind of clarification. He couldn't mean…

Shawn wasn't a… *virgin.*

Was he?

"Oh come on, you have to have like, thought about it or something!" Mel said.

"Clearly, *you* have, Mel! What do you *want* to do to him?" Shawn countered.

Another silence ensued and Jess imagined Mel was too embarrassed to form words. Jess winced. This exchange was painful. Part of her wanted to burst out of the convertible right now and put this poor girl out of her misery.

But another part of her was curious to hear what the man had to say. What *did* Shawn Cobb find sexy?

She felt the car shift as Shawn turned to face his sister, still leaning against the window.

"Look, Mel, you know what I'd want?" He paused, and let out a big breath, "I'd… If I were with a girl… and she were… you know, if she really wanted… well, *me,* I guess… I'd want her to make it clear. You know? Take out the guesswork. Just be direct and clear and give me what she wants to give me."

Silence for a moment, and then–

"Shawn, that's bogus! Christopher *knows* I like him, okay? We're *engaged.* And how am I supposed to know what I want if I don't even know what… what it *is?*"

Okay. That was about enough for Jess. Hiding and pretending to be a naughty teenager again had been fun, but if this was the kind of puritanical naiveté she'd be forced to endure to keep up the charade, she wasn't going to make it another second. She was about to prop herself back up and open the door when Shawn blurted out,

"I don't know, Mel. Give him a blowjob or something!"

Jess froze. Her heartbeat stuttered into doubletime.

This was the weirdest fucking conversation she'd ever over-heard. But she couldn't stop listening.

"With my *mouth?*" Mel squeaked. Jess put her hand to her face.

This girl's unbelievable.

"How… how does that work?"

Once again, Jess found herself torn between all-consuming embarrassment for this girl and her curiosity in hearing Shawn's answer.

"Look, you eat bananas, right?" Shawn asked.

Jess's jaw dropped. He was *not.*

"You know, like that. But not the biting part." He finished lamely.

Jess closed her eyes. Dear God. He *was* actually a virgin.

"Shawn, you have been entirely unhelpful. I guess I'll google it." Jess felt the weight of the car shift and heard the click of heels retreat back into the house.

Jess almost didn't have the strength to sit back up after that. She couldn't believe what she'd just heard. She heard the click of the passenger door and felt the leather of the seat shift as Shawn got back in the car.

They looked at each other. His face was crimson.

"Like eating a *banana?*" she deadpanned, staring him down.

"You try talking to your sister about sex, okay?" he muttered.

Jess's stare didn't wither. She leaned closer to him, and he shrank into the door. She barked out an incredulous laugh. "You've never actually gotten a blowjob, have you?"

His cheeks flushed, impossibly, even redder.

"Jess, I don't–"

"Oh my gosh, you actually haven't!" Jess interrupted him. She covered her mouth with her hands and groaned, "Oh, Shawn, *baby.*"

"Don't call me that!" Shawn slammed his hands down on his knees. "I haven't dated since high school, okay? And I'm not just gonna do that kind of stuff with anyone, you know? It's gotta, like, be special, or something. Don't it?"

Jess didn't answer him. The temperature in the cab notched up a couple degrees.

"Come on, you know what I mean."

Jess didn't break eye contact, but raised her brows. "No. I honestly don't."

Shawn blinked at her. "Well, you gotta, I mean, it…"

She looked at him expectantly, allowing him an attempt to defend himself.

He finally shook his head and groaned, raising his hands to his face. "Jess, I… I don't know. O' course I've *wanted* to, you know, but…"

Her face softened. She didn't need to torture the poor guy.

"What's held you back, Shawn? There has to have been girls who have offered."

Shawn's eyes went wide, "What do you mean?"

Jess snorted. "Seriously? Shawn, you're a great guy. You're hot. You're telling me girls haven't tried to jump you in the past?"

"Jump me?" Shawn leaned back. "Like, mug me??"

Jess pinched the bridge of her nose. "Shawn, I know you know what I mean."

He winced. "Sorry, bad joke." He gazed at the ceiling of the car, and rubbed his hands nervously down his jeans. "I… I've always felt… like there's pressure, you know? I don't have anything against it, but it's always felt like… like it's gotta mean something, I guess. Like with Mel; She's found the one. Christopher. It's gonna mean something for them."

"Mean *what?*" Jess smirked. "Just because they're virgins it's gonna be better or something? Look, Shawn," Jess put a hand on his leg. "I've slept with my fair share of virgins, okay? If Mel's expecting things to be better because she and Chris have waited for each other or some shit, she's gonna be in for a rude awakening on their wedding night."

"Gee, thanks, Jess. Now I *know* my first time's gonna suck."

Jess bit her tongue. *Great job, genius. Way to make him feel worse.*

"Take off your pants."

Shawn jumped in the seat. *"What?"*

Jess rubbed Shawn's arm with the back of her knuckles. Goosebumps trailed in the wake of her touch. Shawn fidgeted.

Okay. Suddenly, Shawn's nervousness over the weekend, the abruptness of his departure, made a lot more sense. He hadn't just been jumpy because she'd had a boyfriend. He'd been scared. It wasn't that he didn't want her, it was that he didn't know how to ask.

I can fix that.

"Would you like a blowjob, Shawn?" she asked.

Shawn looked like he'd just short-circuited for a moment. She gave him a second, and he shook his head and scowled at her. "That ain't fuckin' funny, Jess. You're bein' kinda mean, now. You've got a boyfriend, remember?"

Jess stopped the stroking of her knuckles and laid her palm where she'd been rubbing. She looked him in the eyes, her face serious.

"I'm not joking, Shawn," she said quietly. "I broke up with Kyle." His eyes widened. She cleared her throat. "I'm sorry, I shouldn't have said that about virgins. That wasn't nice."

"Uh… that—that's okay…"

Shawn's Adam's apple bobbed as he swallowed and looked into her eyes. Jess smiled at him gently.

"Would you like a blowjob?" she asked again, not breaking eye contact. She watched as panic flashed behind his eyes.

His light, aquamarine eyes. The color she'd chosen for her bedroom walls.

"You don't have to if you don't want to," she said.

"No, I–" he croaked, then cleared his throat. "I didn't say that."

Jess thought back to what Shawn had said to Mel, before the banana thing. About how he wanted a girl to be clear, direct.

He could have just been trying to get out of talking about sex. But what if that was actually what turned him on?

"Shawn," Jess said, moving her hand slowly up his arm, down his chest, and pausing at his waistband, "I want to unbutton your pants, take your cock out your boxers, and stick it in my mouth."

He sucked in a breath and closed his eyes in what looked like pain. She tilted her head. Maybe that had been too far.

"*Fffffuck,*" Shawn hissed, and grabbed Jess's hand, still poised on the waistband of his jeans. He opened his eyes and stared her down. "Are you for fuckin' real right now?"

Jess smiled widely. "One hundred percent."

He blinked, and then nodded. "Okay."

"Okay?"

"D-do it."

Jess reached down to his belt, and then paused. She wanted to give him the best blowjob he'd ever had, and likely would ever have, for a few years at least. She wanted him to remember this as the bar for all future blow jobs.

But she also wanted to make him work for it.

"So, just to be clear, what do you want me to do?" she asked sweetly, nudging his left thigh toward the back of the seat, so he would let her settle in between his legs on the bench seat.

"What… what you just said you wanted to do," he panted.

Oh God, he was panting. Literally panting.

And she hadn't even *touched* him yet.

"So, you want me to…" Jess looked up at him through her eyelashes. She let the question hang in the air, hovering perfectly still between his legs.

"U-unbuckle my pants…"

"Uh-huh…?" She egged him on, unbuckling his belt and stopping with her fingers on the button of his jeans. He swallowed again, staring unblinking at her hand.

"Unbutton…"

She poked the button through the hole and slowly unzipped his jeans. He moaned. She froze.

"Jess—" he groaned.

"What next?"

"M-my–"

"Your co-ck?" She clicked an extra hard "k" sound at the end of the word.

Oh, she wanted him to *beg* for it.

"Yeah," he breathed, closing his eyes.

"Say it, Shawn. What do you want me to do with your cock?"

"Take it out!" He squirmed against her fingers, and she pulled them away an inch.

"Take what out, Shawn?" she asked.

"My cock!" he said at last, and she pulled down the waistband of his boxer briefs and released the bulge that had been steadily increasing in size while she'd been teasing him.

Now it was her turn to be speechless. Her eyes widened a bit at the length of it, as she carefully pulled it from the leg of his pants.

He was large. Not unpleasantly so, but larger than she'd been expecting. And *hard.*

She gathered herself as she stroked up and down the velvety skin with her fingers, light touches first, before surrounding the girth of it with her whole hand. He hissed and his hips shook a little when she bent towards the tip with her mouth.

And then she remembered their little game. She stopped, and looked at him.

His eyes bore into hers. He'd been gaping at her.

"What would you like me to do with this cock, Shawn?" she purred. He didn't even take a breath.

"Suck it."

She couldn't help herself. She wasn't strong enough.

"Like a banana?" Her mouth opened on a light laugh.

He grabbed her by the back of the head and shoved her onto his cock.

Jess gasped in surprise at the unexpected force, and the head of his cock pushed into the roof of her mouth. She wrapped her lips around him and caught her bearings, humming around him as she took him deeper, his hands loosening immediately as he hissed out a breath above her.

"Oh, *shit*, Jess. I'm sorry, I–"

"Mm-mm," she moaned, cutting him off. She'd felt a gush between her thighs when he'd grabbed her by the hair unexpectedly, and now that she finally had him in her mouth, her pussy was throbbing. She grabbed the base of his cock with one hand and slurped at the rest of his cock with her mouth, swirling her tongue around the head and flicking at the tip at the apex of each stroke up the shaft. With her other hand, she reached up his body, pawing at his surprisingly muscular chest through his t-shirt. She felt his fingers entwine with hers, something she hadn't been expecting, and more heat pooled between her thighs.

Shawn was *fun*.

His hips bucked and he tensed inside her mouth. She pulled back, switching to her hand for a moment so they both could catch their breath. She saw his eyelids droop, and his cock twitched again in her hands.

She wasn't ready for him to come yet, but she also wanted to lick him again.

She slowed her hand, pulling off even more until just her fingertips grazed the tightened skin around his shaft. Then she leaned down and lapped her tongue once, twice, three times at the little ridge around its head.

She felt a shiver scale Shawn's entire body: from his knees

that clenched tight around her hips all the way up his stomach and to his throat where a soft moan escaped.

Her clit was pulsing with her heartbeat, her mouth salivating for him. She was almost worried she was going to leave a puddle on the bench.

With her fingers, Jess tilted Shawn's cock down toward her mouth, and she heard his breath hitch. His eyes met hers, and he practically begged her to take him in her mouth again.

She obliged, relaxing her tongue and throat to get all the way down to the base.

"Oh fuck, Jess, I'm gonna–" Shawn groaned, and tapped her shoulder with his free hand. Jess hummed in approval, still sucking, and flashed her eyes at him, giving him permission to finish in her mouth.

He squeezed her fingers against his chest and held her back with his other hand as his body tensed and she felt his cum shoot into the back of her throat. She clenched her tongue around his shaft and sucked him to the roof of her mouth as he grunted again and again, cum pooling against her tongue with each one. He stilled, panting, the hand he'd placed against her back shaking as he reached up to stroke her hair.

His other hand stayed curled around hers on his chest, and she kept his dick in her mouth for a few more seconds as she swallowed away the evidence of his orgasm, suckling his slowly softening cock as she did.

She almost didn't want to put it away just yet.

She heard a thunk and pulled herself off of him to look up. He'd let his head fall against the passenger window and closed his eyes.

His fingers still tangled in her hair, he scratched her scalp absentmindedly while he caught his breath. Finally, he opened his eyes, and she smirked at him.

"Like eating a banana." She snorted under her breath.

He laughed, and she swore she could see years of tension leak out of his body with each shake of his shoulders.

"When yer right, yer right," he said, straightening and giving her a heart-melting smile. "That was nothin' like eatin' a banana."

CHAPTER 23

Shawn was exhausted. After he and Jess had—well, after *Jess* had…

After whatever had happened there in his parents' garage, all he'd wanted to do was take a nap. Preferably on a bed, and preferably next to the girl who'd just given him something that had sounded a lot more commonplace when he'd heard the guys at the bar talk about it.

But there was nothing common about what Jess had done to him. Just thinking about it, as tired as he was, made his entire lower half go tingly, in a way with which Shawn was at once familiar and altogether inexperienced.

Because now, he *knew*. He knew what it felt like to have a girl make him come. And it was better than he'd ever imagined.

And he'd thought *kissing* her had been amazing.

When he'd finally regained the strength to climb out of the front seat, they'd worked a bit more on the car (which had certainly been interesting), and she'd been all smiles: touching his hand on the stick shift before jumping out of the cab and bouncing her way to the open hood.

Shawn hadn't noticed before how bouncy she was. Her wavy

blonde hair in its perky ponytail swung with each step; her tiny feet, that somehow balanced her wide hips and thighs and huge breasts.

Shawn swallowed. He couldn't look at her the same way now. This was a million times worse than when she'd taken off her shirt after the paint fight. But that wasn't the whole story, either. She'd also been completely straightforward with him, eliminating the awkwardness that had been there before.

And she'd broken up with her boyfriend. *For me?*

Shawn braked a little too fast at the red light coming off the exit toward his grandpa's cabin. He needed a nap. He was too loopy to be driving right now. Drunk, without a drop of alcohol in his system. And he could feel his pulse in his jeans.

Somehow, he got to the country road that led to the cabin and up the winding, wooded driveway. He took lumbering steps to the front door and unlocked it, slamming it closed behind him before quickly stoking the furnace, crashing on the big leather couch and turning on the TV.

He couldn't focus on it, though. In his mind, all he could think about were flashes of him and Jess in the front seat of the Bel Air, with her soft lips wrapped around him. The way her chest was smushed between his thighs, giving him a tantalizing view down her V-neck t-shirt each time she lifted her head off of him and did that light licking thing with her tongue that made electric shocks travel up and down his whole body. How had she known to do that?

While his thoughts had drifted back in time, he'd unzipped his jeans and pulled his dick out, absentmindedly playing with it as the memories replayed in his mind. He was hard, and he knew he wouldn't be able to fall asleep without taking care of himself. But he was also too tired to get the tissues from his bedroom.

He wondered if there was a way to recreate what Jess had done, with the teasing, and the wet warmth of her mouth wrapping around him and squeezing him tight with her tongue and the roof of her mouth. He imagined it as he stroked himself, backing off every now and then to do light taps around the head with his fingers, like he remembered Jess doing with her tongue. He tried to imagine the smell of her hair, the way it would move with each bob of her head. How her tiny fingers wove with his big hand on his chest. The soft pressure of her body stretched along his legs…

He came in a sticky rush over his hand, much sooner than he'd been expecting, and his head jerked as the orgasm consumed him, the replay of him and Jess magnifying the intensity in a way his previous fantasies never had. What was it about her that drove him absolutely crazy?

When he finally finished, he collapsed back down onto the couch, a puddle of white goo on his stomach, too tired to think about cleaning up just yet.

When he did eventually shower and collapse into his bed, he slept better than he had in months.

THE NEXT DAY, Shawn awoke refreshed and determined to find some work. He was going to fix this car if it was the last thing he did.

He posted before and after pictures of the paint job of Jess's room to his Facebook page, being sure to include how meticulously taped everything had been before they'd started. Painting was something that could still be done in the winter time, after all. Maybe he could get a few jobs on the calendar before spring.

A little while later, after he'd taken care of the furnace and finished his second cup of coffee, Natalie called.

"Hey Nat, what's up?"

"Nice post this morning!"

He smiled. Like him, Natalie had a hard time staying idle,

even when there wasn't much work to be had. "But unfortunately, I once again need your help."

Shawn braced himself. "Okaaaay…"

"My kitchen sink is draining really slowly. Could you come check it out?"

Shawn grimaced. It was likely all the paint. He hoped he hadn't messed up her septic.

"Sure thing, Nat. Be right there."

"Thanks, Shawn! I'll make it worth your while."

"You always say that," Shawn teased. He realized with a start that in the past, Natalie saying those kinds of innuendos would have twisted his stomach into knots. But now? Nary a pang.

"Right, but this time Jess bought donuts."

Oh, *there* was the pang.

Right, Shawn remembered, *Jess lives at Natalie's house now.* Shawn's palms began to sweat. "Jess is up at this hour?"

"Haha, she sure is! We're making a morning person out of her!"

"I'm not happy about it!" Shawn heard Jess shout in the background. His heart beat a little faster.

"I guess I'll see you both soon, then."

"See you soon!"

Shawn put his phone back in his pocket and rubbed his eyes. But in the same moment, his stomach bubbled with anticipation at the thought of seeing Jess again.

He grabbed his truck keys and his jacket and headed out.

NATALIE GREETED him at the door with a smile. "Hey you! I feel like I haven't seen you in ages!" She reached out for a hug.

Shawn returned it, and then they walked back to the kitchen. "I guess it has been almost a week, hasn't it?" He paused briefly, wondering at how he hadn't even really missed her. "Where's Jess?"

"She's in the shower," Natalie answered. She gestured to an open box on the table. "Donut?"

"Yes!" Shawn grabbed a Boston Creme and devoured half in one bite. He got out his phone to do a quick search on "paint septic backup" while he chewed. The results weren't good. "Shit," he muttered.

"What's wrong?" Natalie sat down across from him. He counted for a minute in his head.

"How many rooms have we painted?" he asked her.

"Only a few, I thought. The dining room, Jess's room, and Bonnie and I did the living room in December."

"Hmm." Shawn didn't want Natalie to panic. "Is it just the kitchen sink that's backed up?"

"Yeah. The tub and bathroom sinks are okay, or were this morning."

Shawn nodded. "Okay, that's a good sign. Probably not a septic backup then."

"What does that have to do with painting?" Natalie furrowed her brow.

"We shouldn't be rinsing out the brushes and rollers in the sink. The paint can clog up the septic."

Natalie shook her head at him. "How'd you learn all this stuff, Shawn?"

He tapped the side of his head, "Just gotta keep it all organized, you know? You learn as you go."

He finished his donut and made his way over to the sink. He shined a light into the drain. "Well, I'm gonna grab my toolbox and figure this out for ya. Hopefully it's just a clog. If I see any paint in the P drain, I'll take it out and flush it with some mineral spirits."

"Right. Mineralize the P drain," Natalie said.

He rolled his eyes at her. "You're hopeless, Nat."

"That's why you're here!"

He snorted under his breath and headed out into the hallway to get his toolbox, bumping right into Jess.

"Shit!" she hissed. "Sorry, Shawn, I'm in a hurry. Sheila called in sick so I'm working a double today and I'm running late!"

They danced around each other for a few seconds as they both attempted to pass each other in the same direction. Finally, Shawn grabbed hold of Jess's shoulders and physically turned the two of them around. Jess caught his eye, and he smiled at her. "I'll move my truck then. I'm blocking you in," he said.

"Thanks," she said, rocking forward on her toes and lifting her face for a moment, before stopping herself, patting him on the chest, and turning into the kitchen.

Did she almost kiss me?

Shawn spun himself around and out the door. By the time he'd pulled out of the driveway, Jess was in her car and zipping out in front of him onto the road. She waved at him in her rearview mirror as she sped away. Shawn pulled back in and grabbed his toolbox, disappointed that the two of them wouldn't get to talk at all. He'd text her later.

When he walked back into the kitchen, Natalie had set up her laptop on the table. He crouched down to get under the sink and cleared out the cabinet, placing the various cleaning supplies on a dish towel on the floor.

"Not much engagement on your post from this morning so far," Natalie said. Shawn huffed. Last he'd checked, his page likes had increased nominally, from seventeen to just over twenty.

"Doesn't surprise me," he said, "After all, it's still winter. And while it ain't single-digits outside anymore, it's still cold and wet. Nobody wants to think about construction in the winter."

"Have you given any thought to traveling someplace a little farther south for work?" Natalie asked.

Shawn frowned. Something about the way she asked it made him think she was scheming about something. He sat up and looked at her.

"What, like Florida?"

"No, not Florida." Natalie rolled her eyes. "Like… Virginia, maybe."

"What are you on about, Nat?"

Natalie turned her laptop around to face him. "Check this out."

Shawn grumbled as he got back on his feet and walked back to the table to look at the screen. It looked like a website for a winery.

"You think I should start makin' wine?" Shawn scrunched his nose at her.

"No, no, not making wine.This is Lilliette Vineyards. It's the winery that Bonnie took me to last weekend."

"What does this hafta do with–"

"Let me finish!" Natalie interrupted him. "They've got plans to build twenty guest cabins in the next year, as well as a giant pole barn for events. They had a construction company booked for it, but the owner died and they couldn't follow through on the contract."

"That sucks," Shawn said.

Natalie nodded. "Yeah, but now they've already booked the space for next fall, and they need to find a contractor that can follow through on the designs for them. They think they've found someone for the barn, but now they need people that can build the cabins."

Shawn met her eyes. "Like my granddad's cabin."

"And all the lake cabins you've worked on!" Natalie smiled at him, and her eyes sparkled. "Shawn, what if you applied? Bonnie and I talked with the woman that owns the winery while we were down there. She's literally the coolest lady I've ever met: she's the winemaker and heads the tasting room, and runs a burlesque troupe on the side–"

"Woah, woah, woah," Shawn said. "I don't need to know all about her life."

Natalie chuckled. "Right–sorry. Point is, she's amazing. And her vision for the place is incredible. The wine trail down there is really blowing up, Shawn. With this on your resume, you could probably work for any number of places down there. It's only about an hour and a half away–which is a long commute, I know, but maybe you could work out a way to stay there during the week or something? Or even find a place?"

Shawn rubbed his neck. "I don't know Natalie. I've lived here my whole life…"

"But you're so good at what you do, Shawn." Natalie touched his hand. His eyes darted back to the laptop, and he studied the picture of the vineyards stretched out in front of the Blue Ridge Mountains. "Promise me you'll think about it."

Shawn nodded. "I'll think about it."

"Here." Natalie pulled a business card and put it on the table in front of him. She took back her laptop and he picked up the card.

"Leah Cooper, huh?"

"She's the one to call." Natalie said, typing on her keyboard. "Don't wait too long if you decide to go for it. They want to break ground next month."

Shawn flipped over the card and saw the same landscape that had been on the website. He slipped the card in his back pocket and crawled back under the sink.

"Anyone home?"

Shawn stepped over the threshold of his parent's house, listening for a response. Neither of his parents' cars were in the driveway.

"Close the door, you're letting all the cold in."

Grandad shuffled to the end of the hallway with his walker, and Shawn rushed over to give him a hug. "There's the old-timer, speeding 'round the corner! Trying to break a record?"

A good-humored wheeze sounded over his shoulder. "Come for the Bel Air?"

Shawn had accepted that he was at something of an impasse with the car. Jess had promised him that she'd do some research of her own, but she was a professional. If he was going to get the car road-ready, he'd likely have to spend some money.

More money than he had.

"About that…"

"Ah, don't tell me we're stumped!" he gestured for Shawn to follow him into the living room. They sat down, and Shawn ran his fingers through his hair.

"Well, I've got a friend who's going to try to help. But she's–"

"She?" Grandpa's eyes twinkled. "This wouldn't happen to be Ernie's girl, now would it?"

Shawn felt his ears warm. He rubbed his neck. "Uh, yeah. Actually. Jess. She's really good at all that stuff."

"Bet she's good at a few other things, too."

"*Grandad!*" Shawn's jaw fell open.

"What?" he followed a strained laugh with a long drag on his cannula. "I'm old, kid, I ain't blind. It's about time you found a cute girl to show you the ropes."

What is wrong with this family?

"No offense, Grandad, but I do *not* wanna talk about this kinda stuff with you."

"Well why the hell not?" The old man slapped the arm of his lazyboy and narrowed his eyes at his grandson. Shawn shrank back a little, the heat in his ears spreading to his cheeks. "This family don't talk about nothin'! It ain't good for you and yer sister–you think that Christopher o' hers knows thing one about keepin' her happy?"

"Grandad–"

"Now me and yer grandma, we lived together years before she'd marry me. I had to build her that cabin before she'd say yes. Wanted to make sure I could take care of her first, and she was damn smart to do it, too! I was an idiot when I met yer Grandma."

"Wait–you and Gram lived together before you were married?" Shawn leaned forward. "I thought the two of you were super into the church…"

"Eh, that came later. Then the church changed. Really did a number to yer father, boy, tell you what." His breath hitched for a second, and he coughed into his hand. Shawn rose to help him.

"I'm fine, I'm fine," he rasped, taking a few shuddering breaths and waving him off. Slowly, Shawn sat back down, and waited for his grandpa to continue. "Tell me about Jess."

He shuffled on the edge of the sofa. "Well, what do you wanna know?"

The old man chuckled. "Well, for starters, do you like her?"

Shawn thought for a moment. Over the past week, he'd mostly been concerned with how attracted he was to Jess–how difficult it was to hold back around her. How his body seemed to take over when he imagined her lips, her hair, her body. Even as he sat there on the sofa, his heart pounded at the thought of her. She was intoxicating.

But she was also *fun.* Talented. The way she could weave through a crowded bar with a whole tray of Jaeger Bombs without spilling any, the glint she got in her eye when she scanned his Chevy under the hood, the teasing tilt of the corner of her mouth when they flirted… she wasn't just sexy. She was intimidating, challenging.

Mesmerizing.

"Who wouldn't like her?" Shawn sighed. "She's funny, tough, a whiz with cars–"

"Pretty–"

"*Stunning.*" Shawn cut off his grandpa, practically growling. *Where did* that *come from?*

"Oh-ho, well ex-*cuuuuse me.*"

He winced. "Sorry, Grandad, I just mean–"

"You better lock her down, son. Girls like that don't stick around forever."

"But she just broke up with her boyfriend. Shouldn't I, I don't know." He shrugged. "Give it a few weeks?"

Shawn was met with the full ire of Walter Cobb's gray, watery eyes. He swallowed.

"Not for a second. You tell that girl how you feel, or someone else will." Then he reclined back in his armchair and crossed his hands over his chest, closing his eyes for a nap. "Build her a house if you have to."

Shawn stared at him for a moment, before a light snore informed him that the conversation was truly over. Then he pulled out his phone.

ME

You working late tonight?

JESS FROM PBG

Yeah. Double shift.

Mind if I hang out at the bar?

Only if you don't tip ;)

CHAPTER 24

Jess smiled down at her phone, then hastily tucked it away in her apron pocket when Dave rounded the corner. Grabbing her dishrag, she swiped off the condensation rings and crumbs leftover from the lunch rush and prepped the glassware for the earlybirds.

Her mind, however, was across the state line in Shawn's parents' garage, where it had been occupying most of the last twenty-four hours.

That hadn't been the first time Jess had blown a guy in a car, of course (after all, she'd come of age in a mechanic's shop), but she couldn't remember ever having quite as much fun with a guy in a car before. She'd replayed the event in her mind enough that it was almost like a movie, trying to figure out what it was about the experience that was so different from what she was used to.

She'd ruled out the danger factor: the threat of being caught usually did add a little extra spice, of course, and his parents' house had felt deliciously naughty, especially after hearing him and his sister talk about how little experience they'd had in the sneaking-around department. She remembered the conspiratorial glint in Shawn's eyes when he'd shut the door of the car on her after she'd ducked down to hide from his sister.

Yes. Fear of getting caught had added to the excitement. But it couldn't be the only ingredient. Once again, Jess went over the highlight reel. She felt her chest tingle as she recalled the way Shawn had thrust himself inside her mouth when she'd teased him, as if he couldn't wait another second. Again, usually not Jess's thing, but the way he'd immediately apologized afterwards, the panic in his voice–it had been so gosh darn innocent and earnest that it had only made her want to give him even more.

The way he'd held her was different, too. Instead of grabbing her by the hair or holding her head like a watermelon, he'd threaded his fingers in hers, clutching her hand to his chest, and his other arm had reached down to rub her back. She had felt so cared for, so safe, in that moment–the car and the garage and the conversation leading up to it had just disappeared.

For those few minutes, Jess and Shawn had been the only people that mattered in the universe.

The jangle of the bells above the door lurched Jess out of her reverie, and she blinked herself back into the restaurant, where an elderly couple was coming in for the early bird special. She checked the clock above the bar—4:30 on the dot.

She got them seated and took their orders, and refocused on another mystery from her time with Shawn: the Bel Air. After their front seat exploits, Shawn had gotten her a Gatorade and they'd gone through all that he'd done to try to fix the engine problem. Jess had run down the entire checklist with him of things she'd think to look at, and it appeared that he'd been plenty thorough. But why would a car just stop running after 20 minutes? All symptoms pointed to a gas or carburetor issue, but Jess had double-checked Shawn's work herself; everything about the fuel system was running as it should be.

She tapped her fingers on the bar top as she ran the problem over and over again in her mind, trying to isolate each component for weaknesses.

"Order up!" Dave called from the kitchen window.

"Got it!" Jess grabbed the plates and a water pitcher, and walked across the restaurant to take care of her early birds. When she returned, Dave was lingering in the window, studying her.

"You're awfully quiet today, Jess."

"No more than usual."

Dave grunted. "Nah, you're thinkin' about something. Seems like it's got you a little worked up."

Jess blushed. "A friend of mine's got a car problem. It's a real head-scratcher," she said. Technically, it was the truth. Even if it wasn't the exact thing that had her "worked up," as Dave had put it.

"Ah. Did you tell them to take it to your dad's?"

Jess rolled her eyes, "No, my friend's low on cash right now. Can't really afford to take it in. He's actually pretty handy, though." She took a moment to appreciate just how much work Shawn had put into the car himself. It seemed as though he and his grandpa had been working together on cars for most of his life—as he knew his way around a toolset and an engine block almost as well as Jess did—and she appreciated that Shawn wanted a project that was his own. "But he may have to call in a professional. Even I'm having a hard time diagnosing the problem with it."

Dave leveled his gaze at her. "Even you, huh? Sounds like it's no ordinary problem."

Jess set down her tray and leaned forward toward the window. "It's seriously the weirdest thing. Like, the engine runs fantastic for ten minutes, purrs like a kitten, but right around the twenty minute mark it'll just slowly start to bog down and—poof!" She spread her fingers to simulate a puff of smoke. "It stops. Won't start again until it cools down. Dead in the water." She swept a lock of hair behind her ears.

"That is a real head scratcher," Dave said, then nodded toward the door. "Looks like the dinner rush is starting early today."

Jess turned back toward the front of the restaurant, where a group of rowdy college students had seated themselves in the corner booth while she'd been talking. "Right. On it," she said, and snatched a pile of menus.

"Can I get y'all started with–" Jess froze. Smack-dab in the middle of the wrap-around bench seat was Kyle, flanked by the rest of his teammates.

"Hey babe, pour me and the guys a round, would ya? We're bulking this week!"

He shot her a wide, toothy grin, as if he hadn't abandoned her with her furious father nary a week ago.

"I'm not your babe, Kyle. We're finished, remember?"

A chorus of "oooohs" rang up from the table. Kyle smirked. "Oh, look, she buys her own sheets and suddenly she's too good for me."

He and the rest of the team sniggered. Jess put a hand on her hip.

"IDs."

"What?" That wiped the smirk off his face.

"You ordered a round. I need to see everyone's ID's."

"Babe." The guys all shuffled awkwardly as Kyle pressed his way out of the booth. He reached his arm around her shoulder and leaned down, muttering in her ear. "Not everyone here's of age, okay? I said you'd hook us up."

Jess squirmed out of his hold. His eyes widened. "I'm. Not. Your. *Babe.* No IDs, no beer."

She turned to walk away. He caught her by the wrist. "What's gotten into you?"

"Me?" Jess jerked herself around, snatching her arm away.

"You ignore me for a week after saying you need a break, and then expect to come in here and act like we're still a thing? We're done, Kyle. I've moved on."

She stalked away to the bar, and he followed her, until Sheila stopped him at the barrier.

"Employees only, Romeo."

"My bad, my bad!" He gave her an oily grin. Sheila narrowed her eyes. "Jess, look, I'm sorry, alright? If you say we're done, we're done, okay? But you still have clothes at the dorm."

Jess looked up from the pitcher of Pepsi she'd been filling. "What?"

He sidled across from her and leaned into the tap. "You know, those lacy pink panties? Your ratty old Orioles sweater with the holes in it?"

Shit. Her dad had given her that sweater. She'd been wondering where it was.

"Come over tomorrow. I'll give 'em back. We can talk."

She sighed, and handed him the pitcher along with a stack of plastic cups. He grimaced. "Can *I* at least have a beer?"

"Fine."

"Fine to the beer, or coming over?"

She pulled him a draught and plunked it on the bar. "Both. But I'm not staying to talk. I'm just collecting my things and leaving."

He looked like he was about to roll his eyes, but he stopped when he saw the glare on her face. "Alright, alright. You're a real ball-buster, Jess, you know that? It's one of the things I always found sexy about you."

Sheila came around and wrenched the pitcher out of his hands. "Yeah, yeah, tell it to someone who's interested."

Jess watched him trail after Sheila and join the rest of the team. The waitress returned and handed over her order pad. "What's this?"

"I'll take care of the children. You can have my section for the night."

Jess almost cried with gratitude. "You're the best, Sheila."

She flipped her wild, dark curls over her shoulder and smiled. "I know."

CHAPTER 25

*S*hawn beamed at his phone. At the moment, he was sitting at his parents' kitchen island, drinking a third cup of coffee as Melanie and her bridesmaids fawned over vision boards of various color schemes for her wedding. He'd gotten distracted with the Bel Air after talking with his grandpa and hadn't made it out to the bar to visit Jess like he'd planned. But they had been texting a ton.

Melanie shoved a wad of fabric in between his face and his phone.

"Shawn, stop texting. This is important."

"Why am I here again?" He'd arrived that morning intent on

heading straight to the garage, when Melanie and her two best friends had hijacked him in the foyer.

"For the male perspective," Ariel said.

"And an opinion on the groomsmen attire," Charity added.

Ariel, Charity, and Melanie had been friends since their days in the womb, when all the church moms-to-be had started a quilting club to make baby blankets for the expected. The club had stuck together after the children were born, eventually evolving into the tummy-time club, play dates, and then PTA fundraising meetings.

Shawn and Melanie's parents had taken their grandfather to a check-up at the hospital this morning, so he was left on his own to fend off the swatch-swapping bridal party.

"Although your coloring is all wrong," Ariel said, jerking Shawn back into the conversation.

"What's wrong with my coloring?" He shot back. "I always stay inside the lines!"

Mel smacked his shoulder. He winced and rubbed his arm in mock offense. "She's right though. Christopher has more of an olive complexion, doesn't he?"

Charity held a pink swatch up to his cheek. "Yes. Shawn's much warmer."

Ariel giggled and nudged her friend's arm. Charity blushed.

Shawn swatted her hand away and pinched his nose.

"Then why am I here?" Shawn repeated. "Why don't you just get Christopher down here to go over all this stuff? He's the one you're marrying!"

A shadow fell over Melanie's face for a split second; if Shawn had blinked, he would have missed it. She waved a hand and gave a careless roll of her eyes.

"He's useless when it comes to colors. If I asked him his opinion on bridesmaid's dresses, he'd probably give me RGB values instead of names."

"He's *so* smart, Mel. You're so lucky," Charity sighed. "Does Christopher have any single co-workers at his company?"

Mel straightened her back and put on a smug smile. "He's one of a kind, Charity."

Shawn gagged. Ariel stuck her tongue out at him. "And what do *you* do for a living, Shawn? Play with cars?"

Shawn scowled at her. "Speaking of, I've got a project to work on," he said, biting back a harsher retort. He drained the last of his coffee and strode out to the garage, shutting the door behind him.

Once he was alone, he snatched a tennis ball off the floor and threw it against the ground. Each bounce did little to calm his frustration. Normally, he didn't mind Melanie's friends; he'd grown up with them, after all. But since Melanie had started dating Christopher and he'd stopped going to church, he always felt like he was being judged whenever the girls came over. And work had been a particularly sore subject for him all winter–*especially* when Melanie bragged about Christopher and the fancy start-up he worked for.

He pulled a stool over to the Bel Air and lifted the hood again. He got out his phone to use as a flashlight, hoping this time he'd see something obvious he'd missed the last hundred times he'd looked at the engine. As he swiped his screen, he noticed he'd missed a text from Jess.

> Just doing some research. You've made this personal, now ;)

A warm tingling in his chest eased some of the tension that had settled there. He considered how to respond.

He was pretty sure *she* had been the one to make things personal. She'd certainly been the one to escalate things to the next level.

Shawn paused a moment, fingers hovering over the phone screen. What level exactly *were* Shawn and Jess? He knew that it wouldn't be right to start calling her his girlfriend; they hadn't specified in any conversation that they were dating, and she'd just broken up with another guy. But the word "friend" didn't seem to encompass his feelings for her the way it had a week ago. He saw her differently now, thought about her differently. It was almost harder to talk to her now, as if there were higher stakes with each text exchange. But at the same time, he had the nagging desire to tell her everything.

He wanted to see her. He kicked himself for not going to the bar the night before.

> Why don't you come over and do some more hands-on research?

He hit the send button before truly absorbing the greater context of the text. The second it registered as "sent," his heart dropped into his stomach.

Hands-on research. Oh man. Was that too much?

But then, he felt that familiar tugging in his jeans, and it overtook his initial nervousness. He *had* been thinking about the car. Now, he was thinking about the kinds of things that happened *inside* the car. With Jess. With her hands.

His phone screen dimmed, and he saw the three dots appear by Jess's name to let him know she was typing. And then they disappeared.

They popped up again for a second. And again, they were gone.

Once more, the bubble flashed, and then his backlight turned off.

Ah, shit, he thought, *Was it too much? Did I mess up?*

The phone buzzed and the screen lit back to life. Shawn seized it.

> Hmmm... you know, I have wondered about your hands... ;)

Shawn blinked.

She had?

Now the stakes were significantly higher. His mouth went dry as he fumbled in his brain for words, any words. Clever words. Sexy words.

It was like trying to mine for diamonds with a spoon.

You have?

They're awfully big

Shawn stared at the text. She was going to kill him. A million dirty responses pelted his mind like a hailstorm, and once again he felt like he was mining for gold, sifting and sifting and sifting for the one gem of a response that would impress her.

There was the obvious joke there about big hands, of course. But that was low-hanging fruit, and Jess deserved better than that. He held up one of his hands in front of his face. Stared at it. Flexed his fingers. He closed his eyes, and the all-too-familiar memory of her falling into him jumped to the forefront of his mind as he conjured how her skin had felt against his palm. He imagined reaching his fingers further up her body, and suddenly, he knew what he wanted to text back.

But it was risky. So risky. He'd be upping the ante from the implied to the overt, the crystal clear and real.

He took a deep breath. He and Jess had played this game before. He dug deep to access the same strength he'd summoned when she'd asked him to tell her what he wanted, when she'd made him spell out each word for her in the front seat of the Bel Air.

All the better for squeezing those huge tits of yours

The door to the kitchen creaked open, and Shawn jumped a

good foot in the air from his stool, clutching his phone tight to his chest and shouting in surprise. "Melanie!"

"Shawn? You okay?" His sister walked around her parents' SUV and approached him, an apologetic frown on her face. He fumbled his phone into his pocket and looked at her.

"What? Yeah, yeah, I'm fine, why wouldn't I be?"

Melanie wrung her hands. "Ariel shouldn't have said that."

Shawn blinked. Then he remembered why he'd stormed into the garage in the first place.

"Oh. Right." Shawn cleared his throat as his phone buzzed in his pocket. Heat crept up his spine as he used every ounce of his willpower not to take it out and read Jess's response. "Well, We don't have to talk about it."

"You're going to get more work." Melanie's eyes shone at him under pinched brows, and he winced at what he saw there. She patted his knee.

She was looking at him with pity. His sister pitied him.

"Oh God, you actually agree with her, don't you?" He forgot about his phone, his anger rising. "Mel, I'm a grown man. Just because I don't work for some fancy company or have some big degree don't mean I'm stupid."

Melanie's eyes went wide. "Shawn, I didn't say–"

"No!" Shawn cut her off. "You and yer friends have been lookin' down on me for years now. I'm done, Mel. I don't need y'all to save me or tell me I'm not good enough for you. I'm fine, okay?" I've got—I—" Shawn threw his hands up in frustration. "You know what? I'm going home. I don't need to be here if y'all are gonna make fun of me while lookin' at fabric and swoonin' over Pinterest all day."

"Shawn, we're not making fun of you–"

"I'm tired of *playing with cars* today, anyway," Shawn rose and stomped over to the door.

"She didn't mean that–"

"Bye, Melanie," Shawn said, slamming the door behind him.

Shawn wrenched open the door to his pickup, climbed inside, and wrenched the key in the ignition. As he let the truck warm up, he rubbed his face in his hands.

April would mark two years that he'd been trying to get his contracting business off the ground. In the beginning, he'd done fairly well by tackling old projects for family friends, but the word of mouth had never spread far enough to truly launch a successful career. The slow growth, coupled with the fact that he'd traded most of his labor for his biggest client, Natalie, for a vintage car that was proving to be expensive to fix, had been a recipe for disaster. If Shawn's situation were such that he couldn't live rent-free in his grandpa's house, he would have had to find a real job months ago.

He shuffled in his seat and felt a poke in his back pocket. He reached in and found the business card that Natalie had given him a few days ago: Leah Cooper, winemaker and owner, Lilli-ette Vineyards.

He studied the card for a moment, flipping it over in his fingers. The landscape of the Blue Ridge Mountains and acres of grape vineyards taunted him from the rigid paper. He got out his phone, and immediately flipped to the keypad.

"Hello, I'm looking for Leah Cooper?"

CHAPTER 26

*J*ess was in agony.

She shouldn't have sent the picture. She thought Shawn had been ready, but he clearly had not. It had been half an hour, and he hadn't responded.

She bit her lip to keep the water in her eyes from leaking down her face. She'd never actually sent a nude photo to any guy she'd dated, ever. Something inside her felt like it was asking for trouble: putting that much power into a guy's hands, giving him something he could send around to his buddies or use against her when they broke up.

But something about Shawn was different. Deep down, she knew that Shawn wouldn't betray her trust like that. No matter how hard she tried, she just couldn't see him spreading around her photo, even if their friendship were to end.

She looked back down at the topless picture on the screen. She had to admit, she'd done a good job. She'd posed with herself kneeling on the ground, leaning over with her tits sandwiched between her arms, and she'd balanced the phone on the edge of the tub to get the right angle to show off her cleavage. The light from the bathroom window cut across the top of her chest and her face in a bright ray, making her brown eyes twinkle gold underneath her long lashes. The rolls of her stomach weren't poking out for once, and the way she had tilted her head had eliminated her double-chin. She looked hot.

But he hadn't responded.

She pulled at her sweater and looked at her reflection in the bathroom door mirror, scrutinizing herself. Maybe she was looking at this the wrong way. Maybe it wasn't that he was mad at her or turned off by the picture. Maybe, he was so turned *on* that he hadn't been able to keep from touching himself. He might be jerking off at this very second, his phone clenched in his non-dominant hand, fapping furiously at her titillating breasts.

It was a nice fantasy. Even if it was total B.S.

She cursed herself once more. Nope. She'd known she'd needed to take it slow, especially so soon after her break-up. But as hard as she tried, she hadn't been able to. And after the fun they'd had in his car last week…

She met her own eyes in the mirror.

Oh my God. I like him.

The realization struck her like a wrecking ball. Her breath caught in her throat as she once more looked down at the phone, and back at her reflection, and saw her cheeks turn pink.

I just sent a topless photo to a guy because I like *him. A super nice, genuinely good guy who I've been attempting to seduce into a rebound, except now I don't want it to be just a rebound because I have feelings.*

She put her face in her hands, carefully wiping at her eyes so her make-up wouldn't smudge. No, no, no this was all wrong! She wasn't supposed to get a crush on him. She was supposed to be the cool, sexy friend that helped the nice guy get over his fear of sex with the power of orgasms. She was supposed to be showing him that he could have any girl he wanted, and that he didn't need to pine over some old lesbian with a girlfriend.

Or, bisexual person. Whatever.

But now, Jess realized, she didn't want Shawn to just have any girl. She wanted Shawn to have *her*. Otherwise, she wouldn't be fantasizing about him masturbating to a photo of her boobs.

She licked her lips. She liked thinking about him masturbating. She liked thinking about him, thinking about *her,* while he masturbated.

Her phone buzzed, and she seized it, impatiently pressing her thumb to the fingerprint sensor while it unlocked.

BF KYLE

You coming over or what?

Ugh. She really needed to change his name in her phone.

omw

She could think more about Shawn touching himself after she rescued her sweater.

KYLE WAS WAITING on the bench outside his dorm, a cardboard box lying open on the ground beside him. He rose when Jess approached, and spread his arms for a hug.

She reluctantly accepted it, pulling away as quickly as she could. She was fully prepared to fake getting a phone call to end this encounter early if she had to.

"This all of it?" she asked, pointing with her phone at the box. "I've got somewhere to be."

He stepped in front of it, placing himself between her and her things.

"Listen, about us–"

"Shawn!" Jess winced. "I mean, *Kyle–*"

"Shawn?" A flash of anger streaked across Kyle's face. Jess

wanted to kick herself. The photo she'd sent was still front and center in her mind and she wasn't thinking straight. She was horny, dammit. And her tongue had slipped.

"Kyle. Give me my stuff."

"Who's Shawn?" He crossed his arms, still blocking her from the box.

"None of your business." She reached around him, and he shifted his body weight to block her. He was closer now, and his face was only a few inches from hers.

"Were you cheating on me?" He growled.

"No!" Jess stomped her foot, and tried to feign right, but he was too quick for her. "Jesus, Kyle, you were the one that wanted a break."

He continued to side-step her as she reached for the box, until finally he grabbed her arm. "It's been a week, Jess. How long did it take you to fuck this guy? A day? Two?"

She struggled against his grip. "I didn't fuck him, okay? Give me my shit!"

With that, she wrenched her hand back, sending her phone flying across the quad. He lunged for it, and Jess took the opportunity to snatch up the box of her things. Then she turned around to find Kyle attempting to unlock her phone.

"Give it back, Kyle."

"No, I want to see what you've texted this guy." Once again, she reached toward him, but he held her phone over his head and out of her reach.

Kyle wasn't particularly tall, but Jess was only 5'1", and he had at least eight inches on her. She growled.

"Give. It. Back."

"Cheaters lose their phone privileges, babe. You can have this back when you've learned your lesson."

She lunged at him, but with the box in her hands and her inferior height, he had a tactical advantage. He dove out of her reach and bolted to the dorm, and she stumbled over the bench when she tried to run after him. By the time she'd caught up to the entrance of the dorm, he'd already swiped his ID card and slipped inside, and she heard the latch click just as her fingers brushed the handle of the door.

He sneered at her from the other side of the glass, and she pounded on it.

"This isn't funny, Kyle!"

"Neither is cheating, bitch."

She fumed helplessly as he stuck out his tongue and skipped out of sight. With her phone. The phone with her topless photo on it.

Great. Now what?

CHAPTER 27

*J*ess pulled up behind the main shop of Ernie's Garage and took a deep breath. She didn't have any way to reach Natalie or Shawn without her phone, and the only other person she knew to turn to was probably still mad at her.

She and her dad hadn't spoken since she'd moved out of his house. What's worse, he'd been absolutely right to judge Kyle. He was a total jerk, abandoning her the way he did, and was currently ruining any shot she had with Shawn by taking away her means of communicating with him. How was she supposed to tell her dad that: one, he was right about her old boyfriend, and two, she needed help figuring out how to win over her (hopefully) future boyfriend?

If there were one thing she and her dad *could* always talk about, though, it was cars. And even if she couldn't find or text Shawn right now, there was still one thing she could do to let him know how she felt about him.

She and Shawn had gone over every single possibility that Jess could think of, and they still couldn't figure out why his Bel Air wouldn't stay running. But she knew someone who could.

Swallowing her pride (what little was left of it), she climbed out of her car and into the shop.

Beau was the only tech Jess could see on the floor when she walked in. She waved at him as he bent over an old El Camino, and he tilted his chin at her in greeting.

"Is Dad around?" she called.

"Office," Beau grunted. Jess smirked. Apparently, she wasn't the only one stumped by a car. Beau looked ready to pull his hair out.

Jess headed to the office and found Ernie exactly where Beau said he'd be, hunched over the computer in the tiny trailer that served as his personal office and the shop's waiting room. Jess knocked on the open door.

"Can I come in?"

Ernie looked up, and his bushy eyebrows lifted. "Jess! What are you doing here?"

"I was in the neighborhood." Jess waffled in the doorway as she let her sentence fade. Ernie motioned for her to come in.

She sat in the cheap, plastic chair in front of his desk. She wrung her hands as silence stretched between them.

"Well? How's the new place?" Ernie said finally, backing his wheeled chair away from his keyboard and leaning his elbows back on the armrests.

"It's good," Jess said. She smiled at him. "My roommate is really cool."

Ernie nodded, returning the grin, "That's great, Soo-Soo. I— I'm proud of you."

Jess's brows knit, and she stopped fiddling with her hands. "You are?"

"I am." Father and daughter locked eyes. Moisture glistened in her dad's deep brown eyes, and he blinked it away, his mustache twitching. He cleared his throat. "I'm uh… I'm sorry for the way things happened the other day. You're a good ki—

young lady. We may not always see eye-to-eye on the boys you bring home…"

Jess swallowed, a sudden lump in her throat. She wiped at her eyes, not sure what to do with her father focused on her after so many days avoiding him.

"Thanks. But don't compliment me too much. You were right about Kyle."

He leaned forward. "What happened?"

Jess waved a hand. She didn't want to get into all of it, and what's more—she didn't want four angry mechanics storming down to campus to give her ex a piece of their mind. It would only fortify Kyle's prejudice against them. "He's a jerk. I should have seen it earlier."

"Oh, Soo-Soo." Ernie shook his head. "I'm sorry. You deserve someone who'll like you for who you are, you know? Grease and all."

"Yeah," Jess huffed. Hearing her dad talking this way made her uncomfortable. Crank shafts, cylinder heads, carburetor kits—*that* was what she and her dad were good at. Talking about feelings was not the White family's forte. "Speaking of, my friend's got an old vintage hot rod he's fixing up, and he's stuck. I've been over there to look at it, and the thing looks like it should run great, but the engine always cuts out after about 20 minutes. I've tried everything I can think of, and I just can't figure it out."

Ernie's lips turned in a thoughtful frown. "What's the car?"

"A 1954 Chevy Bel Air."

The color drained from Ernie's face. In an instant, it was as if all the air was sucked from the room. It looked as if he'd seen a ghost.

"Fifty four?" Her dad breathed. Jess nodded, eyeing him warily. *What's got him so spooked all of the sudden?* Was he weirded out from talking about Kyle, or…?

He shook his head. "You should ask Beau to help you." He

pushed himself out of his chair and crossed to the office door. "I've got a pick-up I forgot about. I'll see you around."

"Dad, wait, what just—"

But he was gone. Faster than Jess had ever seen him move, Ernie bolted out of the trailer. By the time Jess gathered herself and followed him outside, his truck was nowhere to be seen.

Jess's confusion shifted quickly to anger as she kicked at the dirty ice crust at the edge of the parking lot. She waited, shivering, for a moment, before stomping back to the shop and yanking open the door. She slammed it shut behind her.

Beau jumped, crashing his head against the hood of the El Camino. "Jesus, Jess, again? Every time you visit the shop, I go home with bruises."

Jess ignored his complaint. "Dad just fucking left," she shouted.

Beau studied her, rubbing his head. "Uh… I'm getting the impression you're mad about this."

Jess kicked at a tire in frustration. "Yes, Beau, I'm fucking mad about this. I haven't talked to him in weeks, and then we have a moment and I finally think maybe we're cool, and then he literally runs away when I try to ask him a question!"

She paced furiously back and forth in the shop, her hands shaking and clenched into fists. First Kyle, then her phone, now this. She wanted to punch something.

"Woah, woah, slow down. What did you ask him?"

Jess stopped pacing and threw her hands up in the air. "I asked him about my friend's car! I can't figure out what's wrong with it, and I thought, 'Well gosh, Dad would probably know. Maybe we could actually *talk* about it!' But apparently fucking *not,* because he can't spend more than five minutes with me without bursting into flames!"

Beau scrunched his nose and gave his head a little shake, before holding out his hands and giving Jess a questioning look,

"Wait. So, are you mad about him driving off, or mad about being stumped about the car?"

Jess shot him a hopeless look. "Him! And the car, just—everything!" She resumed her pacing, this time making her way over to the car Beau was working on. "What's going on here? What are you stumped on?"

Beau huffed out a breath, leaning a hand on the roof of the car. "I have no fuckin' clue. The owner brought it in saying he thought it was the carburetor, 'cause it just putters out whenever he turns it on, like it isn't getting the fuel it needs. But I rebuilt the carb, and it's still doing it."

Jess blinked at him. "Fuel lines?"

Beau shook his head. "All fine, far as I can tell."

"Really."

"It's fuckin' weird. Literally, like, starts up fine, and then after about ten minutes it'll sound like it's off rhythm or somethin', you know? And then it'll just… die."

"And won't start until it cools down again?"

Beau stared at her. "Yeah. Exactly. Have you seen this before?"

Jess tilted her head at him. "This is literally the exact same problem my friend is having."

"The one you asked Ernie about?"

Jess nodded.

"And the sonuvabitch ran away??" Beau rubbed his eyes with his palms. "That's fuckin' rich, isn't it?"

Jess slumped all her weight into the back panel of the car in defeat. "Yeah. You're telling me."

Her elbow bumped the gas cap cover and it popped open. She grunted and bumped it again to pop it close, but missed, jamming her funny bone directly into the side of the car.

"Gaaaaaaaah, Christ!" She clutched her elbow with her opposite hand, "Fuck, really?" She turned around and glared at the tiny door. "Fuck you, you stupid thing!" She wrenched it open to see if the flap of metal had maybe gotten caught on the chain that attached the gas cap when she'd tried to close it. But as she fiddled with the chain and tried to twirl the cap, it wouldn't turn.

"What the–" she gripped the cap harder and tried to wrench it open.

"What are you doing?" Beau had been watching her breakdown in amused silence.

"The gas cap is stuck," Jess said, still trying and failing to twist it free.

"What? Lemme try." Beau pushed her out of the way. She shot him a glare as he reached in the fuel hatch and wrapped his hand around the cap. He turned.

Nothing happened. He huffed out a breath and tried again.

"Jeeeeesus," he groaned, also failing to unscrew the cap. "What the hell?"

Jess chewed her cheek for a moment before jogging to the tool chest, where she grabbed a flashlight and an adjustable C-wrench. She slid back beside the car and flashed the light into the hatch.

"It does look a little corroded around the cap. Maybe salt got in there." She held out her hand to Beau. "You got a flathead?"

He handed her a screwdriver. She scraped at the flakes of gunk that clung to the base of the cap, and wedged the end of the tool against it while tightening the jaws of the wrench around the cap with her thumb, until the teeth bit into the plastic. Using the screwdriver as a lever, she wiggled the two tools back and forth, until she heard a tiny hiss escape from under the cap. She gave a hard twist of the wrench and the cap jerked free, popping off the neck of the tank.

She stumbled back with the force and Beau caught her before she fell on her ass.

"Ooof." She scrambled to right herself. "Thanks."

"You got it." Beau propped her back to her feet before

reaching for the gas cap. He bent over it, and Jess shined the flashlight into the inside of the threads.

"The gasket is eroded." He said, pointing at the shiny silver ring lining the inside. "It's been metal on metal. Do you think it maybe made a seal?"

"Like a vacuum?" Jess breathed, poking at the cap with the tip of the screwdriver. "Oh my God, Beau–if the cap sealed airtight to the tank, and air couldn't get in to replace the fuel as it burns—"

"It'd choke the engine!" Beau finished for her. Jess gaped, dumfounded. He stared back at her, incredulous, at their accidental discovery.

"Do you think that's it?? Do you think maybe it's been the gas cap the whole time?" Jess's voice rose in pitch as she bounded to the far end of the shop toward the parts storage. She raced past the rows until she landed in the vintage Chevy parts, scouring for a replacement cap. Finding one, she plucked it off the shelf and raced back into the shop.

"I have to try this. Beau!! This could be the fix!" She reached around him in a bear hug, and he laughed, lifting her into the air. She giggled.

"Wait, wait, wait. We gotta try it to make sure it's actually the problem. Get me one that'll fit the El Camino."

He set her down and she nodded, running back to the warehouse to grab a new gas cap for Beau. As she did, Chuck waltzed into the shop, a large styrofoam coffee cup in his hand.

"Woah, there, Jess!" he crowed. "You're back! What's got you in such a hurry?"

"Beau and I may have just figured something out. We're gonna test our theory."

With the new cap secured, Jess and Chuck flanked the car as Beau climbed in and started her up. Chuck opened the bay door so they wouldn't be choked by the exhaust. Not that it would have mattered. Jess was pretty sure she held her breath for the twenty minutes they waited to see if the engine would cut out.

It purred like a kitten for the entire time.

"That's half an hour," Beau finally said, checking the time on his phone. He laughed in disbelief. "I can't believe it. A new carburetor and six hours of labor later only to find the fix in a four dollar chunk of plastic and a rubber ring."

Jess shook her head. "Shawn is going to be so frickin' thrilled!" She reached into her pocket to text him, when she remembered she didn't have her phone anymore. Her chest tightened as she remembered the last thing she'd sent him before Kyle had snatched it away.

I have to get that phone back.

"Shawn–that's Walter's grandson? The one with the Bel Air?" Chuck asked.

"Bel Air?" Beau turned his head to Jess. "You didn't say it was a Bel Air."

"Ain't that a trip?" Chuck nodded to Beau, and Beau let out a low whistle.

"What? What's a trip?" Jess asked, looking from Beau to Chuck.

"Just, what a coincidence, you know?" Beau shook his head sadly. "What are the odds that you'd be roped into fixing that particular model of car"

"It's the same year, too, ain't it?" Chuck asked her.

"Same year as what?" Jess said, more forcefully. What were they talking about?

"Come on, Jess, don't you remember?" Beau squinted at her, and Jess shook her head, starting to get annoyed. "One of those sat in the junk pile in the back for a decade before Ernie finally scrapped it."

Jess froze. He couldn't mean–

"Yep. A 1954 Chevrolet Turquoise Bel Air. The car that took

your momma," Chuck said sadly, placing a hand on Jess's shoulder.

Beau frowned too, and then his eyes widened. "Wait–Jess, did you tell your dad the model you were working on?"

Tears sprung to Jess's eyes, and she nodded dumbly. She clutched the gas cap in her hand and backed away from Beau and Chuck. "I have to go," she said, as she swiped her keys from the hook by the door and once again climbed into her car.

She had to find her dad.

CHAPTER 28

When Shawn called the winery, he hadn't expected things to move so fast.

Leah had answered after just a couple of rings, swirling his anger into anxiety. But he *had* called, and now that she'd picked up, the last thing he wanted to do was waste her time.

"My name is Shawn Cobb. A friend of mine visited your winery last week and mentioned that you were on the hunt for a new contractor."

He did his best to tame down his twang while he spoke to her. Something about wineries and vineyards just seemed fancy, and Shawn had never been particularly high-brow. He wiped his palms on his jeans while Leah answered him.

"A friend of yours?"

"Natalie Roche? She was with her girlfriend, Bonnie Baker?"

"Bonnie and Natalie!" Shawn could hear the smile in her voice, "That's right, that's right… they mentioned they had a friend that might know their way around a cabin."

"Yes, ma'am," Shawn said. "That'd be me."

"Well why don't you tell me a little about yourself, Shawn Cobb?"

For the next twenty minutes, Shawn sat in the cab of his truck and talked with Leah, learning about her winery and her plans for making it a destination for large events. A few of the things he remembered from what Natalie had said, like their contractor pulling out at the last minute. Finally, Leah mentioned how one of the main draws would be rentable cabins to house bridal parties or family reunions.

"And that's where I'd come in?" Shawn asked.

"Potentially, yes." He heard a shuffling of papers on the other end of the line. "What does the day after tomorrow look like for you, Shawn?"

Shawn didn't have to think too hard. "I've got some availability."

"Would you want to come down for an interview and tour?"

Shawn hesitated for only a fraction of a second, before responding. "Sounds perfect."

HALF AN HOUR LATER, Shawn was pounding on Natalie's door.

"Jess? Natalie?"

Natalie came to the door, still in pajamas despite it being mid-afternoon. Shawn stifled a slight jab of disappointment. "Shawn!" She beckoned him to come in. "To what do I owe the pleasure?"

"I called Leah."

"Leah?" Natalie yawned. "Leah who?"

Shawn rolled his eyes at her, "The lady from the winery?" He tapped the top of Natalie's head with the flat of his hand. "Earth to Nat! What's got you so groggy?"

Natalie gave him a coy look. "I was taking a nap."

Shawn checked his watch. "A nap?"

They had wandered back to the kitchen, where Natalie prepared a pot of coffee. "Yes, a nap."

She filled the reservoir with water and flicked the on button, before finally turning to face Shawn. He raised his eyebrows.

"Okay, Bonnie came over during her lunch break and tired me out, all right? I'm allowed to have an afternoon off, Shawn!"

Shawn chuckled and shook his head. Then he asked, "Jess not around?"

Natalie shook her head. "She left in a bit of a hurry this morning, actually. I assume work?"

Shawn shook his head. "She doesn't work until later–"

Natalie cut him off as she slammed her hand on the table. Shawn jumped. "Jesus, Nat, what on earth–"

"You called Leah!!" she squealed. Shawn's jaw dropped.

"Duh. That's why I came over here!"

"Oh my God, oh my God, oh my GOD! Tell me everything!" She pulled out a chair across from him and plopped into it. Shawn shook his head.

"You just registered that?"

"You woke me up from a nap! Now, spill. What happened with Leah?"

Shawn recounted the whole phone conversation, giving his impression of the winery owner, and to his surprise, he started to feel butterflies in his stomach. Happy butterflies. Natalie poured them both a mug of coffee as he talked.

"And so I'll be going down there tomorrow for an interview and a tour of the place," he finished, taking a sip of his coffee.

"Shawn, that's amazing!" Natalie reached over the table between them and placed a hand on his wrist. "I *knew* it would be a good fit for you. I just knew it!"

"Well, I gotta get through the interview first." The butterflies gathered and settled into a heavy weight. "I mean, it might not pan out."

Natalie lifted her hand from his arm and smacked him across the face.

"Ow! What was that–"

"Now you listen here, Shawn." Natalie waggled her finger at him. "Don't you dare be down on yourself about this. You are a good man, and you've got some good skills. Look at this house! Do you remember the shape it was in before you got your Shawn Cobb hands all over it?"

Shawn looked down at his hands as she said that. Compared to Natalie's, they seemed so large. He felt heat rush to his face as he remembered.

"Do you know when Jess might be back?"

Natalie blinked at the sudden change in subject. "No. But you could text her, I guess."

Shawn suddenly remembered that he hadn't read her message from earlier. He dug his phone from out of his pocket, and Natalie got up to refill her coffee. When he swiped down his notifications, he saw that Jess had sent him a picture message hours ago. He tapped on the banner.

And immediately slammed the phone facedown on the table.

"What?" Natalie startled at the noise, spinning around and walking towards him, "Everything okay?"

Shawn nodded furiously, leaning away from her. He clutched his phone to his chest.

"Shawn?" Natalie's brow was furrowed in concern. "You're practically purple. What happened? Is Jess hurt?"

Shawn shook his head, as he tried desperately to find his voice. He didn't think he could say anything without sounding like a dying frog.

"No," he croaked, and cleared his throat. "No, no, no one's hurt, it's fine." He lowered his phone down to his lap and folded his hands over the crease of his hips. He swallowed. Natalie continued to stare at him.

"Shawn, you look like just saw your parents having sex," she joked.

A strangled wheeze escaped him, and he winced. Natalie's eyes darted to where his hands were clutching his phone.

"Shawn," Natalie said, an impish gleam in her eyes, "what's on your phone there, buddy?"

Shawn closed his eyes. "Nothing."

"That so?"

He felt her body leaning toward him, and he bounded backward out of the seat. Natalie straightened, and the two stared at each other for a second.

"I might know where Jess is." Shawn swallowed, his dry tongue sticking to the roof of his mouth. "I'm gonna go find her."

Shawn about-faced and practically ran down the hall to the front door and out to his truck.

"Bye then!" Natalie called, sounding concerned and amused.

Shawn waved over his shoulder before shutting the door behind him, reaching down to adjust himself once he was sure Natalie couldn't see him. He climbed into his truck and turned the key in the ignition, and as the engine warmed up, he unlocked the screen of his phone.

Jess, beautiful, blonde Jess, stared at him with wide doe-eyes as she leaned forward, a ray of light illuminating the bare, milky-white skin of her naked breasts. Beautifully pert nipples, surrounded by matching, delicate rings of pink flesh poked from the center of each one, pushed forward above the crooks of her elbows, and Shawn literally felt his mouth water as he gaped at the perfection of Jess's body.

JESS FROM PBG

You mean these tits?

Shawn threw his phone at the passenger's seat and hissed out a breath, the previously hibernating butterflies in his stomach having woken into a swarm that energized his entire lower half. He grabbed the phone again and clenched his jaw as the picture once again taunted him.

Where are you?

SHAWN DROVE AROUND AIMLESSLY for half an hour as he waited for Jess to text him back, until he finally pulled into a truck stop at the Virginia/West Virginia border to fill up with diesel and clear his head.

Shawn attempted to form coherent thoughts as he stood at the pump, willing the blood in his body to flow back to his brain from his dick, where it felt like every nerve ending was pulsing with each breath. Once again, he rearranged his jeans, this time tucking himself into his waistband, which, given how hard it was, was really the only way he could comfortably avoid making an idiot of himself at the truck stop.

At last, the pump jerked to a stop, and he parked his truck and walked a loop around the parking lot, passing semi after semi as he worked out his restlessness.

His phone rested silently in his pocket.

I don't think I can avoid it anymore. Shawn kicked a pebble farther and farther down the rows of parking spaces. It felt like he had reached a crossroads of sorts, one that he'd been carefully avoiding since high school. A rite of passage—one of which he'd heard countless stories from his friends, which he'd laughed and joked about, playing the role of someone who knew what it was all about.

But until Jess, he hadn't.

Sighing, Shawn stopped walking and settled at a picnic table nestled in a brown, grassy field mottled with melting snow. He buried his ungloved hands into the pockets of his sweatshirt, and stared off into the tree line, where he could just make out the slight crest of blue of the horizon.

Shawn was tired of being a virgin. His entire childhood, sex had been built up into some big secret, and those who'd had it were members of an exclusive club—or really, one of two exclusive clubs. One consisting of good people like his parents and Melanie, who waited until marriage to have sex, and another consisting of... well, of the kinds of folks that Shawn wasn't supposed to talk to. And yet, that system had broken down slowly as Shawn had grown up and he'd *met* more of those people in club two, people who led happy lives and seemed to Shawn to be just as worthy and kind as the people in club one.

But still, the wall between him and those who knew, those who'd done it, stood tall. Occasionally, Shawn would reach up and peek over, but always, every time he'd had the chance to hop over, he'd found some reason not to. Some reason to run away. And so, he'd walked along the wall, step by step, waiting for some exit sign that might point him toward an answer, a path into the club that made sense to him.

And being with Jess... made sense. Something about her quieted his guilt and fear, pushed the years of Sunday School lessons and feelings of inadequacy deep enough down that his other feelings could take control. Feelings that he'd thought he'd maybe had before: about Natalie, about old girlfriends. But since he'd spent more time with Jess, it was as if all of those crushes he'd had in the past were foothills.

But the way he felt now as he thought about the weekend they'd spent painting her room, the many nights they'd spent shooting the shit across the bar, their texts back and forth parsing out potential fixes for the Bel Air, and, of course, the lesson she'd taught him in the front seat, was as if he'd finally climbed and sat atop the wall that separated him from the rest of the adult world. And he could at last look out and see the full majesty of the mountains. A place where maybe he finally belonged.

He didn't know if he and Jess would be forever. But he did know that he didn't want to go forever without giving the two of them a real try. He wasn't yet sure where he'd end up or who he'd be with when he got there. But when he closed his eyes and imagined the road directly in front of him, there was at last a sign directing him off the highway, and he was ready to signal.

He dug his phone out of his pocket, at last feeling a little more clear-headed, to see if Jess had texted him back. But there was nothing from her.

He hoped he hadn't missed his exit.

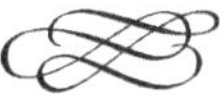

CHAPTER 29

Jess pulled into the driveway of her dad's ranch house. His truck was there, and she knew exactly where he would be.

Behind the driveway, slightly downhill from their family home, Ernie had an old shed. Over the years, it had had several renovations, transforming from a glorified tool shed to a tinkering cave, then a greatest projects gallery, until it entered its final form: "Dad's Sanctuary."

The barn doors, which had never actually made to the upgrade list, weren't quite sealed shut. Jess finished turning the old style latch handle and crept inside. Just as she'd thought, her father sat at his desk in the back corner, where he was looking at an old photo album that Jess didn't recognize.

"Hey, Dad."

Ernie gave a slight grunt to indicate he'd heard her. She padded across the Berber carpet and stood behind his ancient executive office chair, resting her elbows on his shoulders. She tussled the thinning hair on his head. He grunted again.

"Why didn't you tell me that Shawn's car was the same model as Mom's?" she asked gently. Ernie shook his head. He held up a picture over his shoulder, and Jess took it, straightening.

It was from an old disposable camera and stamped with a date on the back. In it, a 30-years-younger Ernie tossed a cocky grin over his shoulder as he leaned over the open hood of a turquoise Chevrolet Bel Air, and a big-haired, doe-eyed woman with feathered hair waved cheerily from behind the steering wheel.

Mom. But this picture must have been taken years before Jess was around. She didn't look much older than Jess now.

"We'd been dating about a year when that was taken," her dad finally said. Jess shifted to a short stool so she could face him as he spoke. "On our anniversary—which I'd completely forgotten about, o' course." He huffed out a wry chuckle, "She corralled Randy into going with her to some auction or other and came back with that to surprise me."

"Randy from the shop?"

Ernie nodded. "He introduced us. Your mother was one of his sweetie's sorority sisters back in the day. He'd begged me to go with her to some dance or other, and from the moment I saw her when I went to pick her up from her parents'… Well, I ain't one to get all touchy-feely about these kinds a things, you know. But I knew."

Jess looked back down at the picture and flipped it around to see the date. May 2, 1989.

"The car was a mess. Real piece of work. It wouldn't even drive off the auction block. Randy towed it all the way back to the shop and the two of them hid it from me for almost a week before she finally showed me. We were workin' on that car for months. O' course, just lookin' at it, I wasn't sure I'd ever quite get it driving again. Frame was bent. The shop was little then, and Randy and I didn't have all the tools we had now… but your momma swore we could get it there.

"Well, it ended up sittin' in our shop for close to ten years.

We'd married by then, had you to take care of, and by about the time you turned five and the shop had expanded some, she'd nearly forgotten about it. Well, one day I turned to Randy and asked him to help me get it on the lift again. Chuck was there then, too, and he helped us weld it all into somethin' we thought might work."

Ernie put his head in his hands then. Jess got off the chair and walked over to him, placing a hand on his shoulder. She didn't ask any questions. It had been years since she'd heard her dad string this many words together, and she feared that if she spoke, she might ruin it.

He took a deep, shuddering breath. "It was our tenth anniversary. We all showed it to her, and of course, she wanted to take it out right then. But the weather weren't too good that night. And those old cars don't got seatbelts in 'em, you know, and…" He trailed off, and Jess just kept rubbing his shoulder.

A memory popped up in her head from when she was little, of Chuck and his wife taking her in for a few days—a memory that had faded far into the back of her mind over the years.

"You both were in the hospital, weren't you?" She said, piecing it together.

Ernie nodded. "I made it out with some scratches and a few broken ribs. But your momma … it was her side of the car that got smashed. She–" His breath hitched, the pain still fresh even fifteen years later. "She didn't make it."

Jess's dad looked into his daughters eyes then, where tears had gathered, mirroring the ones in his own eyes. His shoulders shook, and Jess leaned down to hold him as he continued to quake with sobs, overcome with more emotion than she'd ever seen from him. He buried his head into her shoulder, and she patted his back, making calm *shush*-ing sounds until eventually falling silent, allowing him to grieve as much as he needed.

Silent tears streaked down Jess's own face as she held him. Not for her mother, she realized; she'd lived so long without her that she didn't really know how to mourn the life she could have had. As she stood there, holding her dad in his cracked leather office chair, she cried for *him*, for the man who'd never forgiven himself for his wife's death.

"Dad, it isn't your fault," Jess said at last. "It's not your fault."

"I knew it wasn't safe. I knew the weather weren't right, I knew–"

"You knew that that car was all she'd wanted," Jess interrupted him. "For ten years, that thing had sat in your shop. Of course you wanted to fix it for her. Of course she wanted to take it for a spin. It wasn't your fault."

"Jess…"

She shook her head at him, holding him across from her with her hands on his shoulders. He avoided her eyes, until she gave his shoulders a little shake.

"I do not blame you for mom's death." Her gaze bored into her father's. "I don't blame you."

More water gathered at the corners of Ernie's eyes, and his lip quivered.

"I'm so sorry all you had was me growin' up, Jess. Maybe if your mom was here, she'd have been able to teach you about dating. You wouldn't have been stuck at the shop–"

"Stop it!" They both started at the force of her voice, which resonated in the wooden shed around them. She swallowed, straightened her shoulders, and doubled down. "Don't you dare go and say somethin' stupid like I'd have turned out better if I'd had a mom around. You–you and me–," Jess's words broke on a sob that spilled out of her throat. She shook her head and powered through the tears, "I like who I am, dammit. I'm good at what I do–at all you taught me. We're the best damn father-daughter team in the whole Shenandoah Valley, Dad. And a real man will understand that you and me–that you're–"

She stared at him, trying to figure out how she could say what she was feeling inside. This was the man that had taught her everything she knew. The man that taught her how to ride a bike, how to change the oil in her car, the difference between a V8 and a straight six—all while grieving his own loss. The two of them were family. And no guy should make her choose between her and her family.

She knew her dad wasn't always the best parent, but he hadn't needed to be. Even without a mom, he'd given Jess the tools to teach herself the rest. She'd eventually figured out that Kyle was a loser, and she hadn't needed her mom for that. She'd only needed time.

"You're my *dad*." She finished at last, trying to cram as much meaning into that one syllable as she could possibly muster. "And that's all I've ever needed you to be."

Silence enveloped them as they continued to look at each other. At last, Jess saw something shift in her father's deep brown eyes, and he gave a her a slight nod, before pulling her into a hug.

They held each other for a moment, a dad and his girl, before Jess pulled herself away.

"Now when was the last time you ate a decent meal?"

Jess called off work from the old landline and stayed at her dad's place that night, cooking them a decent dinner with the chicken and veggies she'd found buried in the freezer. When she wasn't cooking, she was filling Ernie in on all that had happened in her life in the past few weeks: her break-up, her new room-mate and her girlfriend, how training the new bartenders was going, and of course, Shawn.

She didn't say anything more about Kyle, though, and she skirted around talking about the Bel Air too much, and the big discovery she'd had with Beau in the shop earlier. She didn't want to continue to dig into the freshly-opened wound of her mother's accident, so instead she focused on telling him about her new crush: his handiness with fixing up Natalie's home, how he'd helped her paint her room, how close he was with his grandpa.

Ernie nodded thoughtfully as she spoke, at one point setting down his fork and giving her a quizzical look over his beer. "Sounds like you feel a little differently about this boy than the others I seen you around with," he said.

Jess noticed a careful lack of judgment in his tone. She blushed.

"Well," she began carefully, "he's different than the other boys I've… hung around."

"Really?"

"Really."

Ernie gave a *humph*, before saying, "And this is the boy with the Bel Air."

Jess's fork stopped on its way to her mouth. She looked at her dad. "Yeah."

He picked at his food. "Well. How's it look?"

A tiny spark of excitement sprung to life in Jess's stomach. "Dad, it's beautiful. It's been sitting in a garage for probably fifty years–barely even been driven. The odometer's just over 20,000 miles, the body looks amazing…" She trailed off, seeing the slightest pain flicker across her dad's face. "But we don't need to—"

"What's wrong with it?" Ernie interrupted her, blinking away any traces of discomfort and replacing it with a face that Jess had seen before—the face of a mechanic with a project.

Jess smiled. "I *think*," she said, "I just figured it out."

THE NEXT MORNING, Jess walked Ernie through the entire diagnostic of Shawn's car, recounting every test and precaution they'd taken to try to assess the problem. By the time she'd recounted her and Beau's discovery at the garage the previous day, she realized it was already almost 10:30.

"Shit!" she blurted, and Ernie raised her eyebrows at her, "Sorry, but I just realized I'm going to be late for work!"

Ernie waved at her with his hands and assured her that they'd finish their talk later, and she ran to give him a kiss on the cheek before running out the door. "Love you, Daddy!" she called over her shoulder.

"Love you too, Soo-soo."

The rest of the day was a blur of activity. Hints of spring were in the air, and as she drove north to the Potomac Bar and Grill, she raced lines of geese that flew above the highway. The lunch rush bustled with table after table of regulars that trailed melting snow in with their boots, and Jess had her hands full managing the orders and the clean up on her own before Beth and Sheila arrived to help her with the dinner shift. She was so busy, in fact, that she didn't have time to think about her stolen phone, or the last text she'd sent to Shawn.

CHAPTER 30

Shawn still hadn't heard from Jess.

The day of his interview dawned, and at 7:00, Shawn woke to his alarm and immediately checked his phone. Still nothing. He tossed it back onto his nightstand and ran a hand down his face.

It was fine. Really. He needed to focus on this interview anyway.

Since Jess hadn't texted him back at all the previous day, and Natalie had said she hadn't come home that night, he decided to find a project over there to keep him occupied until she came back. And that was why Natalie found him measuring siding at 8:25 a.m. when she walked out onto her front porch with a parka on, holding a travel tumbler of coffee out to him.

"You realize it's like, 30 degrees out, don't you?" She shivered as she glared at him.

His breath formed white puffs that drifted lazily between them. "Yep."

"And you're measuring the outside of my house."

"Siding needs replacing."

"Uh-huh," Natalie deadpanned, "And who's paying for this new siding, Shawn?"

"You know, I been thinkin' about that, and I realized the other day that you're datin' a frickin lawyer. Ain't they supposed to be rich or somethin'?"

Natalie's expression was flat as she pulled her parka closer around her neck. "Let me try this again. Shawn. What are you doing outside my house at fucking sunrise when it's below freezing out?"

"I'm measuri-"

"And don't you dare fucking say you're 'measuring siding' again, or I swear to God—" Natalie set down her coffee mug on a tiny table on the porch. "You leave yesterday in a huff looking for my roommate, who is still missing, by the way, and now you're literally kneeling outside her bedroom window. Some-thing's up between you two."

A shiver rippled its way down Shawn's neck. He faced her. "You know what? You're right. It's freezing. Why don't we go inside."

"Let's do that." She grabbed her coffee and marched through the door.

Shawn rubbed his hands together as he stepped into the foyer, grateful for the time he'd spent putting in the electric baseboard heaters that fall. He watched as Natalie shuffled out of her parka and threw it on a chair in the parlor, before stomping her way back to the kitchen. He heard one of the dining room chairs scrape across the floor as he unzipped his hoodie and laid it over her coat, and then slowly walked back to the kitchen.

"Jess still ain't back, huh?"

Natalie scowled at him from her seat at the table as he sat down. "No. I assumed she was with you."

Shawn snorted. "What's yer problem?"

"My problem??" Natalie raised her voice, "*My problem* is that my best friend tricked me into getting a roommate so he could get into her pants. And now she's missing."

"Excuse me?" Shawn bolted upright from where he'd been slouched in his chair. "What are you trying to say?"

"Isn't that why you were so eager for me to get a roommate?" Natalie asked. "'Oh, my friend Jess needs a place to stay.'" She glared. "And you just happen to have a spare key."

"It wasn't like that!" he shouted. "How could you fuckin' even think that, Nat?" He cut himself off and closed his eyes. He took a deep breath to calm himself down.

"You know I don't take advantage of girls like that," he said. "You, of all people, know I wouldn't do that."

Natalie paused, letting his words sink in. She tapped her fingers on her mug. "Then why were you so insistent on me getting a roommate?"

"Because my friend needed help! Her dad was kickin' her out."

"That's the only reason?" She met his eyes. While they didn't hold as much fire as they had a moment ago, he still shrank back a bit under her scrutiny. He shuffled his shoulders and rubbed his neck. "All right, no, it wasn't the only reason. But the other stuff didn't have anything to do with Jess. It was..." he rubbed his neck, not wanting to admit the reason. Especially now that so much had changed, now that he no longer pined over Natalie the way he had.

He was embarrassed by the Shawn that had tried, however unsuccessfully, to keep Natalie and Bonnie apart.

"Look, it was stupid, okay? Does it really matter?"

Natalie didn't answer. She just continued to stare at him.

"I didn't want you moving in with Bonnie, all right?" he blurted after a minute of tense silence. Natalie raised her eyebrows.

This was agony. Pure agony. But Natalie's face was laced with confusion as she looked at him, and he realized there wasn't any going back now. "But it doesn't matter now, 'cause I don't like you like that anymore."

Natalie blinked, and her mouth formed a tiny O. Shawn saw her cheeks redden as she hastily looked down at her coffee cup. He was grateful that he didn't have to meet her eyes anymore, even as he was mortified at the confession.

"Oh, Shawn, I didn't–"

"Stop." He picked up a crumpled napkin and threw it at her. She batted it away and half-laughed. "You knew I liked you. You had to. I wasn't that subtle."

Natalie chuckled in earnest. "Actually, you'd be surprised. I honestly had no idea."

"What?" Shawn shook his head. "Nah, girls know all about that stuff. Y'all can read us like books."

"The fuck we can!" Natalie laughed. "Guys are absolute mysteries to us. Any woman who says she can read a man is lying—certainly any straight woman." She paused a moment, her mug halfway to her lips. "I wonder if Bonnie had any idea?"

Shawn groaned. Natalie took a sip of her coffee, and then her face shifted once more. She looked at Shawn thoughtfully.

"But now you like someone else," she said.

He nodded. There was really no point in hiding it.

"Jess."

He nodded again.

"My missing roommate."

He leaned forward and put his face in his hands.

"Be honest, Natalie. Do you think she spent the night with another guy?" he said through his hands. This was a girl who'd blown him in a car and sent him a nude photo of herself barely a week after splitting up with her boyfriend. Clearly, she wasn't new to this sort of thing. And one doesn't get experienced at being sexual without… well, having sex. Jess was an adult, and they weren't dating. It shouldn't surprise him that she might be doing things with other guys.

Even so, it still hurt to think about it.

"I don't know, Shawn. That would be something to ask her," Natalie said.

He shook his head. "Yeah, that'd be a fun conversation. 'Hey Jess, I know that we kinda been flirtin' some and you sucked my dick that one time but does that mean we're exclusive, or–?"

Natalie placed a hand on his arm. "So you two *did* have sex?"

"Not technically."

"Shawn," Natalie said. "You *just* said she sucked your dick."

Shawn looked at her. "Yeah, but, like, we didn't have *sex* sex."

She rubbed her face. "Did you come?"

Shawn blushed. "Well… yeah."

"That counts," she said.

"Does not!"

"Oh, so you're a romantic," Natalie teased. "Doesn't count unless she comes too, huh?"

Shawn's face went, if it were possible, even redder. "That's not—I mean, *yeah*, I'd want her to of course, but I meant that–" He shook his head, not wanting to sound like an asshole. "Never mind."

"There's more ways of having sex than penetration, my dear." She patted his arm again and got up to refill her mug. Shawn scrunched his face and tried really hard *not* to picture exactly what Natalie was talking about.

"I get it, Nat. You're a lesbian."

"Bisexual," she corrected. "But for the sake of this conversation, sure." She sat back down with her now full mug and nudged his tumbler toward him. He grabbed it and took a sip. "Hey. It sucks that Jess might be with another dude right now. But also, maybe she isn't. Actually, I'm a little worried about her."

"Yeah. She hasn't answered any of my texts."

Natalie sat with this for a moment. Shawn took another sip of coffee. Where *was* she?

"Well, what was the last thing she texted you?" Despite the seriousness of the moment, he almost had a spit-take. He managed to swallow the hot coffee and coughed, trying to recover from the burn of his windpipe.

"Jesus, are you okay??" She handed him a napkin.

He nodded as he gathered himself. "Yeah, just, the last thing she sent me…"

Natalie looked at him when he didn't finish. "Let me see."

"No."

They stared at each other. Shawn kept his face perfectly blank, but even he could feel the heat creeping up his neck and ears.

"Shawn. What did she send you?"

Shawn shook his head. He wasn't going to say it.

Natalie gasped, then covered her mouth with her hand. "Oh my God. It was dirty, wasn't it?"

Shawn debated whether or not to answer. Though he realized that, at this point, it probably didn't matter. The satisfied smile that started to creep at the corner of her lips meant she knew she was right. He gave the tiniest incline of his head.

Natalie squealed, but then her face fell. "Oh. Oh shit. That actually kinda makes this worse, doesn't it? If she's with someone else?"

Shawn nodded. "It don't feel *good.*"

"Hence you being here at 8:00 in the morning to measure my siding." Natalie glanced at the clock. "Or I guess, almost 10:00 now."

"Ten o'clock?" Shawn repeated, looking at the microwave. "Oh shoot. I should probably get going."

"What's going on?"

"My interview with Leah. She said to come by around lunchtime." He scooted his chair back and patted himself down, checking for his wallet and keys. Natalie stood, too.

"Lemme top off your coffee." She grabbed his tumbler, filled it from the carafe on the counter, and handed it to him, before leaning in and wrapping her arms around his waist. He hugged her back with his free arm, leaning his chin on the top of her head. "You knock 'em dead, Shawn. Leah's going to fucking love you. I've got a good feeling about this."

Shawn nodded and gave her a small smile as he let her go. "Yeah. You know, in spite of everything… I do too."

They stepped back and he headed for the door. "Let me know how it goes!" She called after him, and he waved in acknowledgement before climbing in his truck.

He did feel good about the interview. As shitty as he felt about everything else—his car, his sister and her friends, Jess— this might be something in his life that would actually go right.

CHAPTER 31

$\mathcal{J}$ess awoke in her old bedroom, dressed in the previous day's clothes, and desperate for a shower. When she walked groggily out to the kitchen of her dad's house and grunted out a "Good morning," he handed her a cup of coffee.

"Ain't you got an apartment you live in now or somethin'?" he asked her.

"Yeah, yeah, I know, but we were bonding." She rubbed her eyes and scooped her keys off the kitchen table. "I *do* need to get back, though. Nat's probably worried about me. Plus, I need a shower." She kissed her dad on the head. "I'll see you at the garage later?"

He looked at her, and smiled. "Yeah, Soo-Soo. See you later."

Natalie was waiting for her when she pulled into the driveway.

"There you are!" Natalie was standing in the doorway. Jess jumped.

"Holy shit, Nat! You scared me!"

"Where've you been the past few days?" Nat followed her

into the house and to her room while Jess launched into an apology.

"I'm sorry! I was at my dad's, and Kyle stole my fucking phone, and when I tried to check in on you yesterday Bonnie's car was in the driveway, so I stopped by the garage and it was a whole thing…"

A wave of relief flooded Natalie's expression.

"Oh, thank God! Shawn's been looking for you," she said in a rush. "Wait–Kyle? Isn't he your ex–"

"Shawn was here?" Jess blanched. She hadn't talked to him at all since she'd sent the picture.

Natalie nodded. "Yeah, he just left a few minutes ago, actually."

"What happened? What did he say when he was here??" Jess stared at her roommate with wide eyes. Natalie swallowed.

"Well. We weren't sure where you were… and he wondered where you'd spent the night. He thought it might be with another guy."

Jess groaned and held her face in her hands. *No, no, no!* She tried to hold back tears. "It was the car! I figured out the problem with the Bel Air, but then my dad and I had this big fight, and I found out it was just because my mom—" A sob shook her shoulders, and her lip quivered. She squinted, but the tears started to fall from her eyes, "I have to fix it."

"You should probably shower first," Natalie said, her brow furrowed in concern.

"Right. Right, absolutely. But what do I do?"

Natalie gave her shoulder a squeeze. "I'll text him to let him know you're okay. And then you'll have a talk."

"What about my phone?" Jess bit her lip, and she felt hot tears falling onto her chest.

"We'll figure it out. But first, shower. You smell like diesel."

After Jess showered, she got dressed in a fresh pair of leggings and one of her favorite baggy flannels and brushed out her hair, pulling it into a messy bun atop her head. She debated whether or not to put on make-up. She decided on some eyeliner and mascara, and then called down to Natalie.

"You hear back from Shawn yet?"

"Not yet. He's probably still at his interview."

She looked at herself in the bathroom door mirror, tapping a nervous rhythm on her lap with her fingers. Finally, she couldn't take it any longer. She grabbed her bag, double checking to make sure the gas cap was still in it. Then she ran down the stairs, grabbed her coat, and called to Natalie as she opened the door.

"I'll be at the shop. Call me there if you hear from Shawn!"

HALF AN HOUR LATER, she was knocking on Shawn's parents' front door, bundled in her puffy coat and squinting in the bright, early March sun. An older man with a cannula in his nose answered the door, leaning on a walker.

"Hello?"

"Hi there," she said, mustering her best customer-service grin. "Walter, right?"

"Oh," he said, comprehension dawning in his light blue eyes. "You're Ernie's girl."

"That's right! He says hi, by the way."

"Come in, come in. You want some coffee or anything?"

He shuffled down the hallway and she followed him inside, careful not to overtake his crawling pace. A large kitchen and dining room with a vaulted ceiling stretched in front of her.

"Coffee would be great, thank you."

Walter gestured to a full pot of coffee on the counter and took a breath before saying, "The mugs are up above there."

"Got it. Would you like some as well?" She reached up on her tip-toes to open the cupboard and grab a mug.

He smiled. "Yes, thank you."

As she poured, he turned his walker around and sat on its seat at the island. She pulled up a stool across from him and served him his coffee before sitting down. He nodded at her.

"Shawn's out this morning, I'm afraid," he said. "But it's nice to see you. I know the two of you have been working a bit on the car together."

"Yes, that's right." She gave him a tight smile. She tried not to blush at the thought of the last time she'd been here with Shawn. She cleared her throat. "That's why I'm here, actually. I think I figured out the problem with it, and I brought the part you need." She shifted her bag on her shoulder.

Walter started. "Really?"

"Yes! I'd love to test it out, but of course, we should probably wait for Shawn."

"Nonsense!" Walter waved his arm at her. "He's been throwing everything at that damn engine for months trying to get that thing to stay running. Of course we should test it out!"

"Are you sure?"

He pushed back and slowly rose to his feet, leaning on the island. "The garage is right through that door, there. Go on ahead. And open the big door so we can start her up."

Jess paused to wait for him, and once again he waved at her to go ahead. She darted over to the door to the garage and swept down the few steps to ground level. Finding the door switch, she raised the outside door and uncovered the Bel Air.

The front headlights sparkled as sunlight slowly rose across the nose of the car. Her breath hitched as she admired the glossy paint, seeing it in the glow of the outdoors for the first time. She felt Shawn's grandpa approach behind her.

"Well go on! What'd you figure out?"

She hurried over to the side of the car and released the fuel door. "You're not going to believe it."

"At this point, I'd believe anything," he said, zipping a jacket he'd pulled on while Jess had been ogling the car.

She reached into her bag and pulled out the plastic cap, sticker still affixed to it. "At any point, did either you or Shawn check to see if the gas cap vent had gone bad?"

He blinked at her. "You're kidding."

"Nope." Jess grinned, unscrewing the old cap and replacing it with the new one. "Keys inside?"

Walter nodded, and she climbed into the front seat, closing her eyes for a moment as the smell of the leather seats brought back memories. She spotted the key in the ignition and wrapped her fingers around it. She pushed her foot down into the clutch and turned the key.

It roared to life, settling to a clean purr as it idled. She shifted to neutral and engaged the emergency brake, then stepped out of the driver's seat.

Walter smiled. "It sounds good!"

"Well, we'll see if it can last twenty minutes." She walked over to stand next to Shawn's grandpa.

"How on earth did you figure it out?"

Jess laughed, rubbing the bruise on her elbow. "I got in a fight with an El Camino at my dad's shop that was having the same issue. When I tried to hit it back, I saw that the gas cap was all corroded. We replaced the cap, and it was good as new!"

"El Camino, huh?" Walter's eyes glazed as he reminisced. "That takes me back. Pretty sure Shawn's father was the result of a particularly good night in the back of an El Camino."

Jess's face heated. *What is it with this family? Are they* all *this candid about sex?* "O-oh."

"But that's a story for another time. How long has it been?"

Jess prayed that time never came. "Oh shoot, I don't have my phone on me–"

He pulled out an old pocket watch and they observed it in awkward silence as they watched the seconds tick by. Eleven minutes. Twelve. Thirteen...

"I haven't heard a change in the rhythm, have you?" she asked.

He shook his head. "Not yet."

For the first time in as long as she could remember, Jess found herself reciting a silent prayer in her head. *Please, God, let this work...*

When minute fifteen passed with no change to the rhythm of the engine, Shawn's grandpa shook his head in disbelief.

"That poor kid ripped apart this baby backwards and forwards to try to see what the problem was... and all this time it was a plastic cap."

"It sounds so good," Jess said, grinning. She didn't want to celebrate too early, but she was so excited to see it come to life. She side-eyed Walter and noticed that his eyes were shiny with moisture.

"You know," she said. "It's a bit of a shame that he didn't take it to the garage to give it that extra shine and sparkle."

Walter frowned thoughtfully at her. "Shine and sparkle, you say?"

Jess stroked her chin. "Well, I doubt you can do much in terms of bodywork touch-ups or paint in *this* garage, but I happen to have access to a pretty reputable shop around here."

She jingled her keys in her hand. Twenty minutes rolled past on the stopwatch.

"You think this baby could make it to the shop?"

Walter's face split into a wide grin. "I'd say we should at least give it the ol' college try."

JESS HAD OFFERED to take Walter with her, but he'd shaken his head, claiming that it was his job to watch the house for the day. But she didn't want to leave her own car at Shawn's house.

So in the end, she'd used the Cobb's landline to call Beau to drive the tow truck over and pick it up, and she'd followed him all the way back to Ernie's Garage.

She wasn't working until 8:00 that night at the bar, so she had most of the day to get started on the Bel Air. She'd spend all day if she had to–all month–if that's what it took earn Shawn's forgiveness.

As she and Beau pulled into the garage, Chuck, Randy, and Ernie all piled out in front of the shop. Randy let out a whistle.

"It's like a ghost, seeing that ol' thing pull in here," he breathed.

"Nah," Ernie countered, blinking away tears. "Becca's car never looked that good."

He nodded at Jess as his daughter bounded to the door. "It worked," she said breathlessly. "The gas cap fixed the problem!"

"As far as you know," Chuck scolded. "But we ain't lettin' that thing on the road 'til we've checked every last nook and cranny of it."

"'Specially not if you're gonna be ridin' in it with some boy," Ernie huffed. The mechanics all looked at Jess.

"I thought you said this was for a friend!" Beau hit her arm.

"You mean we're gonna be workin' overtime to help you catch some fish you got tuggin' on the line?" Randy tussled her hair.

"Now wait a minute, here," Chuck cut in. He turned to look her in the eye. She met his gaze, making sure not to look away even as she felt him assessing her. "This ain't the one who made you quit, is it?

Jess shook her head.

"This is Walter's boy?"

She nodded. "Grandson, yeah."

"You like him?"

Heat rose to her cheeks. Beau smirked. Randy elbowed Ernie in the arm, and he coughed.

Once again, Jess nodded, and looked down at her feet. She felt a big hand clap her on the shoulder.

"Well, it's about time you found a boy that can keep you happy," Chuck laughed, and he reached around to open the big bay doors. "Come on, y'all, we got a job to do."

ONCE INSIDE, with the Bel Air loaded onto the lift, all the men—even her dad—looked to Jess for direction. She took a deep breath, and together, the five of them got to work. Everything she and Shawn had gone over the past week was double-checked, and she made a list of each detail in her mental notes and divied up the responsibilities. All five of them worked through the safety check, fluid levels, and state inspection checklist, and Jess inspected the body and cosmetics of the car, marking a sheet with each blemish and chip. As the sun set, the five of them lowered the car off the lift and pushed it into the body shop, where she pinned the sheet and her notes to the cork board on the wall.

"All right, guys," she said, turning to face them. "Here's our weekend project. I'm working tonight, but I can be here at 8 a.m. sharp tomorrow to get started on sanding."

"I'll be here," Beau said.

"Me too," Chuck grunted.

Randy and Ernie nodded their assent as well, and Jess clapped her hands. "Fantastic! Guys, thank you so much. I know this is above and beyond what y'all would normally do on a weekend..."

Beau snuck behind her and wrapped her in a big hug. She jumped a little, surprised at the show of affection. But before she knew it, her dad had wrapped an arm around them both. Then Randy, and even Chuck piled on, until they were just a greasy clump of people standing on the floor of the body shop.

"All right, all right, get your greasy hands off me!" Jess gave a muffled shout over an armful of flannel. "I gotta go be presentable in an hour at my other job!"

They all pulled away, save for Ernie, who kept an arm on his daughter's shoulder and planted a kiss on her forehead. She looked up as he pulled away.

"I'm proud of you, Soo-Soo. You do good here, managing a project." He rummaged a hand in his pocket. "I meant to do this three weeks ago, before things got so outta hand…"

He pulled out a keychain with three keys on it, each with a printed label marked "office," "shop," or "files." A big plastic tag emblazoned with the *Ernie's Garage* logo on it poked from between his fingers.

"I know you might have other plans in the next few years," he said, holding out the keys in his palm. "But I want you to know that, if you want it, there's a place for you here as a team lead."

Jess felt her chest tighten, and she looked back at the three engineers standing around them. They nodded and smiled at her, and her dad cleared his throat.

"We all think you deserve it, Jess. You know this place backwards and forwards, you get how we all work and you're damn good at keepin' us all in line and on track. Plus, you're good with the customers." He dropped his gaze to his feet and pushed the keys toward her. "Regardless, these are yours. You've earned 'em. Whether you take the title or not, there's always gonna be a place for you here to come back to."

Jess reached out her hand and wrapped her fingers around the keychain, sniffling a bit as a couple of tears slid down her cheeks.

"Thanks, Daddy. Thank y'all so much." Jess stuffed the keys in her pocket and looked around the room at all of them. Her team.

Her family.

"Ain't you got work to get to?" Beau teased, breaking the

silence. Jess checked the old pin-up analogue clock just under the ceiling.

"Aw, crap, I'm gonna be late!" she moaned, then darted to the door. As she yanked it open, she shouted over her shoulder "Love y'all! See you tomorrow!"

"Bright n' early!" Ernie called back, waving and smiling as he watched his daughter go.

CHAPTER 32

From the moment Shawn stepped out of his truck and looked out over the acres of vineyards spread before him, he knew there was something special about this place. The commute had been breathtaking: once he'd gotten off the interstate and started down the country highways that wound their way through the Blue Ridge Mountains, he'd seen vignettes of villages and farmland spread before him like a patchwork quilt, tucked amidst a frame of green and purple mountains and blue skies.

It was a car ride he could get used to.

Gravel crunched under his feet as he walked across the parking lot into a large, reclaimed wood pole barn, with a huge raised wrap-around deck that overlooked the valleys of grapevines. When he walked inside, floor-to-ceiling windows continued the view behind a long bar that snaked itself around the perimeter of the tasting room.

Shawn had never been to a winery before, but it was much more like a cafe or a restaurant than he'd imagined. Small tables dotted an open floor, where groups of people sat with glasses of wine and cheese plates, and servers flitted behind the bar talking to folks with four or five sample glasses spread among them.

"Here for a tasting?" A young woman with a ponytail approached him with a paper menu. Shawn waved a hand in front of his chest.

"No menu, thanks. My name's Shawn Cobb, and I'm here for an interview with Leah?"

"Oh!" The woman smiled, and looked him up and down, checking him out–and none too subtly. "I'll get her for you."

As she walked away, Shawn returned her inspection with one of his own.

Too skinny, he thought, remembering Jess's strutting backside from their weekend of painting. Then he closed his eyes and looked away, choosing to admire the view from the windows instead. He reviewed his phone call with Leah in his head.

Only about a minute passed before the hostess returned with a stunningly beautiful woman in tow. Even dressed down in mud-caked boots, denim overalls, and a cropped hoodie, Shawn could see that she was a voluptuous powerhouse. Her black hair was pulled back into a spiky, messy bun, and a red bandana secured flyaways from her strong-featured, heart-shaped face. .

Shawn gave her his best polite smile. Leah stuck out her hand, returning the grin.

"You must be Shawn!" He shook her hand, and as he did, he glimpsed a hint of a tattoo peeking out on her wrist below her sleeve.

"And you're Leah?"

Her smile widened. "That's me. Welcome to Lilliette Vineyards!"

Shawn took in the surroundings once more as Leah opened her arms to encompass the place.

"I'm surprised that there are people here so early drinkin' wine," he said. "I thought that was more of a dinner thing."

Leah laughed. "Oh no, not around here. We offer tastings

every day from ten to six, and on weekends, we host evening events: live music, case club parties, that kind of thing."

"Sounds exciting."

Leah's eyes sparkled. "Let me show you what's *really* exciting."

She beckoned him back the way she'd come, and Shawn followed her through a tall wooden door marked "Employee's Only." There was a small landing that overlooked a huge space like a warehouse below them, with giant metal tanks and rows of plastic tubes and shining pipe that ran between them along the perimeter of the space. A mixture of fluorescents and natural light from ground-level windows illuminated the space almost like a weird steampunk laboratory.

"Woah." Shawn heard himself whistle, and Leah waved him down a flight of stairs.

"Oh yeah. I'm gonna show you where the magic happens."

THE TOUR of the facilities and grounds took just over an hour. Leah walked Shawn through an entire explanation of their wine-making process, while they explored several buildings and even walked through the vineyards. Shawn was grateful that it was sunny out, although the winter chill still clung to the valley. Leah donned an oversized Carhartt before the outside portion of the tour, and Shawn pulled a pair of work gloves out of his pockets to keep his fingers from freezing.

Eventually, she led him past one of the vineyards, down the hill from the tasting room, which stood like a beacon as the sunlight reflected off all the windows overlooking the slope. The two of them walked through a wide clearing between the rows, until the ground leveled out at the base of the hill.

Before them was either a small lake or a very large pond, with oak and birch trees lining the shore. A wooden platform with a large picture frame-like arch sat in the middle of the clearing, and Shawn could see tiny wooden stakes with neon ribbons spread in polygons throughout the forest near the water line. One lone cabin was nestled at the end of the row of stakes.

"This," Leah said, turning around to face Shawn and gesturing around her, "is going to be our wedding venue."

"Wedding venue?"

Leah nodded, and in her eyes Shawn could see an entire plan unfolding. "Each cabin plot is staked out along the beach, and this platform here is going to be a covered stage and pavilion." She hopped to the center of the platform, and Shawn watched her clap her hands together, framed by the wooden arch before the lake, the sunlight shining blinding swaths of white along the half-frozen water behind her.

He could see it. His feet carried him into the tree line and he stepped out the staked plots, picturing the circle of cabins and a campfire pit, imagining chairs set out in rows up the vineyard aisle, and in his mind crowds of people gathered to celebrate.

"This'll be where I work?" he asked her.

She nodded, and Shawn could see her attempting to hide the full extent of her excitement.

"And when's your first event?"

Leah took in a breath, and her eyebrows came together just a fraction of an inch. "Well, that's the tough part. We've got our first wedding booked for October."

"October?" Shawn's jaw dropped. "Leah, you ain't even broken ground yet! We gotta haul materials down this crazy hill, we gotta have manpower…" Shawn shook his head and ran a hand over his face, blowing air through his fingers. "That's a tall ask, even for a full crew."

"We'll have a crew," Leah assured him. "But they need guidance, and that's why I need someone who knows what he's doing. It's mostly kit builds for the cabins, which won't be too bad—pre-fab type stuff. The first one was built by the construction company we hired, but we had some of our guys on the build and they said it went up easy. You can take a look if you want. It's the pavilion that's going to take some doing."

"How are we going to get all the materials down the hill?" he asked.

"Tractors and trailers." She smiled. "Which reminds me, you said you work on vintage cars, too, right? Ever tune up a tractor?"

Shawn coughed out a laugh. "You serious right now?"

Leah shrugged. "Worth a shot. I'm always looking for folks who know their way around the antique engines. It's a lotta upkeep to keep this place running."

"So this is a full-time gig, then?"

Leah nodded, "Certainly through the year. Starting as soon as the ground thaws, which the almanac says should be any day now. Which brings me to my next question."

She stepped down from the pavilion and met his eyes.

"How soon can you start?"

Shawn drove home that afternoon with a heavy heart. He'd just been offered the biggest job of his young career, and he wasn't sure what to do. The winery was amazing, of course, and he'd be silly not to take the job.

But if he was working two hours away every day, he'd likely need to find himself an apartment. A roommate he didn't know. In a strange town, a different place, far away from all he'd ever known.

He flicked on the lights as he stepped into the old place and shivered a bit in his jacket. A chill had set in as the sun had descended below the tree line, and he made his way over to the furnace as he'd grown so accustomed to doing over the past few months.

As he crinkled newspaper into wicks and gathered kindling

and wood for the night, he thought about all that he'd be leaving if he took the job. How long would he be gone?

He thought about Jess. Leaving town would also mean abandoning any chance they might have had to be something. Especially since–

Shawn realized with a start that he hadn't even looked at his phone since he'd left to go to the winery. Not that she would have texted him. It had been three days, after all, since she'd sent that picture, and she'd probably meant it for someone else, anyway.

But he had to check.

He waddled back inside with a full hoddle of wood in his hand, dumped it by the wood stove, and dug into his pockets for his phone. He had three messages waiting for him.

NATLIE FROM MCDS

How'd the interview go?

Found Jess! Her asshole ex stole her phone. She's safe!

She just went to her dad's shop. Find her there?

Shawn's heart stopped beating. The guy she was with was her dad? Her phone was stolen? Did that mean she hadn't even seen his messages?

He scrolled back up to review the texts he'd sent her, which, all at once, seemed to paint a desperate and angry picture of him. Granted, he *had* been angry at the time, but now–

And there it was. The picture. In an instant he went rock hard, his mouth salivating at the sight of her perfect tits. *Fuck.*

He checked the time. It was almost eight. Would she still be at the garage? Or was she working tonight?

The furnace could wait. He grabbed his keys and fired up his pickup.

CHAPTER 33

J ess found herself bopping her head along to the bar music when she approached the oak counter with a full bus tub. Sheila raised her eyebrows as she approached.

"Well somebody's in a good mood." she drawled. "I'm glad to see you're feeling better."

"I am. Thank you for covering my shift last night."

"Of course. That's what friends do." Sheila gave her a smile, which twisted into a smirk. "So what's his name?"

Jess rolled her eyes at her. "What makes you think there's a guy?"

Sheila set down the bar rag she'd been wiping glasses with and leaned over the bar. Jess shrank back. The sheer amount of wisdom she could package into one raised eyebrow amazed her.

"Okay, okay, fine. You caught me," Jess confessed, sinking into a stool. "But that isn't where I was last night. I was with my dad."

"Your dad?" She wasn't convinced.

Jess sighed. "And he's helping me fix up a car for Shawn, okay?"

"Softshell Crab Sandwich guy from Valentine's Day?" Sheila's eyes widened. Jess nodded, picking up the bus tub.

"One and the same," she called as she dropped the dishes in the back. The door swung open again behind her, almost hitting her in the face as she and Sheila spun around each other through the opening.

"Tell. Me. Everything," Sheila said, smacking her gum in between each word.

The corner of Jess's lip curled. "Aren't we a bit old for kiss-n-tell?"

Sheila caught the strings of Jess's apron with her finger and tugged her back. Jess flopped backwards into her friend's magnanimous bosom. "Even when I'm old and gray, Jess, I will *never* be too old for kiss and tell. This little biddy's gonna chit-chat with the best of them till the day she dies."

Jess laughed and shook her head, and Sheila hip-checked her back to standing. Beth came around behind the bar with an empty tray slung under her arm.

"Two margaritas for table six," she said to Sheila, before flashing her eyes at Jess. "So how was your date last night?"

"Jesus, does everyone want to know about my sex life??" Jess threw her hands into the air.

"Was it the pitcher again? We had a bet going." Beth wiggled her eyebrows conspiratorially. Jess sunk her face in her hands.

"Nope! It was the handyman! Pay up, buttercup!" Sheila said, plunking the two margaritas on the tray and holding out her palm.

"Goddammit." Beth dug into the pocket of her apron for her tip money and shoved a few crumpled bills into Sheila's outstretched hand.

"Y'all are unbelievable, gambling with a young woman's heart like that," Jess said. But she held her head high. Even if it were a joke to her co-workers, *she* knew that Shawn was different. Special.

And she couldn't wait to see his face when she showed him the Bel Air.

"Speak of the devil..." Sheila nudged Jess's shoulder and tilted her head towards the door, knocking her out of her revery.

Her breath hitched, and she felt heat rise to her cheeks. She couldn't help it. She wondered if she'd ever get over the fluttering in her chest whenever he entered her field of vision.

"Oh shit, she's got it *bad*," Sheila whispered to Beth behind her, but Jess ignored them. Nerves consumed her. She dreaded what he might have to say about the picture, or her silence over the past three days, but her face still split into a goofy grin as he walked to the bar, and she leaned forward to offer him a beer when he called out to her.

"Jess! I gotta bone to pick with you."

Beth gasped, "A lover's quarrel!"

Jess elbowed her. "Lemme get you a beer first?"

She perched both hands on the bar and purposefully pinched her chest between her arms as she leaned toward him. She smirked as the blood tinted his cheeks when his eyes darted to her cleavage and back.

He coughed. "Yeah, I'll take a beer."

"'Kay!" Jess chirped and bounced back on her heels, grabbing a pint and holding it under the tap. "So what's this bone you got for me?"

Sheila snorted, and Shawn's cheeks reddened further.

"Oh, hun, you are too cute," Sheila muttered before Jess swatted her butt with a dishrag. The girls gave her some space.

"Someone has some explaining to do," he growled, bending over his pint as she handed it to him. He stroked his fingers up and down her wrist as he said it, and her heart skipped a beat.

She felt Sheila's and Beth's eyes glued on them. She looked up at Shawn through her eyelashes, and heat simmered between them. She cleared her throat. He let go.

"Maybe we could talk about this somewhere else–"

"Hey!" A male voice interrupted their conversation. Jess glanced over Shawn's shoulder and straightened in surprise when she saw Kyle walking toward her.

Or rather, toward Shawn.

He put his hand on Shawn's shoulder. Shawn turned and looked at the guy. Jess froze.

Shit.

"You touchin' my girl?" Kyle pushed his chest into Shawn's arm. Shawn shot a glance at Jess, who returned it with panic in her eyes.

"Kyle, I'm not–"

"You stay out of this, Jess," Kyle said. Her eyes narrowed. He turned back to Shawn. "I said, are you touchin' my girl?"

Shawn stood calmly, and even though Kyle wasn't particularly short, he had to bend his neck back to maintain eye contact with the man. "I think you have something that doesn't belong to you," Shawn said. "And *Jess* don't belong to nobody."

"Is that what she told you?" Kyle turned to the bar. Jess raised her eyebrows at him.

Oh, so now *you want me to join the conversation?*

"If you're not here to give my back my phone, you can turn right around and leave, Kyle."

"I protected you, Jess!" Kyle's face reddened with anger. "I protected both of you!" He shot a look toward Beth.

Beth walked up to the two of them and placed a hand on his arm. "We never *asked* you to protect us. Now leave, before we call the cops."

Kyle swatted Beth away, his fingers landing in a smack against her cheek. Beth backed away, hand to her face, and Shawn grabbed the collar of Kyle's shirt. He tried to weasel out of his grip. "But first, hand over the phone."

"I'm not afraid of you, asshole."

Shawn raised an eyebrow. "I'm not the one you need to be afraid of."

"You fucking–"

He never got out the end of that sentence. Because in a flash, Sheila launched herself around the bar and sucker-punched Kyle in the face. Jess's mouth opened in shock, and she stared at Shawn, who'd let go of Kyle's shirt when he dropped to the floor. He rubbed his chin, and Beth backed up slowly, holding her phone aloft in preparation to call backup.

"See if I ever get rid of a creep for any of you ever again!" he shouted, his lip already swelling with a nasty purple bruise. "You fucking whores!"

"Get out." Sheila pointed to the door. She stepped forward, and all 250 pounds of her threatened to give him another blow. "You're not fucking welcome here anymore."

He looked like he was about to bite out a retort when Shawn bent down and dug into his pockets. Kyle struggled, Sheila grabbed his arms while Shawn pinned his chest with a knee. At last, he raised an iPhone in a sparkly purple case into the air, and looked to Jess.

"This it?"

"Yes!" She clapped, and Shawn rose and returned it to her. Sheila took over, pressing on Kyle's chest with one hand and pointing to a sign above the bar with the other.

"You see that? What's that say, all-star? It says we got the right to kick anyone outta here for any reason, at any time. Now get. The *fuck*. Out of our *bar!*"

A few of Sheila's regular customers had gotten out of their seats and approached silently in a ring around the altercation. Kyle grimaced, spat on the floor, and turned away, muttering as he shoved past them and stormed out of the entrance.

The second the door shut behind him, a cheer erupted throughout the bar. Beth and Sheila both smiled sheepishly as the patrons whooped around them and a few regulars got up to pat them on the back. Jess snuck around them as they congratulated the girls and headed right for Shawn.

"Hey," Jess said quietly, placing a hand on Shawn's arm. Someone called out for a round of shots, and a cacophony of raised voices and clinking glasses drowned them out.

He jerked his head toward the back room, where the pool tables had emptied out in all the excitement. She nodded, and he grabbed her hand to pull her through the crowd.

He dragged her around the wall and backed her against one of the bumpers, out of view of the bar.

"I liked the picture." He leaned in closer. Jess could feel his breath tickle the sensitive skin under her ear. "A lot."

"Oh thank *God*." Jess giggled, and rested her forehead against his shoulder. She breathed him in. "I've been agonizing over it."

"You know what I've been agonizing over?" He reached underneath her ass and lifted her onto the pool table. Her legs parted and he wedged himself between them, and leaned his head against hers.

"What?" It came out as a whisper.

His fingers squeezed into her hips. Her heart pounded. "All. Of. This."

And then he kissed her. But unlike the wild, unrestrained kiss they'd shared in her room, this one was slower, almost like he was asking for permission.

"All of you," he breathed against her. She nipped at his lower lip, pulling him in for another kiss. He groaned.

"How long til you get off?" he breathed, breaking away from her.

"It won't take me long." Her core was already aching.

Shawn laughed, a low sound that rumbled in his chest. She felt her pussy clench. "I mean off *work*."

"Oh. Right." Heat rose to her face. "Uh—give me a sec."

She braced her hands against his chest as she lowered herself back to the ground. Her legs were wobbly. She sped-walked to the bar, where Sheila and Beth were still pouring shots for the crowd, which had broken out into an out-of-tune chorus of "We Are the Champions."

"At this rate, we're gonna run out of Jameson," Sheila called over her shoulder. A grin spread across her face when she saw Jess. "Well if it isn't Cinderella!"

"Yeah, haha. About that–"

"You haven't left yet?" Beth set a tray of whiskey on the bartop and called over the crowd. "Jame-O up!" Jess ducked under the divider to avoid the wave of patrons. "We thought you left with the handyman!"

Jess blinked. "Are you two okay with that?"

"Are you kidding?" Sheila crowed, "I've never felt so alive! We can handle this crowd. You go get your man!"

Jess laughed. "Aye, aye, cap'n!"

And then she raced back into Shawn's waiting arms.

CHAPTER 34

Through his windshield, Shawn saw Jess step out of her car in the skinny driveway, leaning carefully back to avoid hitting her head against the rough brick of the chimney. He pulled directly behind her, shutting off the truck and not even stopping to think before jumping out of the cab and racing over to her. He squeezed himself in between the side of the house and her car, trapping her between her open driver's door and his body, the latter towering over her. He leaned in, propping one arm on the roof of the car and grabbing her waist with the other.

He bent down, pulled her soft body against him and crashed his lips to hers.

Her mouth yielded easily to his, and he darted his tongue inside of her, needing to taste her. Her plush, soft lips that had pouted so tantalizingly in the photo she'd sent, finally locked with his own. He nipped at them, first the top, then the bottom, before running his tongue along them slowly, savoring their pillowy softness. He had to explore her, keep testing and teasing her mouth until he'd had his fill.

Jess pulled away, panting, and looked up into his eyes.

Shawn gazed back down at her, taking in her pink cheeks and sparkling eyes. Her long, dark eyelashes winked with tiny tears, and he tilted her forehead toward his lips as he kissed them away.

"Let's go upstairs," he breathed against her neck, folding over her and burying his face in the crease of her collarbone. He heard her sharp intake of breath against his ear.

"Shawn, are you sure?" She tapped him on the shoulder and he pulled back, catching her concerned look with his own. She glanced quickly around the driveway, and leaned in closer to him. "I'd be you first, right?" She whispered.

Shawn grimaced. When he opened his eyes, Jess was giving him a gentle look, and her hand was resting on his chest.

He nodded. "But I don't care about that. I care about *you*. Jess, I haven't been able to stop thinking about you, since–"

He cut himself off. Right then, he couldn't even remember the last time he hadn't been thinking about her.

"I need a shower," she said, gesturing down at her clothes, which Shawn was just now noticing had some grease stains. "I spent all day at the shop before my shift."

Shawn pulled her back into him once again, the thought of her naked body slippery with soap suds driving a fresh surge of desire through him. He tilted his lips to her ear. "*Jeezus*, have I mentioned how sexy it is that you work on cars?"

A mischievous grin pulled at the corners of her irresistible lips. "You're absolutely certain you're ready?" she asked.

"100 percent." He'd never been more certain of anything in his life.

She grabbed his hand, and led him up the side steps into the house and up into her bedroom. Their reflection flashed back at them in the darkened windows when she flicked on the light. He closed the door behind them.

She held up a finger at him, telling him to stay still, and walked into the bathroom. He heard her turn on the shower.

An agonizing minute passed as he waited, steam slowly drifting out through the bathroom door and up towards the ceiling of the bedroom. He was about to abandon the bit and storm in through the doorway when Jess's hand poked through it.

She was holding her panties, and she fingered them for a second before flicking her wrist and letting them fall lazily to the floor.

He tore at his jacket, beginning first to unzip it before just pulling it and his polo shirt over his head in one, quick movement. He unbuckled his belt and undid the button of his jeans as he walked into the bathroom, his lower half pulling him forward so he could see the rest of her.

She stood in the middle of the small bathroom, completely and totally naked from head to toe. Her blonde hair draped in soft curls around her shoulders, and the warm glow of several candles she'd lit cast bronze and copper highlights over the locks. He followed the strands down to the top of her chest, and before he knew it, his hand was reaching out to cup the heavy swell of her breasts in his hands.

She moaned at his cool, rough fingers, and he gently pulled them away until he was barely touching her, just ghosting his knuckles down the sides of her rib cage, down the slight dip of her waist, and finally resting on the curve of her hips. He swallowed, their eyes locked on each other.

She gave him a shy smile, and tugged at the shower curtain. "Care to join me?"

He watched her thigh as she lifted her leg over the ledge of the tub and stepped behind the curtain. He shoved his pants and boxers down his legs and stepped out of them, whipping aside the curtain and following her into the shower.

The spray hit his back, and he hissed at the heat of the water. Jess reached for him and wrapped her hands behind his back, climbing her fingers up into the divot between his shoulder blades where the water struck him, and massaged and rubbed the warm water into his shoulders. He heard a groan rumble out of his chest, and he dropped his face into her hair, where the water streamed over both of them. He ran his hands down her back, slowly pressing into her soft skin before sliding down and spreading his fingers over the cheeks of her ass. He squeezed.

God, is this *what I've been missing?*

His cock throbbed against her stomach, and he ached to bury it against her, inside her, anywhere she'd have him. He pulled her closer, digging his fingertips into the flesh of her ass as he pressed himself flush against her, the hard ridge of his cock sinking deliciously into her belly. He needed her closer, he wanted her to surround him, to fall into her again and again and again until he couldn't feel anything else but her body around him.

"I need you, Jess." His husky voice resonated in the close walls of the shower. He felt lightheaded from the steam and dizzy with his desire, all of the blood in his body flooding south, where he pulsed insistently for the woman in his arms.

"I know. Let me clean up," she replied, pulling her arms back and reaching for her shampoo.

"Turn around." He let go of her ass reluctantly and rested his hands on her shoulders.

"What?" She blinked water out of her eyes as she looked up at him. Slowly, he turned her around to face the shower wall, and backed them up so her head was underneath the water. He thread his fingers through her wet hair, pulling the bulk of it aside and leaning down to say into her ear, "Take care of the rest of you. I'll get your hair."

She leaned back, arching her body, and he groaned as her ass brushed against his erection. He steeled himself as he squeezed some fruity-smelling shampoo into his palm and worked it into her hair, digging his fingertips into her scalp and using every ounce of his willpower not to bend her over and thrust himself in between the round, slippery cheeks that teased the length of his shaft. The smell of her shampoo saturated the steam of the shower and he closed his eyes, losing himself in the feel of her as he slowly massaged his fingers around the base of her neck. It took him a moment to realize Jess wasn't even attempting to wash herself anymore. She leaned into his chest and he felt her soft hands reach up to stroke the back of his head, and he let his arms sweep around to her front.

Her whole body was slick with the suds rinsing down from her scalp. He slid his hands around the sides of her breasts, lifting them up and forward before pressing his fingers into them, unable to hold back anymore.

"These fucking tits, Jess," he moaned. He felt them jiggle as her shoulders shook in a laugh.

"You *really* liked the picture, then," she said.

He bent his wrist back and slapped her boob with a wet *smack*. She yelped in surprise, and tried to pull away.

He grabbed her around the waist and secured her against him, smiling into the curve of her neck. He chuckled.

"If you think I'm letting you get away…"

"You'll what?" she challenged, spinning in his arms and shaking out her wet hair.

He stared down at her. She reached up and swept the last of the suds out of her face.

"I think you're clean enough."

"Then let's get dirty."

She bent behind him to turn off the water, and he admired the sight of her ass in front of him. He caught himself against the wall of the shower as his pelvis urged him forward. Jess looked over her shoulder and slowly rose, her hand trailing from her knee, up her thigh, and behind her to her lower back. He felt a noise rumble in the base of his throat as he followed the journey of her fingers.

"You better step out of this shower before I accidentally give you a concussion," he said.

She winked at him and hopped over the ledge, her tits bouncing tantalizingly before she wrapped herself in a towel. He leapt after her, grabbing at the corner of it.

"Oh no you don't." he snatched it away, once more revealing her perfect curves.

"But we're gonna get the bed all wet," she teased. He backed her against the edge of the bed, until she fell back on top of the aqua-colored comforter. He planted his hands on either side of her torso and fit himself between her legs. He sucked in a breath as her soaking wet hair painted a damp puddle beneath her head.

God she's beautiful.

He reached back down to the floor, taking a moment to glance at the spot between her spread legs, and the delicate folds of pink skin that peeked between them. He froze for a fraction of a second, his mind short-circuiting as he took in the mystery of her naked body, open before him, before finally grabbing the fallen towel.

"Put this under you," he choked, eyes not leaving her smooth, pale skin. He tossed it up to her and barely registered the top half of her body as she shifted to follow his command. He sunk to his knees before her, transfixed by her pussy. Jess squirmed.

"Don't you want to–"

"Can I–" he interrupted her, his voice hoarse. He cleared his throat, and raised his eyes to meet hers. "Can I just look at it–at you–for a second?"

Jess nodded, her mouth open slightly, "Yes."

He returned his gaze to the apex of her thighs, and reached forward to spread them further. He felt Jess's breath hitch as his fingers smoothed the velvety skin, pushing her hips open. She raised her legs, scooting back and resting the soles of her feet on the edge of the bed. He swallowed.

The outer lips of her pussy parted before him, and he marveled at the inner folds of pink and red skin that were revealed, glistening with a wetness that seemed somehow different from the beads of water that peppered the rest of her skin. This seemed thinner, slicker, and he breathed in through his nose as he leaned in closer to investigate.

"C-can I–?" He let the question linger, his hand poised millimeters away from her opening.

"God, yes," Jess moaned.

He slowly touched his fingertips to the smooth outer skin, stroking up and down, and listened carefully to the way Jess's breath changed while he explored her. He dipped a finger in deeper, where the skin darkened, and her legs shook.

"Did I–"

"Don't stop," Jess shuddered out, her eyes closed and her head pushed back against a pillow, "Don't fucking stop."

He looked back down at his fingers as they stroked between her folds, up and down. He was right—this wetness was different. It lubricated his hand, allowing it to slip in and out more easily around the layers of her. He reached in with his other hand, and he parted the two innermost folds with his fingers. He heard Jess gasp. He saw, then, with his own eyes, her opening.

He wedged the very tips of his fingers at the edge of her, bracing himself against her thick thigh with his other hand. He could feel her tremble as he scooted closer, circling around the slick entrance with his fingers and watching her reaction.

Each time his finger swiped across the top, her chest rose, bouncing her heavy breasts with subtle tremors. He smiled in awe as he realized that every shiver was his doing. He kept circling her, transfixed as he watched her breath hitch higher and higher, wondering if he should adjust his pace at all to keep up.

"Should I–?"

"Just like that," she said, opening her eyes slightly, the shining pupils glinting under hooded lids. "Oh, God, Shawn, just keep doing that. Maybe–" she stopped herself, as a particularly strong jolt shook through her. "Oh, God, there—there up towards the top…"

He looked down to see where she meant. He saw a slight bud of flesh peaking through where the inner folds parted, where he thought his finger might have grazed when she'd shook just then. He touched it with his thumb.

"Here?" he asked softly.

She arched her back up off of the towel for a second as he grazed it back and forth with the rough pad of his thumb. She nodded, exhaling quickly, and her hips suddenly jerked around his hand and he tried to hold her still by hugging her thigh against his chest.

"Fuck, I'm so—I'm not usually this—*oh!*" She gasped as he dipped his fingers back inside her where the wetness was pooling, and used it to allow his fingers to glide more smoothly against that small puckering of flesh that she seemed to like so much.

He smiled at her, amazed at the reaction of her body. He could watch her tremble and shake around his hand all night.

But then she opened her eyes and met his gaze, and he once again felt the aching pressure in his stomach. He jerked a bit into her thigh, and she returned his smile.

"I've got condoms," she said breathlessly, "In the nightstand."

"Oh. Right. Yes."

He dug around in the drawer beside the bed and found a box of condoms. He fumbled with the foil wrappers, separating one and opening it.

Shit. Which way–?

He shoved the tip of his dick in the stretchy circle and attempted to roll it down, before realizing he'd put it on backwards. "Uh–"

"Here." Jess pushed his hands away, dropping the condom he was holding to the floor and pulling out a fresh one. She ripped open the wrapper with her teeth, then pinched the middle of the condom with her fingers as she fit it on him and rolled it in her hand down the length of him.

She did all of this in the span of a second. His whole body tensed. She reached up and squeezed the muscles of his forearm before lying back on the bed. He followed her with his eyes.

"Shawn, I want you inside me."

At her words, his cock gave a hearty throb. He groaned, pushed her legs even wider and returned his thumb to her clit. Jess panted, and he withdrew his thumb and instead pushed two of his fingers deep inside of her, where he felt the column of muscles there squeeze him tightly.

Sweet Jesus, she's going to kill me, he thought, struggling to curve and straighten his fingers as he stroked inside of her.

Jess's breathing quickened, and she tightened her grip on his arm.

"Shawn, Shawn, I want *you,*" she moaned, batting at his fingers with her other hand, arching her back again as her hips shook.

He leaned over her body and withdrew his fingers quickly. She jerked as they slid out of her, and he straightened himself and he propped her ankle on his shoulder. He lifted his fingers to his mouth. He needed to know what she tasted like.

"*Ohhhhh,*" he groaned, losing himself when her tangy juices hit his tongue.

"Get inside me, Shawn!" She bounced her hips against him.

He lined himself up with her opening, gripping under her ass with one hand as he stroked his cock in between her folds with the other. He shuddered with desire as he felt her soft skin around him, and suddenly, instinct took over.

He thrust himself inside her, faster than he'd intended, pushing her back further onto the bed before grabbing hold of her hips with both hands to steady them. Her wet channel pulsed around him, contracting around his hard, thick shaft, and his vision went black for a second.

"Fuck, you feel amazing," he grunted, pressing into her hips. Every muscle in his pelvis contracted and he grimaced, squeezing his eyes shut and praying not to lose himself in his first thrust. Slowly, he pulled back, relishing the smooth pressure of her pussy around him, before he pounded back inside of her.

Jess moaned, and he opened his eyes to look down at her.

Her blonde hair, still dark from the shower, tangled underneath her head. Her eyelashes clumped and smudges of mascara ringed her golden brown eyes. Her lips and cheeks flushed crimson against the pale white of her skin, and her body jiggled with every single thrust.

She was stunning. His mouth watered as her tits bounced up and down to his rhythm, and at last he focused on her eyes, which fluttered open and closed while she lost herself to the feeling of him inside her.

"Fuck, Shawn," she gasped. "You can come, you can–ah–"

Her hands balled into fists into the comforter beside her, and he felt her pussy squeeze around him. His breath left his lungs as he pushed himself into her a few more times, tension coiling in his stomach, her ankles bouncing wildly against his shoulders as he once again buried himself inside her.

Deep in his abdomen, he felt his muscles seize and clench tight, stars bursting behind his eyelids. Pressure built within his cock as Jess's pussy gripped around him, spasming tighter and faster until at last he heard her cry out as she came. A sudden, dizzying shudder ran through him at the sound of her voice, and he felt himself follow her into his own orgasm, shooting his release into her core as he grunted over her, panting heavily. Her legs finally relaxed against his chest and fell to his sides, trembling occasionally with little tremors that raced up her body. He tried to watch them travel out from her center to her fingertips and toes, wanting to cherish every single second of her pleasure, but his eyelids drooped with the thrill of his own release, and then with exhaustion. He slowed himself with his arms as he collapsed on top of her, leaning on his elbows to allow her space to breath.

He felt himself begin to soften inside her, and he pressed his lips to hers. She returned his kiss, and he carefully pulled out, tossing the condom in the trashcan by her nightstand. Then he climbed beside her and gathered her in his arms. They held each other there for a long time, softly exploring their mouths with lazy kisses.

He settled his hand in the crease of her waist, curving his palm over the rise of her hips. She ran her fingers up and down his thigh, and they stared at each other.

"That was amazing." Shawn said quietly, disbelief in his eyes as he took in the beautiful woman in front of him. Jess smiled.

"It really was," she chuckled, and squinted her eyes at him. "Are you sure that was your first time?"

He laughed as he rolled onto his back and folded his hands behind his head. "Trust me, I'd have remembered if it wasn't."

She sat up and walked toward the bathroom. He jerked upright.

"Where are you going?" He asked.

"I'm texting the guys to let them know I'll be late tomorrow," she called over her shoulder. Then he saw her messy-haired head poke through the door frame, "And then I'm going to break you in with another round. You've got some catchin' up to do."

CHAPTER 35

Shawn woke to the smell of strawberries. Strands of blonde hair covered his face, and as the memories of the previous evening floated over him and he realized that he was smelling Jess's shampoo, he breathed out a contented sigh.

He snaked his arm under the covers and around Jess's waist, pulling her in closer to his body. He knew she could feel his morning wood poking against her ass. She pretended to be asleep still as he lazily stroked his hand between her breasts.

"Good mornin'," he murmured against her shoulder. He kissed the divot of her collarbone.

"Mmm… mornin'," she slurred back. "What time is it?"

Shawn's stomach growled. Loudly.

"Time for breakfast, I think," he answered. "We skipped dinner last night, didn't we?"

He felt Jess's smile when her cheek pressed against the side of his face. "I was too busy getting seconds on dessert."

"And thirds…" Shawn rubbed his hand down her side to squeeze her thigh. She giggled.

"But yes, I think breakfast is in order," she announced, throwing the covers off of them. Shawn blinked at the sunlight streaming through the window and reflecting off of her white sheets, then marveled at the rays as they bent around her body. His cock twitched.

"But maybe just one more bite of dessert first?" He asked, tightening his grip on her hips and pulling her into him.

"No!" Jess laughed, scrambling out of his arms, "This pussy needs a break! I'm still sore from last night."

Shawn's face went serious. "Are you okay?" He sat up, and his hand grabbed his neck as he looked her up and down with concern. "Did I hurt you? Aw, man, Jess. I–"

"You didn't hurt me," Jess assured him, turning around and kneeling in front of him. He relaxed a bit, and his gaze darted down to the sway of her tits as she leaned forward. He gave her a mischievous smile.

"Well, what about these?" He took his hand and lifted one of her breasts, savoring the weight of it while teasing at the nipple with his thumb. Jess squirmed. "Did I hurt these?"

She batted his hand away. "You might if you keep rubbin' em with those callous-y hands of yours."

He pulled away and looked at his fingers. "You don't like my hands?"

"Oh no, I like your hands," she said, weaving her own smaller fingers in between his, "But I'm getting you a tub of that No-Crack stuff that the guys at the shop use for your birthday. Your hands need some love."

She leaned in and kissed him gently on the lips. She smiled at him. "Luckily for you, I'm a pretty tough girl. I can handle some rough contact."

Shawn growled and pushed their hands behind her back. Jess gasped and fell backwards, losing her balance, and Shawn lorded over her, keeping her hands secured behind her with one hand while steadying himself with the other. She raised her eyebrows at him.

"Do you... like it rough?" Shawn asked.

Jess almost laughed at the earnestness of his question. His boyish face and southern twang were hard to take seriously, even with her hands behind her back. She smiled.

"Sometimes."

Shawn returned a sheepish grin, and released her. They both sat up. "I'll keep that in mind."

Eventually, they were able to get dressed and make it downstairs to the kitchen. The smell of coffee wafted over them, and Natalie sat at her laptop at the kitchen table.

"You're up," she said, eyeing them suggestively over her reading glasses. "Both of you."

Shawn rubbed his neck. "Hey Natalie."

"Good morning, Shawn." her lips tilted up in a knowing smile. "I take it the two of you worked things out?"

Jess snorted as she sauntered over to the counter by the coffee pot and filled two mugs. Shawn tore his eyes away from her swaying hips to sit across from Natalie and attempt to hold an actual conversation. "Yep. Just a misunderstanding."

"You know, Natalie, I doubted you," Jess said, pulling out the chair between them and handing Shawn his coffee. He accepted it, and looked curiously at Jess. "When you said that sex could be life-changing?"

Natalie and Shawn both blinked at her.

"Oh?" Natalie tented her fingers.

"Mm-hmm." Jess nodded and swallowed her sip of coffee. "But you know, last night I might have been convinced."

Shawn felt his face burn with embarrassment. He shot Jess a panicked expression.

"Is that so?" A suppressed laugh colored her voice. He refused to meet Natalie's eyes as she studied him.

Dear Lord, strike me now. I have had a taste of heaven only to be thrown in the flames...

"Yeah. Shawn might be coming over a lot more. I hope that's

okay." Jess carried her coffee toward the stairs. "I'm gonna get ready to head to the shop. I'll talk to y'all later!"

Shawn held his breath as his eyes bore a hole into his coffee. Natalie tapped her fingers on the table.

"Well, I guess that explains all the noises I heard last night."

ONE SLIGHTLY AWKWARD BREAKFAST LATER, Jess was heading out the door to work on her surprise for Shawn. She kissed him goodbye, and leaned herself against him in what started as a sweet press of her lips, but soon evolved into a lingering exploration of each other's mouths. Natalie coughed, and they pulled away from each other, blushing slightly. A smirk tugged at the corner of Shawn's mouth as he watched Jess prance away to her car.

"So," Natalie said when her car had at last pulled out of the driveway. "Didn't you have an interview yesterday?"

It took Shawn a moment to remember what she was talking about. "Oh right!" He said finally, hitting his palm to his forehead. "It went great! Leah wants me to start ASAP."

Natalie's face split into a giant grin. "Shawn, that's amazing! I knew you'd be a good fit there!"

"I think so…" Shawn trailed off, and his face fell a little. "But you know, it is a long drive. I'm wonderin' if it makes sense to take it."

Natalie furrowed her brow. "What do you mean?"

"Well, for starters," Shawn attempted to organize his reservations in his head. "It's gonna take a lotta gas goin' back and forth everyday."

"You wouldn't just find a place down there?"

Shawn rubbed his neck. "Well, that would be the other option." he sighed. "But things are just getting started with Jess…"

Natalie pursed her lip a bit as Shawn spoke. She seemed to

be deep in thought, considering. "You really shouldn't let that get in the way of this opportunity, though. People make long distance work."

They shared a look. Natalie sighed.

"I know I'm not really one to talk about staying somewhere because you fall in love," she said. "But do you think you and Jess are really in this for the long haul?"

Shawn sat back down at the table and rubbed his palms on his jeans. "I don't know. I don't know if she'd want me long-term."

Natalie rested her chin on her hand. "Hmm. Something tells me her desires aren't really what's in question."

Shawn felt his ears go hot. He cleared his throat.

"Either way," she continued, "the thing is, you both are still pretty young, Shawn. This is the time when you're finding your way, figuring out who you are. I've always been of the opinion that it doesn't make sense to assume you know where you belong in the world until you've actually seen some of it."

Shawn thought about that for a moment. Then, he remembered something Leah had said to him during their interview. He hopped up from his chair.

"I just remembered I gotta make a phone call," he walked over to Natalie and hugged her. "Thanks, Nat. For everything."

Natalie gave him a wary look as he pulled away, and he headed for the door. "Uh, sure! Anytime, Shawn."

As he hopped into his truck, he smiled to himself. He had a good feeling about this.

An hour later, Shawn pulled into the perfect cement driveway of his parents' beautiful colonial-style home. He was positively lighter than air as he bounced up to the front steps, and knocked on the door. A minute or so passed, and Melanie finally answered.

"Shawn!" Her eyes widened. "We weren't expecting–"

"I know, it's a surprise visit. I have some really good news." he cut her off, stepping inside. "Where's Mom and Dad?"

"They're at work, Shawn. It's 1:00 on a weekday."

"Oh," Shawn said, the air blowing out of his sails a little. "Then what are you doing home?"

Melanie blushed a little. She shuffled her feet. "Um… well, Christopher and I took the day off together…"

Shawn's eyes widened. "Oh! Uh—*oh.*" He paused, taking a moment to actually look at his sister.

She was wearing a fluffy bathrobe, and her feet were bare on the hardwood floor of the foyer. He heard grandad snoring in his chair in the living room. He lifted his eyes to her face, which now resembled a ripened tomato.

"I—uh, I see," he said awkwardly. "So um… I take it the two of you…"

"Yep!" Melanie squeaked. "We talked, and um… figured some things out!" She gave an awkward laugh. The two siblings looked at each other, and he burst out laughing.

"*Shawn!*" Melanie hissed, hitting him on the shoulder, "*Quiet down!* You'll wake Grandad–"

He backed away from her attack as he covered his mouth, attempting to quiet the laughter bubbling up.

He couldn't believe it. Despite their parents' and the church's best efforts, it looked like both Melanie and Shawn were a couple of heathens after all.

"I'll distract Grandad. You go back to your man," Shawn whispered, wiggling his eyebrows at her.

Melanie attempted to hold a scowl, but silent giggles eventually overtook her. "'Kay!"

She bounded back up the stairs.

Shawn wasn't planning to dwell on the idea of his sister having sex upstairs while he was in the house, but he took a moment to be proud of his little sister. He shook his head as he made his way to the kitchen and snuck a glance at his grandad, still snoring away. He walked over to the door to the garage, figuring while he was here he'd get some work in on the Bel Air.

But when he stepped out onto the landing, he froze.

The Bel Air was gone.

"Grandad?" Shawn called, bolting back into the kitchen and across the house to the living room. He lightly shook his grandfather's shoulder. "Grandad! Wake up!"

Walter jolted awake, his cannula knocking askew as Shawn grabbed his shoulder.

"What? What's going on?" He said blearily. He blinked as he reached over to the TV tray for his glasses. "Shawn? Is that you?"

"Yes, Grandad, it's me. Do you know what happened to the Bel Air?"

Shawn towered over the old man as he slowly gathered his bearings. Walter took a few breaths, the hiss of the oxygen tank punctuating each one. Shawn tried to calm down, remembering that he was dealing with his grandfather, and not a burglar.

"Sorry, Grandad. Here," he handed him his cup of water. Walter took a few sips from the straw. "Do you know what happened to my car?"

His grandad nodded, swallowing. "Yes. Ernie's daughter took it with her."

"Ernie's–you mean Jess?" Shawn felt a lump form in his throat.

Walter drew in another labored breath. "Jess, yeah, that's the one. She's a pistol!" He coughed out a laugh and landed his twinkly blue eyes on Shawn. "I think she might have taken a shine to you."

Shawn cleared his throat. "Where did she take it?"

"To get it fixed, of course." His gray eyes glittered. "She figured out the problem."

"She did?"

"Yep. Smart cookie, that Jess."

Shawn straightened, wanting to race immediately to Ernie's Garage and find out what Jess had done to his car. But just as he was about to head to the door, he heard the creak of a floorboard from upstairs.

Dammit. I said I'd keep Grandad busy, he thought to himself, remembering his promise to Mel.

"You gonna take off again and check it out?" Walter asked.

Shawn shook his head, quickly pulling out his phone and sending a text to Jess to ask about the car. He looked up at his grandad, and suddenly remembered the reason he'd been so excited to come over here in the first place. "Nope, I'll handle that later. But right now, I've got some good news for you."

For the next few hours, Shawn told his grandpa all about the winery and the new job offer. They went over his reservations about moving away, his excitement for a steady paycheck, and his grandad reminisced to Shawn about building *his* cabin. As they talked, the doubts Shawn had had about taking the job faded away. It was the right place for him to be.

He and Jess would make it work. He'd make sure of it.

Shawn was so immersed in the conversation that he had totally lost track of time when Melanie appeared behind the couch.

"Aw hey there, Mel," Shawn drawled as she approached. "You finally done bein' anti-social?" He shot her a knowing grin.

She glared at him from behind their grandad's chair. "Yes, dear prodigal brother, I am," she said tightly. "Are you planning to grace us with your presence for dinner?"

He looked over at the clock on the microwave. It was almost 5:00. His parents would be home soon.

"You know what? I think I am," he said. "In fact, why don't I order us all some pizza for dinner? I've got an announcement to make."

. . .

His parents and Melanie were just as excited as he was when he shared the news with them over pizza. Between his grandad's recovery, Melanie's engagement, and Shawn's new job, the whole Cobb family was in the highest spirits they'd been in years. He said something about it, as he and Melanie cleaned up the dishes while their parents and Grandad settled in the living room to watch TV.

"You know," he said, "I don't even remember the last time we all had dinner like this."

"We have family dinner every week, Shawn."

"I know, but..." Shawn thought for a moment as he rinsed off a plate. He handed it to Melanie to dry. "We all seem happy, I guess. It's been a while since we've all been happy, huh?"

Melanie pondered that for a moment. He handed her another plate. "Maybe... maybe it has. I mean, Grandad was sick for a while, and then you moved out, and I was in school. A lot was changing, you know?"

Shawn *humphed* thoughtfully. Melanie chuckled.

"You sound just like Grandad when you do that, you know."

"I do not!"

"Do too."

He narrowed his eyes at her. Then he flicked her face with soapy water.

"*Shawn!!*"

"Kids! Quiet down!" Their dad called from the couch. Shawn and Melanie shared a look, and they each suppressed a laugh.

"So," he muttered, just beneath the sound of the faucet. Melanie leaned in to hear him. "How was your day with Christopher?"

Melanie's face heated. She straightened the towel in her hands before accepting a wet mug. "Quite... productive," she finished lamely.

"For both of you?" he asked impishly.

"Yes."

Shawn nodded. "Good. I'm happy for you." He nudged her with his elbow. Melanie smiled shyly to herself. "You deserve it, you know. A good match."

"I'm happy for you too, Shawn." She nudged him back. "This job… it sounds really awesome. Even if you are going to be over two hours away." She paused, rubbing the towel over the same dish for a little longer than necessary. "I'm gonna miss you."

"Oh, Mel, you ain't gettin' rid of me that easy." He drained the sink and rinsed off his hands. He put a dripping arm around her shoulders, and she grimaced. "But for now, I think I've had about all the family time I can handle. I'm headed out to the bar."

"The bar? But it's late!"

"Can't be helped, Mel. I gotta talk to a girl about a car."

Jess paused, her hand poised on the handle of the side door of the shop with her keychain dangling from the lock.

"Are you sure you're ready to see this?" she said, knowing what his answer would be. He'd stormed into the bar and hounded her for her entire shift about her stealing his Bel Air. Now here they were, at two in the morning, because he refused to go home without seeing it in action.

"Jess, I swear to God if you don't let me see my own fucking car–"

She shoved open the door and flicked the lights on, hurrying out of his way. He stepped past her, eyes widening and feet slowing as he let out a low whistle.

"You painted her?" He looked over his shoulder in disbelief.

She nodded. He turned back, approaching gingerly and reaching out to ever so lightly caress the chrome. "She's *beautiful*," he whispered. Jess felt a glow in her chest as he circled the car, and she positively beamed at his approval.

"And it runs?" He asked, his voice choked with emotion.

"It runs."

He shook his head. "What was the problem? I thought I tried everything!"

Jess hopped over to the car, trailing her fingers along his back as she slid around him, flicking open the fuel door. She unscrewed the cap and tilted it toward him, turning it so that the new plastic glinted in the light.

He blinked at her.

"Every now and then, the vents in these old gas caps will go bad," she explained. "I never woulda thought of it, until Beau had an old El Camino in here last week with the same problem."

"And you put two and two together, huh?" Shawn had an unfamiliar gleam in his eye. Jess replaced the cap and crossed her arms under her chest.

"I did."

He snaked his hands around her waist and pulled her toward him, and she lifted her chin to meet his lips in a lingering kiss. He didn't pull away when their lips parted, instead tilting his head and leaning his forehead against hers. "You are some kinda genius, you know that?"

A laugh bubbled in her throat, and she twisted up for another kiss. They stood like that for a long moment, wrapped in each other against the side of the Bel Air, when Shawn suddenly ended their make out session with a wet *smack.*

"Oh! Shoot! That reminds me!" He stretched his arms and held her by the shoulders, forcing her to look at his face. "I got a job!"

"A… job?" Jess stuttered, still a little dizzy with the heat of their kiss.

"At a winery. I've been hired by Lilliette Vineyards as head contractor for their events venue and campground!"

Jess gave him a dazed smile. Her forehead wrinkled with confusion. What did this have to do with the car?

"Um, congratulations! That's… good?"

"It's awesome! It's just over two hours away, down in Virginia, in this neat little town…"

He kept talking, but static filled Jess's ears after he'd said 'two hours away'.

Two hours?

Jess's mind went numb as she realized what he was trying to tell her. He was leaving.

Her breathing became shallow, and she felt her chest constrict. She looked up at Shawn, trying to listen, trying to be supportive, but in her chest, her heart was weighted with failure.

"Jess? Whaddya say?"

"What?" She jerked back to the present, and Shawn pressed his hands more firmly into the small of her back.

"To the mechanic job."

"I thought you were contracting?" She stammered.

"Did you hear a word I said? Jess, Leah needs a mechanic. You should apply!"

Shawn's light blue-green eyes sparkled at her, reflecting the sheen of the paint of the car behind her and wide with excitement. It took a moment for the full meaning of his words to sink in.

"You mean, apply to work at the winery? With you?"

"Mm-hmm." he hummed into her neck, bending over her against the car, pressing their hips together. He whispered a kiss against the base of her ear.

"As a mechanic?"

"What job do you think you'd apply for? You can't possibly think I'd want you to just pour wine your whole life."

Shawn kissed his way around to her lips and smiled against them. She smiled too, her lips pulling back as a giggle escaped from the back of her throat. He chuckled too, and their laughter grew in volume until she threw her hands around his neck and crashed her lips to his. He grabbed her hips and hoisted her up between him and the car, and their kiss deepened, tongues swirling around each other as she wrapped her legs around his waist. She pulled away for air.

"So you aren't leaving me?"

He leaned his forehead against hers. "Not if I can help it. I'll drive back and forth every night if I have to."

He kissed her again. And this time, it was him that popped up for air.

"After all, what good is it having a sexy hot rod like this without a sexy woman to drive it home to?"

She nuzzled against his chest, lips stretching in a smile against the flannel. Then she bucked against him, sliding over to the driver's side door and wrenching it open.

"Who says I'm gonna let *you* drive it?"

"Hey now–" he reached forward, blocking her from closing the door.

"You coming or not? I thought we were gonna take this beauty for a spin." She rubbed her hands along the plastic of the steering wheel. Shawn rolled his eyes.

"It's the middle of the night!"

"You'd rather break it in another way?" She grinned at him, scooting further into the cab and leaning against the passenger window.

His blue-green eyes sparkled as he crawled between her open legs. "*Now* you're talkin'."

EPILOGUE

$\mathcal{S}$hawn swept off the deck boards of the Lilliette Vineyards Event Pavilion, pausing to admire the view of the lake from center stage. He didn't have long to take it in, however, before the shrieking bridezilla that was his sister barrelled down the hill.

"You'll ruin your hair, honey," he heard his mom call feebly, before catching sight of Melanie, wrapped haphazardly in a short satin robe and nude-colored bike shorts, stomping toward him. Her hair did, in fact, look on the edge of ruin.

"Shawn Ezekiel Cobb, what in God's name do you think you are doing??"

"I'm sweeping off the stage," he said, gesturing around him. She stalked closer, and he could hear her labored breathing as she pounced on him.

"The ceremony starts in eighty-seven *minutes, Shawn!*" she screamed. Shawn would have laughed if he hadn't feared for his life.

"*And,*" she added, voice approaching banshee levels, "*your girlfriend is missing!*"

Shawn grimaced. He figured he knew exactly where his girlfriend was, as he'd heard the big tractor backfire the day before in the vineyard when the crew had been out picking the cabernet franc. He squinted into the sun behind Melanie's head.

"And you're filthy! Where's your tux??"

Finally, their mom arrived at the foot of the pavilion, where she reached toward her daughter. "Melanie, honey, everything is going to be perfect. Shawn is leaving *right now,*" his mother glared at him, "and everyone is going to be exactly where they're supposed to be in time to line up for the procession."

"But they missed the champagne brunch!" Melanie whined, moisture gathering around her false eyelashes.

Shawn snuck away when their mom gave him another pointed look, and he climbed around the stage out toward the cabins, where the whole wedding party was staying for the weekend.

Melanie had positively flipped when Shawn had shown her the initial sketches for the event pavilion. She'd immediately wanted to book her and Christopher's wedding there, despite the fact that it wasn't even close to finished when he'd shown her back in May. But when he'd been joking to Leah about it, she mentioned (ever the savvy businesswoman) that if Melanie would be all right with it, Leah could use the earlier wedding as an opportunity to take marketing photos to advertise the space for the next season.

Not that she'd needed to. No sooner had they cut the ribbon to the facilities than the phone started ringing off the hook with reservations well into the following year.

But now that the wedding photos were being used for marketing purposes, Melanie was even more insistent than she would have been about every detail being absolutely perfect. She was going to be a beautiful bride, he was sure, but she was an *ugly* bridezilla.

Shawn passed the cabin that he and Jess were sharing for the weekend (to his grandfather's amusement) and headed instead up the lakeside trail to the vineyard workshop, where all the land managers and pickers kept their tools and the tractors. There, he found Jess exactly where he knew she'd be: elbow deep into the side panel of a Ford 3000, covered in grease.

"Ah, jeez, Jess, before the wedding?" He ragged on her, slumping against the nose. He admired the way the soft light peeking in through the old wooden siding made lines across her skin. Gold highlights winked in her blonde hair as she turned on him.

"It's harvest season, Shawn!" She poked him in the chest with an oily finger. "Dad just got the part last night. *Your* job might be done here, but mine's just getting started!" She dove back into the engine, levering a wrench in between the various components. "Almost… and… there!" Her arm jerked back and a nut flew out from inside and almost whacked her in the face.

"Shit!" she yelped, jumping back, "That was a close one!"

"Can you imagine sportin' a black eye in all of the photos cause you took a nut to the face?"

Jess glowered at him. He sniggered.

"The guys all washed the Bel Air, by the way. It should be all ready to go for the ceremony."

When Shawn had proposed that Jess apply to work at Lilliette Vineyards, she'd seen more than just a job opportunity. She and her dad had identified a need in the growing wine industry for antique tractor mechanics. They'd offered a deal to Leah, and she'd been so happy with their work that they now had three other service contracts with different wineries across the Shenandoah Valley. Jess still worked for her dad's shop, but she'd made a new position for herself as their traveling machine technician.

Which meant that, more often than not, she spent the night with Shawn.

"Grandad will be thrilled. But Melanie's panicking that we won't be ready in time."

"Fine, I'll stop for now," she huffed, shoving the wrench into his stomach, "But I'm coming right back out here after pictures,"

"You're not going anywhere, little missy," he shot back, catching her around the waist and spinning her into his arms. He was suddenly very grateful he was still in his work clothes. He wouldn't have been able to squeeze her like this if he'd already gotten dressed for the wedding. He buried his face into her messy hair and breathed in the scent of oil and gasoline mixed with the strawberries of her shampoo. He sighed contentedly, and he felt a familiar stirring in his jeans as her rear end pressed against his front.

"Melanie says there's only 87 minutes left until the ceremony," he murmured into her ear. He felt a shiver race down her spine.

"Well, that seems like plenty of time." Jess leaned into him, tilting her head back. "Almost too much, really. We'll need to figure out how we're gonna fill all of it."

He smiled against her lips. Her tongue darted out and caught his, and he kissed her back deeply, rubbing his hands up and down her filthy clothes.

"I can think of a couple ways to fill it." Her breath hitched as he jerked his hips against her.

The outline of his cock in his jeans rubbed insistently against her ass. She moaned, bending forward to rest her hands on the lift arm. She raised and wiggled her ass tantalizingly before him. He scowled.

"Goddammit, Jess, I can't fuck ya like that when you're wearin' overalls!" He smacked his hand against the outside of her ass, and she jumped, flipping her hair in his face as she quickly stood.

"Well then, let's get me out of them." She winked at him over her shoulder as she sauntered toward the big barn doors, exaggerating the sway of her hips while he stared her down.

He started to chase her, and they raced down the trail back

to their cabin, where they wasted no time stripping naked and getting cleaned up for the wedding.

Well, maybe they wasted a *little* time.

DESPITE THEIR BEST EFFORTS, both Jess and Shawn made it to the ceremony on time, walking down the aisle to stand on either side of the groom, Jess in her jade green floor-length bridesmaid's dress that she absolutely hated, and Shawn in his slate gray vest and green-and-blue paisley tie. As the wedding march began, Grandad crested the hill in the Bel Air, where he delivered Melanie, a vision in white lace and tulle, to meet their dad at the top of the aisle so he could give her away.

Shawn and Jess beamed at each other over the altar. *These pictures are going to be phenomenal.*

At the end of the night, they shared a tiny bag of sprinkles to toss after Melanie and Christopher as they raced out of the winery and into their waiting limousine. As they sped away, Jess leaned against Shawn's chest, and he clasped his hands around her stomach, enjoying the warmth of her body in the evening chill of the late September night.

"I don't know why you hate this dress so much," Shawn said. "I think you look pretty dang beautiful tonight."

He felt his girlfriend smile against him, and she tilted her chin to look at him.

"Do you think that'll be us someday?" she asked.

"Think what'll be us?"

"Bride and groom, climbing into a limo and riding off into the sunset?"

Shawn stared into her golden brown eyes, smiling to himself as he imagined their wedding day.

Wedding Day.

Just a few months ago, he'd been adrift: pining over a woman that didn't love him, struggling to find work, and pulling his hair out over a vintage car he couldn't afford to fix. Now, he had an amazing job, a sparkling 1954 Bel Air, and a woman in his arms that could rev his engine like no other. "No, I don't think so."

Jess's shoulders sagged, and her eyebrows pinched together. "You don't?"

"Nah. When we drive off into the sunset, it'll be in a hot rod."

THE END.

WANNA HEAR Shawn's and his sister's garage conversations from Melanie's point of view? Check out *Here Comes the Bride* on Kindle Store!

ACKNOWLEDGMENTS

Holy Shit. You know, you start the first book on a whim. What the hey, you think to yourself, it's 50,000 words, NaNoWriMo, it'll be fun. No big deal, right?

Then you finish it. You send it out to friends. They love it. So you decide to publish it. And then you think, well, what the hell, I'll write a sequel.

Six months, 100,000 words, 90+ Amazon reviews, a dozen facebook groups, and a viral TikTok video later, you find yourself hiring an editor to help you figure out if there's any hope for your second novel. Turns out, there is.

And here we find ourselves.

First of all, I find myself once again in the debt of Mary Adams-Legge, my former English Teacher and current editor, without whom I wouldn't have a novel resembling anything close to a contemporary romance. Congratulations on your retirement: and here's to wishing you many golden years of relaxation (Provided you'll still edit my books, of course)!

And Sue, you little shit, here it is. THANK YOU. You happy now? Happy that I've listed you BY NAME this time in the acknowledgements? As if I WASN'T grateful for my amazing Mother-In-Law and *wasn't* including you when I thanked my "precious family" in the back of my last novel? Well, here ya go. Thanks. And I don't wanna hear another word about it!

But seriously. You are the actual best, I love you so much, and without you raising your incredible son, I never would have met the inspiration for every love story I write. Thank you for reading my books and sharing them with the people you love.

As for my biological family, I love that me embracing writing and self-publishing has brought you so much joy. I know romance novels aren't really y'all's thing, but it truly means the world to me that you power through them anyway in solidarity. And that photo of Daddy reading *Betting on the House* at the kitchen table is one of my all-time favorites. I love you all so much. Thank you.

Emily, you are a scholar and a saint. You were totally right about the condoms, and I will never be able to put into words how much I treasure your face and your insight. And your haircut is BOMB.

Karli. Where the hell do I EVEN begin??? You are the most supportive friend a girl could ever ask for. You are sweet and caring beyond words, and your feedback has kept me going through thick and thin. Thank you so, SO much.

Michael and Zach, thank YOU for being my experts and research assistants, and letting me know that there's no such thing as a gear shaft. And then, after reading through your advanced copy in which I said there was no such thing as a *crank* shaft, correcting me yet again (So for those keeping track: crank shaft—does exist. Gear shaft—doesn't exist). I cannot state how much I depended on your knowledge; I likely wouldn't have attempted this book if we weren't such good friends.

To all my RomCom Facebook darlings: you have kept me sane, have spruced my blurbs, have laughed at my jokes and given me a much-needed release valve while wading through the pressure of self-publishing. I am so grateful for you. And for all of my TikTok friends, thank you for enjoying my random thoughts and musings, sharing them with friends, and helping me find a community in a scary new social media platform.

To my herner, my squeeze, my muse, my flame: thank you

for finally starting my first book! And you know, for supporting me, loving me, and every moment of every day you've gifted me. You and Ogun remain my world. I love you, more and more, each and every day.

And finally, to Mary Ann and Pesto, who are giving 'em hell in Heaven right now. Your sass is unmatched, and I trust you two to take care of each other up there. Thank you for teaching me that you are never too old or too young to appreciate a good love story.

Cassandra Medcalf is a writer, narrator, audio engineer, food enthusiast, wine taster, do-it-yourselfer, and an amateur film critic (despite barely having seen any movies). She lives on a future vineyard, in a future dream home in upstate New York with her adorable husband and their even more adorable dog. You can follow her and her family's hare-brained schemes and lofty pursuits on her website, cassandramedcalf.com (or, if you're just here for the smut, on TikTok @Cassandra-MedcalfVO).

facebook.com/CassandraMedcalfVO
twitter.com/voiceofcass
instagram.com/CassandraMedcalfVO

ALSO BY CASSANDRA MEDCALF

In the Fixer Upper Universe:

Betting on the House, Book #1

Betting on the Bird, Book #1.5

Hot Rod Hookups, Book #2

Here Comes the Bride, Book #2.5

Find them all at cassandramedcalf.com/books !